STORM RISING

STUART WHITE

PENOBI PRESS

Ice Farms
Alpine Forests
Corena's Village
Fort Lorn
Ghondulon
Smugglers Bay
Loch Liten
Loch Mikill
Silver Wood
Midtown
New Swort
Washing Bay
Eagletown
REJIK
Symport
Radiation Belt
Sulphur Swamps
Death Bay
N
W
E
S

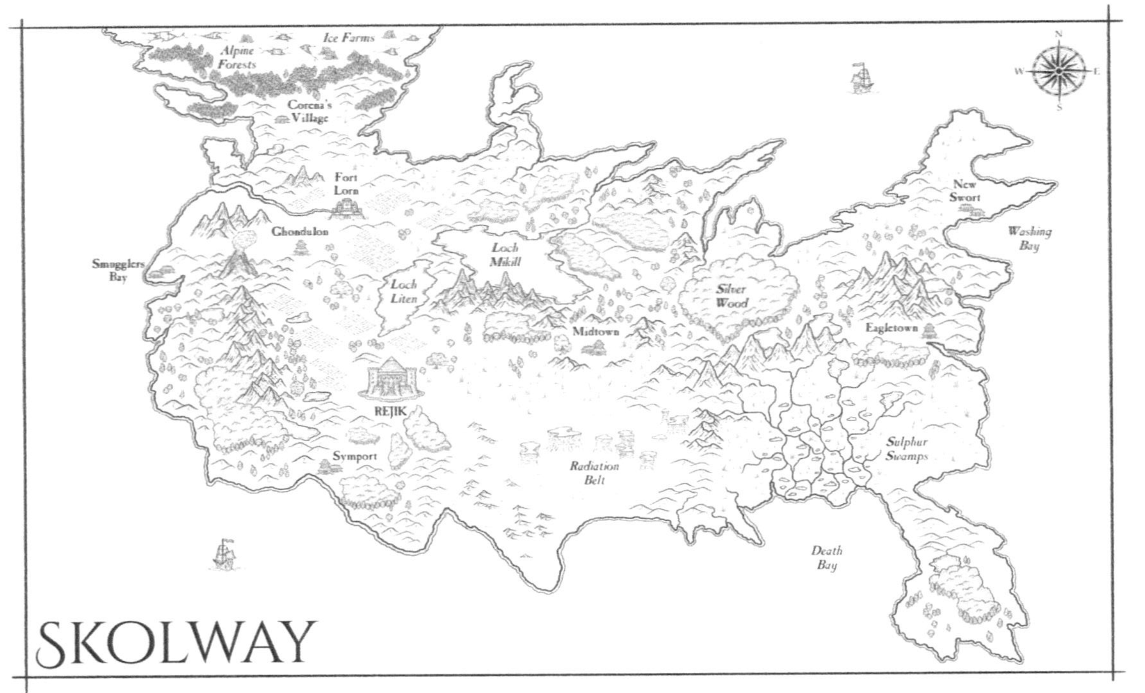

SKOLWAY

CHAPTER 1

If I'm not hanged for being Wiccan, I'll probably be hanged for this.

'What if we get caught?' I move my lips closer to Asta's. 'What if the Klerik finds out?'

An owl hoots from a branch lined with evening frost. I pull away and snap my head around. Nothing. No-one.

The forest is the perfect place for secrets. Only the old church and the hanging dais sit out here, well away from the village.

'Shut up and kiss me.'

I lean closer, my head edging towards hers. Our lips slowly part. Her head tilts, and I close my eyes.

Asta's lips are soft. Much softer than a boy's. As she brushes them against mine, she strokes my cheek. A small drop of melted snow splashes on my nose. I tremble and pull my furs tighter around me.

'Wow.' I pull gently away from her. But not too far. 'How...how was it?'

'Fine.' Her gaze darts around the forest. 'Want to do it again? Longer?'

I nod and close my eyes. The excitement of the moment sizzles down my arms and my chest tightens. Tingles wriggle across my thighs.

Asta's lips are harder this time. Her hot breath ignites a furnace of desire. It scorches my body, from the tip of my tongue to my frozen toes.

She pauses for a second and runs her fingers through my hair. 'As white as snow. It's beautiful.'

Something touches my back, and I tense, slowly turning. The mossy rope from the hanging platform swings like a scythe with the winter wind. It's so rotten I reckon it would snap under my body weight. I relax my shoulders and turn back to Asta.

We kiss again.

Small flakes of snow build up on my forehead. Each one melts against my skin. Her shivering hands move across my body. I edge closer.

The owl hoots louder this time.

As her hand moves down, I grab it instinctively.

She stares at me, her eyes narrowed. 'What's wrong with you?'

'Nothing. Just...please don't.' I release her. Nobody can know what I'm hiding. No one could love me, once they know what I am.

'Sinners!' A gritty, shallow voice echoes through the forest.

Asta jumps back, pushing me away.

Klerik Anticus shuffles into sight from behind the church. He raises his small gas-lamp and squints towards us. The surrounding trees light up.

'In the name of the Ten, stop that unnatural behaviour right now.'

The owl takes flight, screeching as it soars into the night.

I knew we shouldn't have come anywhere near the church. Even though part of me was excited at being so close.

He limps closer.

Asta moves away and stands beside him. 'She forced me to do it, Klerik. I didn't want to. She made me.'

What's she talking about? She kissed me back. It was her idea...wait...

'You set me up?' A frost forms inside me where moments before there was fire. A large lump of snow crashes to the ground behind the Klerik.

He steps back, staring up at the tree.

A second lump falls from another tree. But this time he doesn't look at the tree.

His eyes rake me. Sharp, clear and intent.

He suspects.

I dig my nails into my palms as the surge of power reaches my hands. Don't lose control. Don't ever lose control again.

Asta turns to Anticus. 'It was awful. So disgusting. So unnatural. Will the Gods ever forgive me?' She fake-retches.

He pats her slowly on the back, his face softening, along with his voice. 'Yes, Asta, my child. They will forgive you. But you must pray.'

The snow illuminates him against the darkness of the forest behind him, deepening the creases in his face. His gaze fixes on me. 'Corena Storm. You've sinned once again. Come inside and pray to the Ten for forgiveness. You can't continue to behave like you do. The Gods lose patience.' His words make him appear taller, the way he does at his sermons.

'Can't you see she's tricking you? She kissed me. She sinned, too.' I hold my arms up to the Gods I'm sure aren't there. If they were, they'd never let something as abnormal as me live in their perfectly ordered world.

'The only trick here is you deceiving your nature. The Gods state woman shall love man. You defy Mama Killa herself. It's unnatural for a woman to love a woman.'

'I hardly love her.'

Asta sends me a sarcastic smile, just out of Anticus' view. Damn, I like that smile. 'And even if I did, why is it unnatural?' I ask the Klerik.

'Because the Gods say so. They're beyond question.' He looks to Asta, who switches quickly from a grin to a pout. 'You go home, Asta, and let your parents know what happened. I'll take Corena and deal with her.'

'Thank you, Klerik.' She saunters off, giving me a last, triumphant smile.

I can't believe I thought she liked me.

'Given your previous...mishaps, I'm going to have to report this to the Kurikon...and to your parents.' The Klerik shakes his head, looking toward the dark sky. 'You behave like neither boy nor girl. And your unnaturalness...you have no place in this world. If it's the wrath of the Gods you want from this life, then you have it.'

'I want to be myself and not receive self-righteous lectures from intolerants.' I know it's too much the second I speak, but I've been bursting to say it for so many years.

Klerik Anticus creases his lined face and points his crooked index finger at me. 'You've crossed the line, Corena Storm. Your mother will be ashamed, and your penance will come. And sooner than you may think.'

The mention of my mother is too much. The dam I've built in my mind to hold back my powers suddenly bursts and shards of ice plummet from the tall trees around and fly straight for the Klerik.

At the last moment I regain control, and redirect them so they all miss him.

Except one.

It only grazes the side of his scalp, but the deep red that sprinkles on the surrounding snow signal that I've really gone too far now. I've hid my power for so long, but I've shown it in front of the worst possible person.

If he recognises what I am, that I caused those ice shards to attack him, then I'm done for.

Within an hour the Kurikon will receive an eagle with a note.

And I will be taken.

I stomp through the village, the lecture from Klerik Anticus fuelling my strides, kicking one of the 'Wiccans Wanted' posters that offer big rewards.

I tried to convince him the shards were natural, but I'm not sure he believed me. He's always been suspicious of me since Gullan died.

Apparently, I'll burn at Ka-Ferno's Gate.

Apparently, none of the Gods, not even the trickster Susanoo-no-Mikoto, will let me ascend.

Apparently...

Asta strides towards me.

I ignore her. I don't want to lose control in sight of people, as everyone's out for season changeover tonight, but she grabs my arm.

'Please listen.'

'We're done. I can't believe I actually liked you, even a little bit.'

'But I had to, Corena. You know what it's like, we'd both be sent off to be reformed.'

'So better me than you, huh? Coward.' I try to give her my evil stare, but those goddam perfect curls and that scar on her left cheek just make me realise how much I do like her. I *did* like her.

'I'm sorry.'

'Yeah, not as sorry as I am. Or will be, no doubt.' I pull away and continue down the main road, just wanting to get home and not think about Asta.

Or that kiss.

The street gets busier as I approach the village centre and the food, noise and music, almost make me U-turn. Especially when I see the Enforcer that everyone whispers has no face, and their friend, hammering more 'Wiccans Wanted' posters into the trees that line the road.

There's rumours about those two, especially the one without a face. I mean, I've never seen it behind the mask, but apparently he murdered thousands, and a Wiccan took his face. All the kids run away from him, screaming.

They spin around and stare at me through their blue masks. I turn away, not wanting any more trouble today.

But then I see my brother.

Pat waits for me outside the Blacksmith's barn, his white hair emphasised by the blazing oil lamps that light up the main road. His face glows, and he sprints over once he sees me, slamming into my embrace. He's way too old for cradling but is small and light for a twelve-year-old.

'Seriously, Pat, you know you really need a bath.'

I release him, and he bounces beside me as we pass the bustling village hall.

'Where you been, Rena?' His wee cheeks burn red against his pale skin. We Storms are whiter than the snow that surrounds us.

'Nowhere.'

'Why were you with the Klerik, then? I searched everywhere, and that's the only place you could be coming from. They going to send you away this time?' He grabs my hand, and I squeeze back as we pass a large building to the right. My workplace. Snow thaws upon the roof, small clumps falling on the built-up ice beneath. The stalactites are melting.

My fellow ice-farmers have shelved their tools and are sharpening their axes instead, as we do at the end of every winter. I have tonight off, but I should be working. We need the money. I thought Asta was worth it.

'No. It was nothing.'

'Don't believe you.'

'Would I lie to you?' I give him a wink.

He nods fast. 'Aye, you would,' he says with a laugh, and I join in.

In front of us, a large crowd has gathered on the road. There must be thirty villagers huddled together, silent and staring our way.

No, not now. Not today.

I notice the music has stopped. The noise gone. The smell of roasted hog and ale is still strong in the air. The one time of year we can afford such luxuries. But nobody is attending it, they've all got bigger prey to hunt.

Even some of my closest workmates have moved across the mud track to join them.

'Do you know what this is about?' I ask Pat.

He shakes his head, steps in front of me and positions himself between me and the crowd. 'I won't let them be nasty to you again, Rena.'

I squeeze him in a hug. 'It's fine, I can handle myself. Run home. Go the long way.'

'No, I want to stay with you.' He resists my release.

'I know.' I bend down and pull his collar tighter around his neck. 'But you'll go home and tell Mum and Dad you couldn't find me. Got it?'

'Aye.' He shakes his head and runs to my left, towards the surrounding forest. But then he stops, turns, and runs back.

'Go home now, Pat.'

'We Storms stick together. You wouldn't leave me.'

I bite my lower lip...if he gets hurt, Mum and Dad would kill me, even if this mob doesn't.

I grab him by the arm, the worry squeezing my throat. 'Under no circumstances will you get involved. No matter what they do to me. Got it?'

He nods. I shake my head, wanting to turn him away, but he's promised. I let him walk with me.

'Fine evening.' I stride towards the crowd. 'Did I miss something? Village meeting? Annual play?' My shaking voice belies the false confidence I try to project.

'You know exactly why we're here. We've had enough of you

and your...blasphemous behaviour.' It's one of the old carpenters. Ira. As the eldest in the village, he acts like he's in charge. He's nothing but a stoolpigeon to the Klerik.

'I'm going home. I mean no harm.' I pull Pat tighter to me and march towards the middle of the group, raising my chin and looking beyond them, hoping they'll part.

They don't.

I try to walk around. Several of the villagers move into my path, and I notice Asta's dad is one of them. As they surround us, the stench of sweat and smoke overpowers. Eyes and faces bore into me.

'You've infected my daughter with your...ideas.' He spits at me. It lands on my cheek, warm and stinking of ale.

I wipe the pathetic spittle from my face and then smile. 'Trust me, those ideas were all hers.'

Fresh manure splatters across my face and into my eyes. A hard lump of compacted snow hits my cheek. I lift my arms to defend myself and move closer to Pat.

'Unholy abomination!'

Every time something hits me, a surge of energy flows through my arms.

'Leave! Take your sorcery with you!'

The same surge I fight every day.

'Queer witch!'

Every day since I last lost control.

'Stop it!' My screams rip from my throat. '*Leave me!*'

But none of them listen. They close in, forming a ring around us. Pat moves in front of me, taking abuse. A rock strikes him. Then a potato, rotting with mould and covered in maggots.

'*Don't dare hit him!*'

'She-devil! Return to Ka-Ferno where you belong!'

The barrage forces me to grab Pat and kneel, protecting him from the worst of it with my back and arms. My furs are plastered with filth and reek of manure.

Holding him close, I feel Pat's muscles tensing. He's about to fight back. I want to calm him, but my own power flows through my arms. It's either him that get's in trouble, or me. And they already know about me. The force slips beyond my control, and I release Pat.

My palms become the mothers of two small splinters of ice. The daughter shards grow long, as my rage peaks. *No. No!* I centre my focus on stopping the weapons from forming, but the urge is too strong. *I don't want to be the monster they think I am.*

The sharp edge of a rock splits my forehead, and I growl at the feral face of the thrower. It's the Klerik's aide, Plock. Hot blood runs into my eyes.

My right arm thrusts forward. I can't stop it. A long, sharp shard of ice propels from my hand and jets through the crowd towards him. Plock's face whitens and falls slack.

Then it runs red.

I've hurt him, now, another man of the Kurikon. I'm a dead girl breathing.

People stop attacking and run to his side.

I spot a gap in the crowd and sprint, as fast as my raging body will drive me through the snow, dragging Pat behind me.

The shouts and projectiles are soon behind us.

I wish I could live my life in peace. But people will never accept me or leave me alone.

They want me to be normal. To be like them.

But I'm not like them.

I am something else.

CHAPTER 2

The way they look at me, it's like I'm no longer their daughter. Or son. Or whatever the hell I am.

Unnatural.

Something else.

We sit at the table. Mum's hands shake. Her hair sticks to her forehead. Dad's quiet, his fingers clasped beneath his chin, his eyes closed, doubtless praying.

My brother eats his porridge. 'Why's no one talking?'

I stop chewing my nails.

Mum looks at Dad. His eyes remain closed.

Water drips onto the table from our poorly thatched roof, like blood dripped from Plock's head. I hope I didn't seriously hurt him. He could be dead. I just couldn't control it.

Again.

'Why is that roof always leaking?' Mum slams a bucket down beneath the drops. But it topples, rolls across the table and clanks on the ground.

After a few more seconds of silence, Pat goes back to his porridge.

'I'll work overtime this weekend and trade the wood for straw.' I stare at the leak. 'Maybe I could show Pat how to thatch?'

Mum shakes her head and snatches up her bowl, dropping her spoon onto the straw-covered floor. Dad crosses his arms and tuts at her. When she picks it up, it's covered in mud. A fly crawls onto it, the buzz boring into the silence.

'What did you learn with Klerik Anticus today?' I smile at my brother. I'd be long gone if it wasn't for him. Who knows how brainwashed with Kurikon ideals he'd be if I didn't teach him the opposite every night? Luckily, he's better at not being openly defiant. But he still needs to careful. He can't end up like me.

'Nothing. As usual.' He shrugs. 'Just reciting the Ten Gods and their powers.'

He didn't say a word about the villagers to Mum and Dad when he got home. He never does.

'And who are they?' Mum asks.

Pat rolls his eyes but obediently recalls them. He's so much cleverer than me. Than anyone in the village actually. Mum and Dad have high hopes for him to eventually leave us and study with the High Klerik. That's why they have hid what I am for so long; worried that I could tarnish Pat's prospects.

But I know he's not interested in that life.

'Well, there's Eingana, Mother of All, creator of life. She was the first. Then Suijin, Goddess of Water and Ice. She watches over our village and keeps us blessed with eternal snow for the Ice-Farmers.' He nods to me. 'Prithvi, the Goddess of the Earth, who keeps our lands in the south fertile.'

He pops another spoonful of porridge in his mouth. 'Ra, the God of Fire, who keeps us warm in the north. Ha, God of the Desert, who watches over the capital and the surrounding lands in the south. Mama Killa, Goddess of Fertility, who keeps us blessed with healthy natural, children. Fei Lian, the God of Wind, who keeps our ships sailing and our seeds spreading. Kami-no-Kaze, the God of Speed, who gives us the swiftness to hunt and to defeat our enemies in battle. And Ka-Ferno, the devil-God, Guardian of Death and keeper of sinner's souls.'

Mum stares at him as he speaks, her face glowing in the fire-light. She's never given me that look. Not since I killed Gullan. Her first born. My brother.

'And there's Susanoo-no-Mikoto, who is my favourite.' He beams at me.

'And what happens when a person steals a God's power.' Mum loves to hear him talk religion. She's the most devout person in the village. She must be so ashamed to have me as her child.

'Any Wiccan who steals a God's power are hanged, so that it can be drained and returned to the God from which it came. This is why Queen Freya ordered the Kurikon to hang all Wiccan almost a decade ago.'

Dad glances at me. He spreads his hands flat on the table. His index finger drums on the wood. They love to remind me that they've protected me from the Kurikon for ten years.

Mum leaves the table, whispering something in Dad's ear as she passes.

'Excuse me,' she says to Pat and me.

She disappears beyond the curtain, to their bedroom. Hopefully, she's gone to bed. She's clearly tired. But Dad still hasn't moved. Patrick starts humming.

They must know about the kiss with Asta. It only happened two hours ago but news travels fast. Especially about me. Why haven't they said something about it? Dad loves any excuse to shout at me.

And if they find out about Plock...

I chew my hair again.

But they continue to be weirdly quiet.

I lift the water jug and pour another glass. Beneath the potato bowl, an old, torn parchment catches my eye. Only the words 'reward' and 'Wiccan' are visible, but I know what the rest of it says.

'Why is that here?' I ask, pointing to the parchment.

Dad still won't look at me. I can't stand the silence any longer.

Ramming the water jug back down on the table, sloshing it everywhere, I scream at him. 'WHY?'

He finally looks up. 'I've made a deal. The Klerik insisted...it was the best I could do.'

'What deal? For what?' I smash my fists onto the table.

Silence.

'Actually, I don't care anymore...I can't stand you or this village...'

Four heavy knocks club our door. The fragile wood almost gives. Through the cracks, three lamps outline three shadows.

I leap to my feet, moving towards the large axe sitting above the mantelpiece.

'We are Royal Enforcers. We were sent to this er...house, at Klerik Anticus' request. Open immediately.'

My muscles tense, and my heart speeds up. He's threatened so often, I never really took him seriously.

'Damn, they weren't meant to come until the morning...' Dad shakes his head. 'I wanted more time to be sure...' But he opens the door and three figures march in. They push past him, their royal blue coats soaking and dripping onto the floor.

'Is this Corena Storm?' the shortest Enforcer asks. Her eyes are sunken and dead. They drag across my face, then my body, before she turns to Dad.

'Yes, this is her.' Dad doesn't look at me.

'And does she know?'

'No. Her mum and I...we discussed it with the Klerik and decided...it's for the best...' Dad glances at me for a second, his eyes narrower than usual, before walking into the bedroom.

'What's for the best?' Pat asks.

My stomach churns and a thin film of sweat builds on my forehead.

'Your sister is to go to the northern branch of the Kurikon. There she will have a trial. For being Wiccan,' the smallest enforcer tells the room.

Patrick looks from me to our parents.

'Stop it!' he shouts. 'Don't let them take her!' My brother leaps to his feet and shouts at my parents. 'Help her.'

I've never heard him shout before.

One of the tall Enforcers gently pushes him back into his seat. His arms shake.

'Pat, it's okay.' I nod to him and face my palms to the ground. Our signal to focus on controlling our anger.

I slide out of my chair and away from the Enforcers.

'We'll give you a moment to say goodbye,' says the small one, taking a step away. The two men stand behind her, towering and silent. Both wear blue masks.

Mum's voice draws me into my parents' bedroom.

I rip the manky curtain away and glower at them. They're sitting on their bed, hugging and consoling each other, silent. Pat runs over and grabs my arm, begging them to intervene.

My whole body shakes. 'This is how you're going to end it? You disgust me. Even more than the Klerik, or the Kurikon and their stupid Gods! You should fight for me.' I step forward, pointing a finger at him, then her. 'A parent should always fight for their child, no matter what they've done. No matter who they are.'

'This is the only way.' Dad stands and walks away from the bed, rubbing the back of his neck the way he always does when he's arguing with Mum. I'm shocked it's not red and raw by now.

'It's for her own good.' Mum addresses Dad, not me. 'We've done all we can. If she doesn't change her ways, the Gods will strike her down. And us with her. I can't let the rest of us continue to be tarnished by her ungodly actions. Blizzards, plant-killing frosts and kissing girls, for Gods' sake. Not to mention what happened with Gullan...'

Mum starts ripping at her hair. She usually only twirls her hair when I'm in trouble. 'And they have a specialist... he can *remove* things that are *unnatural*. Maybe that will set her free.'

'This all about what happened with Gullan...he was always your favourite...because he was...*natural.*'

'It's nothing to do with you tearing my boy away from me. It's about you stealing the power of the God's. It's about respecting the laws of our land and about trying to help you...'

'I don't need help...'

'You do. And I can't lose another son. Pat is still innocent and can be saved, without you around. So, we've made a deal...you agree to have the surgery...the correction...and they won't hang you. But you do owe a life of servitude to the Kurikon. And if the surgery doesn't remove the stolen God's powers, then you'll be hanged.'

My throat is completely clamped. I want to scream at her. I want to strangle her. I want to make her feel the way she makes me feel every day.

But it's done. I realise it now. They've hid me for ten years, but they will do it no more.

I turn away, squirming at the list of my past *sins*, walking into the main room. Pat comes with me, his back to our parents.

'Rena...' Mum's voice is a wraith to me. 'Forgive us...'

I want to scream, but I close my eyes instead.

'Can I pack a bag?' I say to the Enforcers, struggling to stop my hands from shaking. I open my eyes, taking a long breath.

The small one nods. What she lacks in stature, she compensates in authority. Her jet-black hair is tied straight back, the only thing I can see beyond the blue mask.

Patrick runs to me and hugs me around the waist. 'Sorry, Corena. I didn't know. Honest, I didn't.' He looks up to me, his eyes swimming.

I ruffle his hair. It's silly as he's nearly as tall as me now, but it reminds me of when he was younger.

He starts smoothing it back into place. He likes it over to one side.

I turn to my tiny bed next to the fireplace. I've always hated sleeping there, but at least I had the heat of the fire at night. The only warmth in our house. Patrick and I used to tell each other scary stories in front of it, once Mum and Dad were in bed.

My first ever memory is being rocked by my grandmother, singing to me by the fire. I've never forgotten those cold but loving hands. Mum said she died when I was young.

I open my small chest, which I carved from wood I chopped. I rummage around, to take my mind off what's going to happen, removing a small bag and packing it with clothes. Like I'm going on a hunting trip with Dad or Pat. Only I'm not returning.

And lastly, I put my carved Hete figure into the pack, hiding it amongst the clothes. The Kurikon would burn it if they found it. Gullan carved it for me when we were young and it's the only thing I have left of him.

I take in the room one last time. Patrick crushes me as he gives me a final hug. At the doorway of my parents' bedroom, Mum is holding onto Dad.

'You know I would've left, if you'd just asked. If you said it was to help Pat, or because you could never forgive me, I'd have gone long ago. But I thought I was helping by staying.' The words are like poison in my mouth. I hope my parents can hear the truth in it. I hope it hurts them as much as it's hurting me.

Pat stands in front of me and I squeeze his shoulders, wringing in the last bit of love I can.

Mum tries to stand, but Dad holds her tight around her waist. Neither of them speak.

'Love you, Rena,' whispers Patrick.

'You too, Pat,' I say. 'I hope I'll see you again...someday.'

I turn to the Enforcers. 'I need to go to the toilet before we leave.'

'Be quick. And don't try running. Some of them do but we always catch them. Always. And that journey to the Kurikon will be that much crueller if you do.'

I pick up my bag, wrap myself in my furs and slide out the

door, immediately covered by the heavy snow that's falling. Dampness worms throughout my shoes as I kick through the drifts and travel towards our toilet. It's next door to our place. Handy if you really need to go, or if it's cold like tonight, but the stench evens things out.

I take a deep breath as my lips quiver. Just outside the toilet door, I stop. The small Enforcer is watching.

This is it. Goodbye to my family and my home, never to return. My parents don't want me because I don't act like the girl that they or the Kurikon want me to be. This all started because of one kiss.

One stupid kiss.

One amazing kiss.

Another loss of control.

And although they don't ever talk about it, I know it's actually because of something that happened a long time ago. One accident, one weird event, and I'm a freak of nature.

Unnatural.

If I was born a boy or a girl, all this would be different.

People wouldn't have provoked me, and I would be able to hide my power.

But I wasn't, and I'm not.

And I never will be.

Not in their eyes.

I open the door to the toilet and close it behind me. It takes a few seconds for my eyes to adjust to the darkness, but I feel my way to the third cubicle. I helped Dad build the toilet shed years ago, so I know a spare axe sits in a unit above it.

When I was twelve, a wolf walked into the shed. I was on my own, so hid in here until Dad came to find me. He chased the wolf away, and the axe has been here ever since.

My fingers search through cobwebs and dust until my hand caresses the smooth, varnished handle, and I cut my index finger on the sharp edge of the metal. Here in the north, we keep our axes sharp and our eyes sharper. It has been known for the

MegaFauna of the extreme north to occasionally wander our way.

My hands shake as I prepare for an escape. I face the closed door, expecting the Enforcer to have followed me, and for it to open any second.

This is probably stupid, but there's no way I'm going to the Kurikon and letting them cut me up. Like they think removing a part of me will remove my power. I'd rather run north sand fight the MegaFauna than serve the Kurikon for rest of my days.

I kneel and push aside a loose piece of wood, next to the outflow pipe. And I crawl out of the far side of the toilet. Fortunately, the angle between our house and where I stand means they can't see me, but it won't be long before they come after me. So I start to run.

I'm in the woods behind our house. These woods are my real home. I know every tree, root and sapling. I smile more widely at the sight of them than I do when I see my own parents.

What does that say about me? What does that say about them?

I spot a movement in the shadows, but I don't wait to see who it is.

I run on my tiptoes, relying on the awful wind and sleet to cover the noise of my escape. But I can't go too far tonight. Not in this weather. Even us Storms can't survive this far north with no food or supplies.

Not unless it's actually life or death.

I'm almost at *my* tree, the tallest in the woods, the one I sleep in when I can't stand to be at home. At the base, I put my toes into the first foothold and begin to climb.

'Rena? What you doing out this late?' Deren asks. His deep voice is so familiar to me after years of scolding and failed flirting.

'Just getting some firewood.'

'Firewood? Up a tree during a storm? Whatever you're doing, just go home. I'll have no nocturnal absconders on my watch.'

He starts to walk back to the village, expecting me to follow, but I remain.

'Come on, you really want to stay out in this?' He holds his shivering hands up to the sky.

'I can't go home.'

'What have you done this time?'

I can't believe he's not heard. Either that, or he's just playing the fool to get me down.

'Nothing. They just don't want me.' The panic writhes up my throat, clawing at my words. If I'm caught because of Deren... Deren? No, that can't happen.

'Now, now, Corena. We've all put the past where it belongs. We all agreed we'd forget about it and move on...'

'You think they've moved on? Deren, I'm begging you. Just leave me. Just for tonight, please? I promise I won't get you in trouble. I won't tell anyone you saw me.'

He squints and comes closer. 'You've done something big this time, haven't you?'

'No.' I jump to the ground, ready to run.

'You smell awful. You look frightened, Rena. I never thought that would be possible, but you do. Tell me or I'll report this. Your mum and I were *very* close once. I won't lie to her.'

The thought of him and my mum being together causes a surge in my right arm.

He takes a step closer. His left arm slides inside his cloak.

I sprint. Before I hurt him. My feet squelch in the mud as I leap logs and duck beneath low branches. Running without thought or direction. Eyes down.

I can't be a Kurikon slave.

I can't let them *remove* anything.

I won't.

It's part of me and it's what makes me, me.

When my legs start to burn, I glance back. I've lost Deren. For now. I slow a little to catch my breath and work out where I am.

I've gone too far north, so I realign my path west towards the Rushing River.

I open my mouth, using the rainwater to wash it out, and clear the poison from my last conversation with my parents. I close my eyes and enjoy the falling water, rinsing my hair and skin.

As I jog through the mist, angry thoughts about my parents seep in, but it's too painful and energy-sapping, so I think about Patrick.

I hope he's okay.

He's annoying, but he's the only one who has ever accepted me for what I am. The only one not terrified of the things I've done. Or the choices I've made. And for that, if nothing else, I love him.

My breath clouds the air in front of me and low-lying mist makes it difficult to see the river. Until I'm in it.

My feet splash to a stop, and the arctic chill of the water bites into my skin. The iciness travels quickly up my body and my teeth are chattering so loud, I'm sure the whole woods can hear.

I walk downstream. If I stick with the river, I'll be in Hullspire by morning. I could get away on a ship and start over somewhere else. Somewhere where the people will never have heard of me or the things I've done.

That thought makes me stumble, slow, then stop.

I've spent years suppressing memories and powers I can't explain. Frightened the Kurikon will punish me for them. And now they've punished me anyway. Maybe I need to stop running away. Maybe I need to go to a place where I can discover why I'm here.

What was the Gods design for me?

I stare up, beyond the sky.

Am I here to scurry in the shadows or am I here to blaze light upon everything the Kurikon want to keep in the dark?

People like me. Wiccans. We're different, but we're still people and someone needs to stick up for us.

Loud, crunching footsteps approach from the woods, so I

paddle over the river and slip behind a bush on the far side. I can't see their faces, but several people stand on the opposite shore, looking around.

The mist lifts and Patrick, Deren, and the three Enforcers search all around, the small one with a knife to my brother's neck.

'We know you are out there,' shouts the smallest Enforcer. 'Listen to me. You are a lost soul, Corena Storm. You belong to the Kurikon. Come with us now, quiet-like, or your brother will take your place. I get paid either way.'

I can't let them take him.

No matter what happens to me.

CHAPTER 3

My heart's tight, my blood thumping. I won't let them hurt Patrick.

I grit my teeth and clench my fists. But I walk towards them.

'There she is,' shouts Deren, and their eyes are back in my direction.

He aims his crossbow, and I raise my arms as I approach. The small Enforcer keeps her knife close to Patrick's throat. A small line of blood slides down into his

shirt.

I take a deep breath, long and slow. It would do no good to lose control now; I must allow them to take me. But once Pat's safe, they'll pay.

'Let him return home.' I address the small, female Enforcer. 'You have me.' My axe bumps against my leg, hanging from the belt, well hidden under my cloak.

'We do have you,' she says, licking her lips. 'This sort of defiance and deceit isn't tolerated in your new service.' She lowers her knife. 'Warden, take the boy back home.'

As Deren drags him away, Pat begs the Enforcers. 'Please don't take my sister.'

They ignore him.

'Take care of yourself.' My words are dry, and I fight the urge to grab him and hold him forever.

'I made you something for your birthday,' he says, his shoulders shaking. 'Maybe I can send it to the place you're going?'

He remembered. The only one to remember. My throat tightens, and I almost chase after him.

Deren pulls Pat into the mist, and he's gone. Each step away shreds my heart.

I might never see him again and the thought extinguishes the small blaze which had been inside me. My arms go weak, and I allow the two tall, silent Enforcers to haul me away. Even the small one's quiet as they take me back through the woods.

The air gets colder.

How could they do this to me?

My teeth chatter. My arms shiver.

Their only daughter.

A silver layer forms on the ground, obscuring the bases of the trunks.

Now, they're dead to me.

The bird song quiets, and the fog thickens.

I slip on a patch of frozen ground. My arms shake as the two Enforcers holding me tremble.

We stop. They throw me to the hard earth.

'Get wrapped up,' instructs the small Enforcer, glancing at me. 'Strange it's come on this quick.'

They wrap up warmer, putting on gloves and an extra coat.

They give me nothing. But I still have my furs, soaked as they are from the river.

Every inch of me is freezing, my fingers struggling to work, but the cold is exhilarating. My heart thumps and my mind is clearer than it's ever been. I bend down and touch the sheet of ice covering the ground and a surge of energy travels up my arm and then back down.

My power is usually related to my emotions. But it's never been this strong before.

'Get up,' says the small Enforcer, kicking me in the stomach.

I lurch backwards, winded. A wave of rage floods me as my head smacks the solid soil.

An icicle falls from the tree next to us. I close my eyes, knowing what's about to happen but unable to stop it. A deep, guttural scream rakes through the frigid air. A screeching harmony. Horror rips at my chest as I process what's happening. But I can't stop it.

I'm losing control.

Again.

I open my eyes and stare at my vengeance. Blood blankets sheer white. The icicle went deep into his leg, sharp as a blade. Turning onto my side, I retch and retch.

Finally, when nothing comes, I spit until my mouth is dry.

It was an accident.

No.

No, it wasn't. I did it.

I wanted it to happen. But not to him. He didn't seem cruel. To the small one. And now I've hurt someone. Badly. For no reason. Just like before.

Gloved hands grab my hair and haul me to my feet. They tear off my hair band and cast it into the pool of blood. I stare at it, soaking in the innocent blood.

'You murdering, little witch!' The small Enforcer punches me on the cheek.

The energy that flowed in me a moment ago is gone. Spent.

'Move.' The small Enforcer pushes me in the small of my back, but I don't move. Then she slaps me across the face. I fall backwards.

I face her, eyes unblinking. The ground has become slushy, the ice pooling in puddles. Drips fall from the trees above us, sticking my soaked hair to my head.

The big Enforcer crouches over the injured one, checking his pulse.

'I'm getting my hair band,' I say, focussing on anything except what has happened.

The small enforcer moves in front of me. 'You're a slave now, awaiting trial for your Wiccan ways. You'll do as we say from now on. If you argue or defy, we'll hurt you, then your family. And we'll punish you for this.' She points to the bleeding body, which whimpers weakly.

I try to run past her, but she pounces on me, wrestling me to the ground. She presses her knife against my cheek. The sting comes, then the blood.

'Yes, I'll spill your blood. Like you spilled Graf's. I know what you are, and you don't deserve to live.' She stands but remains ready to pin me again. 'Sorg, carry him. If he survives the journey, we'll take him to the Klerik for healing. If not, his soul ascends to the Haven and his body to the wolves of the woods.'

The tall Enforcer, Sorg, lifts his wounded comrade with ease and stands beside his chief. 'We can't let him die, Hiro.'

'Blame the Wiccan if he does,' the small enforcer, Hiro, replies.

Sorg moves closer. His mask is now removed.

My breath sticks.

Where most people have eyes, a nose, ears and a mouth, there is nothing. Not even the shape or outline of where they should be.

His head is almost perfectly spherical, like an egg.

I try to say something, but I can't.

Tears run.

They stare at me, both shaking. The temperature has risen again, but they continue to shake. Rage? Or fear?

The tall one spits at me, his saliva landing in my hair.

I couldn't even see where he spat from. There aren't even any holes in his head. How does he hear? Or speak? Or see? Or spit?

I shudder.

Hiro sneers. 'We should take her to the Queen. Make her suffer for longer than if we kill her now. Plus, we haven't had a Wiccan trial in years, so this could be the thing to get us back in the Queen's favour. Yes, could be the thing. Just need to get the Kurikon to agree. That could be tricky.' She turns to the one she calls Sorg. 'Tie her up this time...'

'You sure you don't want to punish her now,' says Sorg. His arms still shake. He wants to strike me. I step back.

'No, we need her alive. The reward would be...well, imagine having your face back? And serving our Queen, like we once did? And if we did her now, the Kurikon would fire us, too. No point in being in the bad books of the two most powerful things in this world.'

The faceless man nods.

'Good, I'll bind her.' Hiro reaches into her pack to get the rope.

As she does, I dart across the ground. But the pressure of Sorg's heavy body crushes mine.

A mouthful of blood, mud and slush muffles my scream. He's hurt me. A broken rib or perhaps worse. But I'll tuck the pain away. As long as Patrick is safe, I'll take whatever they give me.

I've had to my whole life.

Weird.

Different.

Freak.

Unnatural.

I hate them all.

The shaft of my axe presses into my pelvis. As they rip off my furs, they find it and toss my weapon into the woods. I try not to shiver, but it just makes the shaking worse.

Maybe my parents were right to let me go.

Maybe I'm a danger to them and Patrick.

But I do know one thing.

I owe it to Pat, and to others like me, to try and break the shackles of our oppression.

One day we will rise from this dark place.

And the Kurikon will wish they never tried to extinguish our light.

~

Sorg, the faceless man, drags me through the village square, his mask now back on. One final humiliation before I leave. Perhaps it's vengeance for hurting their compatriot. Perhaps it's the Klerik or even my parents' idea. But they're not here.

Deren stands among a small crowd which has gathered despite curfew. I suppose it's the most exciting thing to happen since... well, since my ...incident...ten years ago. I've been the outsider since. An outcast to all the other children who were once my friends.

As I walk through, Asta lurks in the shadows. She looks nervous, not keen to step forward and jeer at me like the rest of them, but she couldn't stay away either.

Did she even like me? Perhaps Anticus forced her, but why then did I feel something in her kiss? I scan her pretty face and spot no hate or fear. Her eyes follow me.

I look away.

This chapter of my life is ending.

A small group of people around my age step forward into the road. I knew them in my old, Gods-fearing life. They point and make comments to each other. This kind of thing used to annoy me, but now I'm numb to their cruelty. I'm numb to almost everything.

'Burn at Ka-Ferno's gate!'

'Good riddance, you never belonged here, Wiccan!'

'Go elsewhere, freak!'

'Monster!'

'Leave and pray to the gods that the Kurikon can make you normal!'

Even if they can make me normal, will I ever feel normal?

Is normal even something to strive for?

The young girl in me whispers yes. The person I've become screams no.

I won't change what I am for them. I can't go back to living a lie.

So, I'll take whatever they do to me.

They throw snowballs at me but none of them hit.

They can do what they want because right now, nothing can hurt me.

I'm a Storm, even though the name is now emotionally dead to me.

And I will rise.

CHAPTER 4

Sorg drags me along like a horse, leading me with the rope. The friction burns my neck.

But I don't say a word to him. Every time I look at where his face should be, and see only smooth skin, I shudder all over. He'll never forgive me for killing Graf, who I think was his brother or partner...I wouldn't forgive anyone if Pat were killed.

At least the diminutive scutter - Hiro - speaks to me. Even if it's just to throw horrible insults my way or taunt me about what's coming when we reach Rejik.

She seems convinced the Kurikon will let them take me all the way to the Queen, for some reason. But if I know that will help them, I'll do whatever I can to make sure we don't get there!

They threw away my pack days ago. My feet have gone through four stages of blistering. On day two I discarded my shoes before my heels wore to the bone. The open wounds could be infected, but at least there is still flesh there.

A scream pierces the air. In one of the fields, two women hold down a young girl. They are robbing her, even removing her clothes. I surge towards them, but the rope tugs on my neck.

'We should help her.' I glare at where Sorg's face should be.

'No,' says Hiro, moving between us. 'We know the only reason you want to help her.' She points at my face. 'As if being Wiccan didn't make you enough of an aberration!'

My arms shake and my neck strains as I pull on my collar, which is crushing the lump in my throat.

Hiro laughs. 'We must continue. No more distractions.'

The girl is now lying, almost naked, while the two robbers divide the spoils.

'Perhaps we should intervene,' says Sorg.

Hiro turns on her compatriot. 'We must get the slave to Fort Lorn, and then onto the capital. She is worth our freedom. Or even more. I could be reinstated to General. You could get your face back. And I'm sure you want compensation for Graf. Don't you want something to show for his death? If we don't make this work, his murder is for nothing.'

'What happened to Graf was an accident. I loved him more than anything in this world, but the Wiccan did not deliberately hurt him.'

'You believe that?'

'Doesn't matter what I think. He's dead. She will be soon. We'll all die sometime.'

'I am sorry about Graf.' As I say it, the rope tightens for a few seconds but then slackens.

Sorg nods to me but does not reply.

'But we need to help her.' I stare at Sorg where his eyes should be.

'Hiro?' He turns his head towards his peer. 'We should help. It's the right thing to do.'

'You're a bigger fool than I thought.' She turns to the victim in the field. 'You want to help people and be a hero? Heroes don't live to see tomorrow. I intend to. Now move.'

Hiro walks past us and doesn't look back. The girl from the field screams again.

'I can't believe you're going to let it happen.' I strain to see. 'What kind of Enforcers are you? You're supposed to help people.'

This cannot be the world I live in.

Sorg just lowers his head and walks on, pulling me behind him. 'We cannot help everyone.'

The faceless man seems to have also lost all he cares about. His face is empty but his soul beneath is an abyss of apathy. He knows the right thing to do, but he doesn't have any fire left in him to act.

A few miles further along the ride, two men charge along the road behind us. When they reach us, they stop, catching their breath.

'What's wrong?' I ask.

'Gory Fire-Wiccan attacked us back there.' When the man speaks, I recognise him as one of the attackers from the field.

'Serves you right, I saw you robbing that girl.'

The one who spoke glares at me. He notices the chain.

'Hardly in a position to judge us,' he says. 'What's this one done?'

'None of your business,' says Hiro. 'Move along. Be glad we're not arresting you.'

The man considers arguing, but just nudges his partner and they start to jog ahead.

'What did the Wiccan look like?' I shout after them.

One of them stops. 'Just like you, actually.'

'We'll stop here, Sorg. Tie her up next to the horses and give her one of their apples. She can drink from the trough.' Hiro flashes her little beaver teeth and grins at her own wickedness.

'Trough water's my favourite actually.' I return my best smile. It's usually reserved for the rations boy, who distributes the Queen's clemency in the village square. My mouth waters at the thought of the stale bread or the bashed fruit he used to bring every Sunday.

Hiro spits on me, then kicks over the trough.

She must hope I'm dehydrated enough to drink it from the ground. But I keep my eyes on her, even when Sorg jerks my rope. Finally, Sorg puts on his mask, and they enter the inn.

I used to think the men in this world were awful, but between Hiro and Asta, I think women are not much better. Sometimes, it makes me glad that I'm neither.

The door opens, then closes, and the smell of boiled potatoes and garlic wafts towards me. My stomach crumples in on itself.

And that's it. I can't take it anymore. Hitting the deck, I lick up the water from the earth. I taste grit, horseshit, and other debris.

'I tried ground once, but I much prefer tatties.'

I look up and see a man tying up his horse. His wide smile immediately morphs into a familiar look of pity. It's the slight extension of the lower lip and the upturned eyebrows. The same one we get from all the rich people when we sell them wood at the market.

But even by my usual standards, I know I'm a disgraceful sight. Dirt covers my hands, muddy water drips from my face and my clothes must stink beyond measure.

'I don't know; the dirt adds a little texture to the water.' I hope he doesn't complain about me inside the bar. I don't need to give the Enforcers any more excuse to beat me.

He laughs and rummages in his side-pack, producing a small canteen of water. He hands it to me, and I grasp it for a moment, turning my head to look at him. He doesn't blanch or turn away or say anything.

I turn the canteen upside down and drain the contents in one go.

As I pass it back, a small smile starts to develop on his dark face. He displays some teeth; brighter than snow and much whiter than any I've ever seen. He disappears into the inn without a word.

I sit beside the horses and eat my apple. It's old, and when I bite into it, it's brown and bitter. But I eat the whole thing and take two more from the horse's pile, finishing them just as quick.

My mind drifts to the Wiccan that attacked the robbers and saved that girl. A Wiccan that looks just like me. Wild thoughts run through my head, including me being able to be in two places at once. But that's ridiculous. Even for a Wiccan, that seems unlikely. And then the idea that I like the most begins to take set.

Pat.

But he doesn't have powers. They said a Fire-Wiccan.

I hope I'm right and wrong in equal measure. If it's him, and he's following me, protecting people, I'd be so proud of him. But if he's following, he's also going to the one place I'd not want him to.

I try to undo the rope, but the knot's an unfamiliar one. And even if I could get the rope off, where would I go? Escape doesn't work because they'll just go back and punish my family.

I could try and find Pat, send him home. But that's if it is him. And the longer I think of it, the more I begin to doubt it. How could he get away? How could he track us? Mum would never let him leave.

The sun is now at its highest and I'm soaked beneath my cloak and clothes. I'm dressed for the colder north and every step south makes my clothes less and less suitable.

They stick...down there...and I have to adjust myself inconspicuously.

I think of sitting by our fire at night, hugging Patrick and trying to keep the cold away. The smell of cooking fish circulates the house. But even a stoked fire couldn't keep out the frostiness of my parents. In the same way, the heat of the south is unable to thaw the icy heart they nurtured in me.

I wake to a kick from Hiro.

'Up, move.' She gives me a second kick before moving on.

I take it because I'm too tired to do anything about it. I'm saving these up, storing them deep inside me for the moment when the tables turn.

And I'm terrified if I use my powers again, I might kill someone else…

Above me, Sorg belches and I get the smell of ale and garlic from his breath. He unties me and pulls me along behind him. I walk unsteady for a few steps then my legs give way. I've nothing left.

Hiro is on me in a second. 'Get up, slave, or I'll drag you the whole way to the Kurikon, then to the capital.'

'Why are you being like this?'

'You have a dirty little Wiccan secret. I've seen one or two of your kind in my time and you're going to get what you deserve.' She turns to Sorg. 'And our reward will be…well, worth more than a freak's life. We just need to convince the High Klerik she's worth taking to the Queen. That she's beyond rehabilitation.'

Sorg shakes his head.

'You still don't believe she's evil? That's your problem, Sorg, you always see the best in people. But I can see her true nature. And it's dark.'

Honestly, Hiro, you have no idea.

She smiles widely before turning back to me. 'So, get up and do as you're told. We'll give you some food if you start walking. Now.'

The thought of food is enough to get me up, but a few yards later, I trip over my own feet, and I'm back down.

'It's no good, I'm too weak.' I can feel my body eating my muscles.

'Fine, give her a potato, Sorg.'

The tall Enforcer throws a potato at me, making sure it hits the soil before I can catch it. But I don't care; I scoop it up, chew and finish in less than a minute.

'Right, move,' Hiro commands.

The rope is taut most of the time. Sorg is well fed and fit and his legs are longer than mine, so I'm dragged like a horse, but at least I'm on my feet.

We walk for an hour in the baking afternoon sun; the land becomes drier, green landscape much more common. The cold north, the only place I've ever known, is now well behind us.

My soaked clothes are chaffing everywhere. I pull a bloodied hair band from inside my cloak and place it on my head, pushing the dirty, sweat-soaked hair from my face. It's a temporary relief.

My right leg goes. I hit the dusty road hard. My head spins and I'm so dizzy I almost vomit. 'Water,' I say, my voice cracking. 'Please.'

'GET UP!' Hiro gives me another kick in the ribs. They still hurt from Sorg suffocating me in the woods and I curl up, clutching my middle.

A second kick to the back cause me to arch the opposite way for a moment, before curling up. Hiro spits on my face three times. 'Get up, slave. I'm going to count to three, then I'm going to...'

'How much for the slave?' I recognise the voice.

'She's not for sale, sir,' replies Hiro, turning to the speaker.

'She is a slave, no? Aren't all slaves for sale at the right price?'

I squint at the speaker, who is on a horse and framed by the sun. It's the man from the inn.

'Not this one, sir. She is special. She is going to the Kurikon, then to the capital.'

'Special, huh? I can see that. I'll pay you handsomely.'

I watch him dismount and move closer, a large moneybag jingling.

'It's not about the price. She is worth much more than coin, sir.'

'Well, what do you want for her?'

'Nothing you can provide, sir.'

'I assure you, Madam Enforcer, I can provide much. In case you know of me not, I will introduce myself. I am Terra Scorpa,

Prince of Haras, and I assure you my favour and my money will be as good as the person's you intend to sell this girl to.'

I watch the negotiation, knowing whoever this Prince is, he'll treat me better than my current slavers. I pray, for the first time in years, they can strike a deal.

Hiro and Sorg both bow. Though he is not their Prince, he is still royalty and it's wise to show some respect. Even I know that.

'I'm afraid this girl is destined for the Queen herself, Prince Terra. We take her first to the Kurikon at Fort Lorn, then to the capital.'

'I understand. I've met the Queen...a great lady...my respect for her is countless and I will not interfere with her business. But perhaps I can ride with you for a while? I've never seen this Kurikon at Fort Lorn. And I'm planning to stop at Ghondulon, then Rejik. Perhaps I could speak to the Queen and change her mind. It seems our paths may bind together.'

'Prince Terra, let me assure you this slave is not worth pursuing.'

'And pray tell me why? You seem adamant that you know my taste in slaves better than myself.'

'I did not mean offence, Prince Terra. But it's not a matter of your taste in slaves, but more her nature that would displease you.'

'And what would displease me about her nature? For it seems to me it's your nature and your treatment of slaves that is question-able right now. How can you chain any person, slave or nay, to a horse post and make them drink trough water from the ground? In my kingdom, I would have you flayed and executed.' He looks from Hiro to Sorg. His hand drifts towards his sheathed sword.

Do it. Do it. Please do it and release me from them. And finish Hiro for me as well.

'Prince Terra, this slave here is a dangerous Wiccan and a murderer. For thousands of years, they have stolen the power of the Gods and if given the chance, she'd kill us all. Luckily, we have a bargaining chip – she cares far too much for her brother, and I hope she remembers that if she considers any of her magic.'

'And you are certain she is a Wiccan?'

'Oh yes, I am sure. I know the signs. I've seen one before, and I'm lucky to have survived it. Fifty killed by that Wiccan before she was subdued. It's in her eyes, too.'

They all stare into my eyes, like they have Wiccan written on them.

I want to shout back at them, to deny it, but I can't.

Hiro is right that I am Wiccan. But she's wrong about one thing. I won't use my powers, even if I had the energy. I won't prove her right.

CHAPTER 5

Prince Terra rides alongside us, which is a distraction and no mistake. But his presence also seems to have curbed the cruelty of my slavers. Now I'm getting water from a canteen and the odd scrap to eat.

'So where are your roots, slave?' the Prince asks.

I ignore him addressing me as 'slave', especially as he's a Prince. To be honest, I can't believe he's talking to me at all.

'In the north; my village is several days north of here.'

'What is it like there? I've never travelled that far.'

'Cold. Very cold. And dull.'

'And the trade?'

'Wood mostly. We farm a little, but the ground is frozen much of the year, so we usually trade wood for crops with the neighbouring villages to the south. We also farm and sell ice to rich lands farther south.'

'So, you were a slave to woodcutters?'

'No, I was a daughter to woodcutters. I was a woodcutter myself, and an ice-farmer, until three days ago.'

'So, you were free?'

'I was.'

'Then how do you come to be here?'

'My parents let the Kurikon take me. To be become one of their *slaves*. They used the word reform. It means the same thing with the Kurikon.'

Silence. The Prince doesn't look at me; instead, he looks off into the distance.'And this is normal amongst your people?'

'I don't think so. My parents just didn't want me around. I'm not so sure they ever did.'

'My parents are cruel, also. But even *they* would not sell me as slave to the Kurikon.' His shakes his head, his hand slipping inside his cloak.

Hiro and Sorg have their heads turned a little, as they walk ahead of us. But they know my story. Or most of it.

'It was for my brother's sake, I think.'

'No, no, no. Sell the cow, sell land, sell wood, but do not sell the daughter. This is not how it should be done.'

'Well, that's what happened. Though I'm not sure sell is the right word. Gave up is more the truth.' The words, the story, they are already becoming dull and true to me. I want to change the subject, but I'm not sure I should be asking questions to a prince.

'How did you end up in the part of the world, Prince Terra?'

'Ah, now that is a very good question, with a very interesting answer.' He looks down to me with a smile. 'I have a blood debt to settle. You know a blood debt?'

I nod.

'A man borrowed much coin from my father and fled here. I must find him before I can return home. But I lost his trail a few days ago. All I want is to travel this world, but I must be the dutiful son.'

'Then why don't you just travel. Surely your father would understand. You are a prince, surely you can do whatever you like?'

He looks at me for a few seconds before trotting ahead and leaning down to talk to Hiro.

I stumble after them, struggling with Sorg's latest pace, but fuelled by the cooked lamb and wine at our last stop. I got the fat of the lamb.

As we move further south, not only has it become warmer, drier and the roads better maintained, we also see far more life. The towns we stop in have a greater number of people and houses, large expanses of farmland, growing acres of crops and endless vineyards. I guess this is how they supply the millions in the cities. And what they use to trade with our people for wood and animal furs. And my specialty. Ice.

My exposed, reddened skin blisters, particularly on my neck and face. My once shiny white hair is now a dull, crispy grey and my clothes are hanging off me.

During the late afternoon, my legs begin to wobble again. I attempt to tell Sorg, but my throat and tongue are so dry, it hurts to try.

I fall.

And the pain of it brings a welcome relief from the screaming agony brought by each step.

Dried dirt from the road puffs up and into my mouth and nose, choking me. But I do not lift my head.

Sorg notices me spluttering but continues to drag me. 'Get up!'

I can't. My hands grasp the rope around my neck and pull at it to stop the pressure but he yanks it again, crushing my throat.

'Get up, slave. We do not stop yet.'

The sound of hooves is followed by a release in rope tension. I glance up to see Prince Terra jumping from the saddle, taking the rope from Sorg and kneeling in front of me.

'Come girl, you shall ride for a while.' He helps me mount his horse.

We have few horses in our village, so I've never learnt to ride, but the Prince uses the rope that was around my neck to lash me to the saddle.

'I will lead the horse, you just need to stay upon him,' he says, nodding and giving a half smile. 'His name is Pegasus.'

'Prince Terra, she is a slave and not worthy of riding upon this horse. Make her walk.' Hiro points to the ground.

'She is a young girl, whatever else she might be, and is exhausted. No good to your Queen or to you if she dies on the road.' The Prince puts his hand inside his cloak.

'It is beneath a Prince to walk while a slave rides,' Sorg replies.

'I believe it's princely to put his people first and to value all lives, slaves or noble. Wiccan or not.'

'But she is not one of your people. She is one of ours and our Queen would be horrified to see this.' Hiro's face begins to redden.

'That may be but ride she shall. And that is the end of the matter.' The Prince opens his light, velvet cloak and rests his hand upon his sword hilt. 'Are we clear?'

Hiro nods. 'Yes, *Prince*.'

He leads us forward, leaving the Royal Enforcers in our wake.

'So tell me, dangerous, murderous Wiccan, why these two want to take you to your Queen so badly?' He smiles, clearly mocking Hiro and Sorg. He really thinks I'm not dangerous.

Although part of me is unsure, I decide to be partly honest, with him. A tiny, loose snowflake of hope of escape floats inside me.

'I did kill someone. It was an accident, but that part is true.'

'I have also killed,' adds the Prince. 'Mine was less accidental but in war, you don't have a choice. Fighting for what you believe in can often come at a cost. Killing itself does not reveal you to be a bad person. It is the reason that counts.'

'Is anger a good reason?'

'Sometimes it's the only reason. I suspect your captivity has not been kind with these two. I will try to make it a little better while I am here.'

I can't help but smile, despite the pain in my cracking lips.

He's the first boy...man that I've ever felt this way about. Maybe I do like men but I've just never met the *right* one. Or maybe I'm confused because he's so kind and handsome and he sticks up for people, like me, in a world where nobody else does.

Even though my fortunes have improved, the nagging thought at the back of my mind tugs away.

I'm a Wiccan slave.

He is a Prince.

What does he want from me?

CHAPTER 6

By early evening, I'm walking again. The Prince gave me water and some of his food rations as I rode. Fortunately, we're about to stop. I can see the *abyss of hope* just ahead.

'Prince Terra, we approach the Kurikon. You'll not be admitted entry,' says Hiro, smiling. 'Because you worship those false gods in your country.'

Prince Terra places his hand on his sword hilt. 'I'd like you to speak more respectfully of my country and its religion.' His hand moves back to his reign. 'Fortunately, in my land we have more tolerance for other's beliefs, and I will forgive your ignorant comment.'

Hiro nods, a small sneer visible on her lowered face that the Prince misses.

'I will make a small camp here and await your return. If the girl is to go to the capital, I will escort you. If not, then we will part ways, and I will resume my blood debt hunt.'

'Fine.' Hiro turns away.

I watch him unload his pack on his horse and get ready to settle in. I've no idea why he's suddenly decided to delay his mission to accompany us. Perhaps he's just a good person, watching out for my welfare. Or perhaps he wants something else from me.

As we put more distance between us, an urge to remain with him builds. An instant affinity I've rarely felt before. If I can get away from this place, I'll do whatever it takes.

My eyes also drift back down the road we've taken, lingering upon the distant horizon, hoping against hope that I see a white-haired boy following us.

It's a fool's hope, but I've so little else left that I cling to it.

'Let me do the talking, Sorg. Everything rests on us convincing the Kurikon that the Queen needs to see her and that we should be the ones to take her. It will be a hard sell, but neither of us can go on with this life. We were once so important, and I can't stand the shame anymore.'

For a second, I almost feel sorry for Hiro, but the memories of her cruelty are still too close. She's like me in some ways, she's an outcast from her people, just trying to find a way to be accepted. I suppose we all are.

Fort Lorn is the grandest, richest, and most beautiful building I've ever seen. That shabby place we worshipped at back home is like a shed compared to this.

Ten tall towers, thin and sharp, ascend towards the sky. One for each of the Gods, I suppose. They remind me of the ice-shards which formed in the forest. They surround a monstrous semi-sphere, about half the height of each tower, but built entirely of glass. Hollow and brittle, like my starving body.

This doesn't seem at all like a place of worship. More like a palace.

We move along a black brick road, smooth and wide. Flanking the road on either side are fields of crops to our left and the most beautiful flowers to our right. A rainbow of colours transcends my view. After years of white and brown, this is almost overload. Nothing nearly as magnificent grows back home.

A honey aroma drifts through the air, reminding me of Gullan. He worked trade with some of the farmers further south. He'd always bring home a little honey each month for us to share. I'd forgotten about honey.

A small creature lands on my arm. Its wings are as stunningly colored as the flowers, but it's the patterns that seize my affection. Many more fly around from flower to flower, small groups floating along gracefully and making everything they land upon even more gorgeous.

I devour the wide range of colours, scents and varieties as we move towards a large house beside the road. Outside, sit several Enforcers. They smoke their pipes and barely acknowledge our approach.

'Good evening,' says Hiro, as she pulls up alongside the Enforcer-house.

'Evening. You bringing in a newbie?' asks one Enforcer, taking a step closer to us.

'Yes, sir.'

'Fine. Take her to tower three.'

'She's not a normal one. We need to see the High Klerik.' Hiro stands a little straighter as she says it.

'The High Klerik is at feast. He has a royal audience. Take her to tower three.' The Enforcer turns back to his colleagues, and they resume their chatter.

'Can I speak to you?' Hiro asks the chief Enforcer. 'In private.' She dismounts and moves to the opposite side of the road from the house.

The Enforcer follows her.

They chat quietly and I don't hear any words, but I do see her slip something into the Enforcers hand that looks a lot like coin.

'Sammer. Ride ahead and let the High Klerik know about our

arrivals,' instructs the chief Enforcer. He returns to his spot outside the house and picks up his pipe.

The one called Sammer shakes his head, but he must be junior, because he doesn't argue. He saddles up and races down the road ahead of us.

Hiro nods to the chief Enforcer as we move up the black brick road once again.

Now Prince Terra is no longer with us, Hiro has the collar back on my neck, but I allow it. I'll bide my time. Exposing myself here would not serve me.

When she shoves me in the back, I spin round and face her, eyes inches from her face. So tempting.

'Oh girl, you better perform when we tell you to. I just shelled out a whole load of coin I can't afford. If the High Klerik doesn't agree to send you to the capital for a trial, then I'm going to go back to your little village and make sure that brother of yours has an *accident*. And you'll never get to see your new admirer, either. So just keep that in mind when we go in here. Move.' She shoves me forward and the tension falls from my shoulders.

Sammer rides back to us, just before we reach the main building.

We sit just beneath one of the mammoth towers and their height dizzies me when I stare straight up at the top. There's also a mammoth granite statue of the Queen, arm in arm with the High Klerik.

'His aide will see you initially. He'll decide if you get to see the High Klerik himself.'

Hiro nods to Sammer, who rides past us to re-join his smoking buddies back at the house.

The semi-spherical glass building is out of this world. We reach the bottom of the steps leading to the front door, the evening sun reflects off the entire building, nearly as beautiful as a sunset by the frozen river back home.

'Close your mouth girl and drop the act. I won't buy it and neither will the Klerik.'

'It's just incred—'

'Shut your mouth! Or are you deaf, too?'

The anger bubbles but I force it away. It will only make me do something I'll regret. I relax my shoulders and let my arms hang loose.

A short man, wearing a long, white robe rushes down to meet us. He reminds me of a rabbit. We stop half-way up the steps.

'Follow me.' He turns and bounds back up the stairs.

The doors to the glass semi-sphere swing open in time with his return, seemingly unmanned.

As I pass beneath the twin chunks of stunningly sculpted birch, my feet purr at the smooth, green marble beneath. Chills shoot up my legs towards my heart, where they rest. I try to calm myself.

I'm an iceberg. They will not break me.

A glass arc covers the rest of this massive Kurikon facility. Just ahead, we pass into a secondary semi-sphere, smaller than the outer glass one, this one composed of more traditional woods and metals.

We walk along a long, narrow corridor, the marble beneath my feet replaced by comforting, familiar wood.

The aide turns right and takes us through a much smaller door, into a side room off the corridor. It's small, dimly lit by two candles, but luxurious in its contents.

'Please, sit.' He indicates two tall chairs which sit opposite an oak desk.

Hiro sits but Sorg remains by my side.

The aide takes his seat, facing the three of us.

'So, you requested an assessment of the girl?'

Hiro nods. 'She is accused of being Wiccan. We have seen her power. It is beyond reform. She needs to be taken to the capital for a trial.'

'A Wiccan?' The aide raises his eyebrows. Then his eyes narrow on me. 'We haven't had a Wiccan trial in years. They were hunted and destroyed by our glorious Queen, relieving this world of their unnaturalness.' He stands and walks round his desk, moving to within a foot of me. 'Evidence?'

Hiro spins round to face me as she speaks. 'She killed an Enforcer. And the local Klerik in her village said there have been other unexplained events in the past.'

'How?'

'Ice.'

'An ice-Wiccan? That's a new one. Not sure I remember any of those from the dark days. Still, I will treat your claim with the respect it deserves.' He walks away from me and returns to his seat. 'She will be tested immediately. I'll inform the High Klerik. Take her to the large doors at the far end of the corridor. Give the Enforcer this note.'

He hands a small piece of parchment to Hiro.

'Thank you,' she replies, bowing slightly. She turns to face me. 'Now, we'll see exactly what you are, girl.'

CHAPTER 7

My naked front is cold against the stone surface.

My breasts are small and flat, which right now is a blessing. I thrash and pull, but my hands and ankles are pinned to the slab. Two male Enforcers stand at the door, their eyes drinking in my body, making me shiver.

They left my bottoms on, luckily. Not sure the Enforcers would be so keen if they could see down there.

The High Klerik stands to my right, along with his aide and my two Enforcers. He looks like a winter swallow in his grand, fine dress. Rimmed with Godsgold by the looks of it. Probably worth more than anything my family will make in their entire lifetime of selling wood.

Another boy stands just behind the High Klerik, slightly in shadow. He also stares at me, but not in the lecherous way the Enforcers do. His eyes gleam yellow in the mirk.

'Girl, you are to be given the Wiccan test.' The voice of the High Klerik is sonorous in this large chamber, echoing as he announces what's to come. 'You shall be whipped until you reveal your Wiccanness. Ten usually did it, though it's been a long time since we had to do it, but we're permitted by the Gods and our Queen to use as much force as is necessary. If you've stolen a God's

49

power, it must be returned immediately. May the mercy of the Ten be with you child and make this swift.'

I turn my head away from them all. I won't let them see me hurt.

CRACK.

The first lash almost makes me pass out. My back arches and I bite the edge of my tongue. Once I unclench my teeth, I spit the blood onto the stone. It's like a sword had sliced open my spine.

CRACK.

My teeth grind, my jaw locking. Tears pour from the edges of my tightly closed eyelids.

CRACK.

I scream out through my clenched teeth.

'Wow, wait a moment.' The voice interrupting the whip is like a God's to me.

I take a long, whimpering breath. My body shakes, the pain deeper than any I've ever experienced before. I'd say anything to stop them doing it again.

'Isn't there a less painful way to do this?' The saviour asks. His voice sounds young.

Of course, there isn't another way.

'No. We appreciate you're close to the Queen, and here on her behalf, but this is none of your business, Bolt. You may stay if you remain silent. If not, leave. We can conclude our business later if you don't have the stomach for this.'

I turn my head to see the boy looking at me, but slowly shaking his head. 'Okay, but you stop if she confesses.'

'Not if she tells us. If she shows us.' The High Klerik nods to the whipper.

I close my eyes and bite down.

CRACK.

The air exits my lungs, my body becoming rigid as frozen oak. I don't want to take another breath, to experience another moment in this pain.

'STOP!' I shout, spit flying from my mouth. 'STOP! I'm Wiccan!'

'Not good enough, girl. They all say that after a few whips. Show us.' He nods again.

CRACK.

Flecks of blood splat the side of my face, a small line running into my eye. The hellfire on my back blanks out all other sensations.

'I'm Wiccan. I can do stuff with ice. I can show you. Just stop.'

'Show us,' the High Klerik repeats, his face bored.

I try to summon up that tingling feeling I had in the woods. But when I move, the pain sears my back, and I lose focus.

CRACK.

This time the lash whips my eyes wide open. Through the blur, I can see Sorg has turned, Bolt too, and even Hiro looks a little uncomfortable, shifting from foot to foot.

'Is this making you happy?' I scream at her. 'Is this what you wanted?'

Hiro shakes her head but doesn't look away.

'Keep going,' says the High Klerik. 'I don't have the time to wait. If something happens, come and find me.'

The whipper must nod, but I can't move to see him. The High Klerik floats from the room, his aide and the boy, Bolt, following him out. At least the Enforcers have got the stomach to watch what they've brought upon me.

CRACK.

My breathing becomes super slow. The room becomes dark.

CRACK.

My eyes fly open, and the dim light of the room is blinding compared to the darkness of before. The flesh on my back burns, the stone beneath me now slick with blood.

CRACK.

Dizziness and darkness.

CRACK.

That one didn't hurt.

CRACK.

Or that one.

The wounds have become cool and less painful. I try to turn but my whole torso is immobile, fixed to the stone.

'IN THE NAME OF KA, HOW DID THAT HAPPEN?' The voice of the whipper echoes around the chamber.

His feet splash across the wet floor and out the door. Hiro and Sorg move close to me.

'That's a good girl,' she says, coming closer. 'Knew it all along. Although, you did last longer than I thought you would. Impressive mental strength. Hopefully the Queen will be equally impressed with us bringing you.'

'What if the High Klerik decides not to release her to us? He might want to keep her now. Pass her to the Queen himself.' Sorg's hand wavers between his side and touching me.

'What's going on? Why can't I move?'

'Your entire back is covered in thick ice. Massive shards were growing right out of you, sharp as needles. Surprised you didn't take an eye. You are a powerful Wiccan. And you are ours.'

CHAPTER 8

This prison stinks worse than I do.

Three walls and a set of bars. A small line of light filters down the rounded window on the surface many feet above. Cells encircle an open pool of excrement, including ours.

'How can anything smell this bad?' I cover my nose with my arm.

'I've smelt worse.' Hiro rattles the bars we're stuck behind. 'Sorg and I used to guard the methane farms to the north of the capital.'

'I wish the smell was the worst of our worries.' I kick shit-spray onto the wall.

She smiles widely at me. 'You mean your worries. Not ours. This is just a mix-up. They won't keep us here for too long. Then, I'll convince the High Klerik that we're the ones to take you to the capital. Yes, just imagine what the Queen would give us if we handed her a Wiccan, huh Sorg?'

The big Enforcer looks away, disinterested.

'You do realise we're in a messy situation here? We've been in here for three days. Stuck down a shit-soaked prison, locked in a cell, awaiting death most likely, no way of escape. And that water level is definitely rising.'

'Gotta keep your options open, girl. Improve your prospects for further down the line. That's what I'm about.'

'Prospects? Looking pretty glum right now, huh? You're delusional if you think the High Klerik is going to come in here now and hand me over to you to deliver to the Queen.' I glare at her.

She has nothing redeemable about her. She is the most selfish creature I've ever encountered. She makes my parents look like saints.

I look past her to the open circular space beyond and the circle of cells. There's a small splash, but I can't tell from where. The water is definitely rising. The flow of sewage must be blocked.

Silence settles. We all face a different wall, dealing with our own thoughts and worries. I rub my back, still amazed at how quickly my back healed. I've had cuts in the past, particularly when I was wood-cutting, but none of them healed half as fast or were half as deep as these ones.

I crouch, splashing a little shitty water onto my face. A frisson passes through me.

The sound of the drips of water from the metal bars is magnified. The small currents are clear to me. I sense the movement of the leeches and maggots beneath the surface.

The water has amplified my senses. But only on or beneath the surface.

The wave of energy passing through me is the same as when I created the frost that speared Graf. Or in the whipping chamber. Or all those years ago when I killed my brother.

'I can help,' comes a wheezy voice from another cell.

'Who's there?' asks Hiro, clenching the bars and peering out.

'I'm No-One.'

'Why have you not spoken before now? Why are you down here?'

'Same reason as you. These people took a dislike to me.'

'Be specific?' asks Sorg, who has now moved to the bars beside Hiro.

'I killed some people, darling.'

'You are a murderer?'

'No, I'm an assassin. I get paid, so I'm a professional. It's my job. Don't worry though, nobody has paid me to kill you three.'

Silence hangs in the air. Whatever any of us are, this woman is dangerous.

'Okay, No-One. Tell us how you can help?'

'I'll help on one condition,' they whisper.

'What's that?'

'You take me with you when you escape.'

Hiro looks around. Sorg shrugs. I do nothing. I don't like it, but what other choice do we have? I'm not ready to die. And unless we act pretty soon, this place will fill up and drown us. Or we'll be at the mercy of the Kurikon. Not sure which is worse.

I nod.

Hiro turns back to face No-One's cell. 'Deal.'

'Good. Now, you must do exactly as I say. Two of you lift the cell door from either side at the same time. It needs to be a sharp lifting motion. The door will come off the hinges, but it's extremely heavy, so the other must help stabilise the weight and place it down gently. If you drop it, they will hear and come down to investigate. Got it?'

'Got it,' replies Hiro. She turns to us. 'Sorg, help me with this. Wiccan, get ready to help.'

Sorg surges through the ankle-high pool of filth and stands at the other side of the door. In unison, they jerk the bars up, but they won't budge.

'What now?' Hiro asks, leaning in close.

It's so dark in that cell, I can't see our assassin accomplice.

'I told you how to do it, darling. Not my fault you don't have the strength. If you do get your door open, do open mine, too, then I'll tell to how to escape from the prison.' She goes silent.

'That's it?' Hiro bangs on the bars a few times. They won't

budge. 'That's all your help? This place is filling up with sewage. We might not be alive tonight. We need to get out...now.'

Time passes and the sewage levels rise.

'Does this happen a lot, No-One?' I ask, trying the bars again.

'Every so often, darling. It gets blocked, I think. Never been this high, though. Must be completely clogged.'

Then the door crashes open.

A white-haired boy leaps into the prison, grabbing me tight, through the bars.

'Pat?' My arms begin to shake.

'It's me,' he says, stepping back and smiling. 'I followed you. I couldn't let this happen to you.'

Prince Terra barges in, holding his beautiful sword aloft, the dripping blood illuminated by a flaming torch in his other hand.

'Prince Terra!' Hiro's shout is so loud, I worry she'll have woken half of the Kurikon.

As the Prince stumbles in, I'm certain I'm hallucinating.

'It is I. I've come to rescue you.' He turns to me and smiles widely.

I nod to him but then focus on Pat. 'But how? How did you get all this way yourself?'

'You taught me a lot, you know, Corena. And I suppose Dad did, too. I stole a bunch of food and stuff from Klerik Anticus, as well.' His smile grows as he says this.

'I'm afraid we have little time for talk.' Prince Terra interrupts us. 'We fought our way down here, but most of them were Kleriks, not Enforcers, and now they know we're here. We are unlikely to be able to fight our way back out against reinforcements.'

'That's okay,' says No-One. 'I have a way out.'

'Who are you?' asks the Prince, staring into the dark cell.

'No-One.'

He looks at me, confused.

'Are you sure we can't go back?' I ask. If he and Pat have risked their life for me, I have to do something to get us out.

'Definitely not. I kill many people.'

'Hold up,' says Hiro. 'Before we think about getting out of the Kurikon, should we not be thinking about these cells. We're all going to drown if we don't, rescue or not.'

She has a point.

Terra starts lunging at the bars with his sword, but each stroke is deflected and soon he is completely exhausted.

'Maybe you should go, Pat.' I grab the bars and squeeze my face between two of them.

'Don't be thick, Corena. We're here to save you.' He places his hands on top of mine, which are still clutching the bars.

And it gets cold. Very cold.

'What's happening?' Pat asks.

I watch the bars become white with ice. And whiter still. And even whiter.

'Is this you?' he asks.

'I think so. Hold on.' I grab the bars tighter.

When I can't stand it anymore, I let go. I expect my hands to have frostbite or something, but they are fine. Pat stares at his hands, too. But neither of us is hurt.

'What now?' Pat asks.

'Stand back,' says Prince Terra.

And we do, well away from the frosted bars. He swings his sword at them, and they explode into thousands of small, metal pieces.

'Wow,' says Pat. 'That...was...awesome!'

I laugh and so do the others. Even Hiro smirks.

'Okay, let's get out.' I grab Pat into a tight hug again. 'We stick together from now on, huh?'

He nods. 'Absolutely.'

'Okay, lovely reunion and all, but how do we get out?' Hiro knows how to spoil the mood, but she's right.

'Open my cell and I'll tell you.' It's No-One.

I do the same thing to her cell as we did to mine, Terra

smashing the bars apart. We stare into the darkness of the cell, now open. No-One remains silent and does not move. We edge forward, listening.

A huge wave of water flies towards us and soaks us. A quiet, but clear laugh follows.

'Thank you. I've been in here for a long time.'

'How long?' Hiro asks.

'A long time, darling. Maybe three years. But now I'm free. Well, almost.'

'So how do we get out of here without a rope or a ladder? Or out the front door guarded by Enforcers.'

No-One steps forward from the shadow, thin, black, and stinking. 'I was hoping the Wiccan might help us with that.'

CHAPTER 9

'Just beneath the surface, there is a pipe which brings the waste in here. And another, on the opposite side, which takes it to the sea. You can take either.' She points to where the pipes sit beneath the pooled water.

'Which is shorter?' asks Sorg.

'I don't know. I've never been out of my cell. Or I'd have escaped through one of them already.' She shakes her head and frowns at Sorg as she says it.

'I'm not sure how I can help,' I say. 'I'm not a good swimmer.'

'I don't give a flying pixie...if you're not Wiccan and you can't swim, you may as well be dead to me.' She splashes past me, her shoulder colliding with mine, towards one of two parts of wall with no cell.

She falls to her knees and moves her hand back and forth beneath the surface of the mirk. For a few seconds, we watch her or look up, expecting the face of a guard to appear. But nobody appears.

'Okay, so where's this pipe, No-One?' I ask.

'It's Elera, darling. Just call me Elera. Now that we're doing this together, you may as well know my name. I don't get down on my knees for just anyone.'

While we wait, Pat hugs me again. I didn't think I'd see him again, but my elation quickly dissipates. Him being here is a big risk to his life. And mine. And the water level continues to rise.

'Did anyone see your face and get away?' I ask him.

'A few people.'

'Anyone here? Anyone in the Kurikon?'

He nods and gives me a sheepish grin.

'It's not a game.' I grab him by the shoulders. 'I'm so happy you're here but this world hates me. They won't tolerate what I can do. If we get out of here, we're going to have to get somewhere safe. Understand?'

He shrugs.

Footsteps echo down from a few corridors away.

'Quickly,' says Terra. 'Hiro, Sorg, help me secure the door. Pick up the remains of the metal doors and we'll block the corridor to keep them out.'

The prince and the enforcers work together to place both cell doors against the main prison door. The footsteps get closer. Many of them.

'Come on, Elera.' I start pacing restlessly.

'Found it.' She stands, a wide smile on her dripping face.

'Okay, who's first?' Hiro asks, looking at Sorg and Elera.

'Not me, I'm the biggest, so if I get stuck then nobody gets through. I should go last.' Sorg says it, not out of cowardice, but apparently out of genuine concern.

Hiro nods. 'Fair point. How about you?' she asks Elera.

'Do you think I'm going to swim blindly into a pipe which may or may not lead somewhere, when I don't even know if it's blocked, or I'll be able to breathe?' She turns away, laughing.

'I'll go.' Pat kneels, ready to submerge, but I grab his shoulder.

'No. I'll go first. We don't have time to argue.' I give Pat a quick hug, then take a long breath out and close my eyes.

I fall to my knees and feel around for the opening. Faeces, urine, stale beer all hit me. I gag and dry retch. When I recover and find the pipe, I notice there is no current or suction. The edges are slimy, but it seems wide enough to squeeze through.

Something small swims over my hands.

When I pull them back out of the water, several small maggots crawl on my fingers. As I flick them back into the water, I notice a large leech attached to my left wrist. I pull it free, leaving a small, bloody patch.

'I think it's blocked.' I turn to the see Hiro close, with her arms crossed.

'Well, get in there and unblock it then.'

I want to hit her, but I take a few deep breaths and turn away, retching again.

Pat's voice is the last thing I hear. 'I'll be right behind you.'

I prepare for the plunge by placing my hands on the upper edge of the pipe and taking in a massive lungful of stinking air. In one quick movement, I hold my breath and pull myself down and then forward, lying low beneath the sludge.

The stone pipe is slippery and hard to grip, so I scramble forward slowly. The pipe is hardly much wider than I am, but I gradually slide onward. I open my eyes for a second, but immediately close them. It's dark and the slop stings them.

For ten endless seconds I haul myself onward, gripping who knows what and sensing there might be no way through.

As I think about being trapped, I take in a mouthful of sludge.

It's so foul, my mouth opens again to vomit it out, but more flows in as I close it again. My arms and legs begin to thrash against the slimy stone, and I try to turn, but there's no room. I can't.

I blow out some of the sludge from my mouth knowing I only have seconds of life left.

I pull myself forward again.

A gentle pull of current comes from ahead. But only gentle.

My arm hits something hard. I move my hands over it, sensing if it's moveable or not.

It's not.

It's like hitting the sturdiest tree with my bare hands.

I punch it over and over, but very little happens. It's clearly built up over a long time. If only I had my axe. But like everything else in this world, I'll never see it again.

I'm going to die.

Drowned in a shit pipe.

My body relaxes, the lack of air shutting down my muscles.

My heartbeat feels slow now.

My mouth screams to open.

And I can't stop it.

My heart becomes ice cold.

Followed by my fingertips.

This is it.

My end.

CHAPTER 10

Finally, my mouth opens.

I expect the cool rush of sewage down my throat, but instead it's cold air. Glorious air, filling my lungs and keeping me alive. At least for a moment.

My opening eyes see a strange sight. Ice. It surrounds my head.

A filthy layer lies beyond, straining to crack the frost.

The breath out is cloudy, but warm.

I am alive.

But how? How has this happened? I clearly know nothing of my powers or their extent.

I move my arms and legs, now operating with much needed oxygen, but both feel longer and colder.

My hands sweep the blocked part of the pipe and while I can, I repeatedly hit it. If this is a brief respite from Ka-Ferno's Gate, then I'll use every last second. There is no sensation in my hands as I strike the blockage time after time. But my arms are driving forward, making some progress.

Crack.

The ice around my head is breaking. Small streams of dark, oozing liquid filter into my ice helmet. I only have seconds before it shatters and I'm back to being in the dark, so I take in a deep, long breath.

Crack.

The temporary life-saving helmet disintegrates. Grime smothers my face and I'm back in blackness. I thrust my arms harder than ever, hoping I'm almost through.

My air runs low again and my arms fatigue. I still can't feel my hands but know they make progress as I move, inch-by-inch along the pipe.

When I'm at the point of exhaustion and I must take another breath, I pray for another ice helmet, but it does not come. I open my mouth, simultaneously thrusting my arm forward one last time.

I fly forward. My chest scrapes along the stone base of the pipe, but I gain speed. Liquid rushes around me, eagerly escaping the top of the pipe, its prison and ours.

I open my eyes, but they sting as sludge covers them. After I wipe it away, it's still dark and I'm still picking up speed. I hope the pipe doesn't toss me out the other side onto a stone floor or even worse, another dead end.

I stare at my cold hands and notice all my fingers locked together in an ice spear, projecting from the tips. That must have been how I broke through the blockage.

As the pipe rounds a corner, the tunnel lightens. Far ahead, brightness rubs out the edges and I'm hurtling towards Illumination. Wiccan don't ascend to the Haven, so this must be the sun.

I brace myself for the impact of the exit. I close my eyes, the sunlight hurting after the time in the darkness. Then I'm weightless, floating through the air with no resistance; no sludge, no pipe, no rope tied round my neck. Freedom.

Thump. I land on my left side and I'm winded. My ribs ache and my left elbow hurts. But not as bad as they should from that fall. Salt licks my tongue as I gasp. Then I cough out something small and hard, which coats my mouth and my face, as well as my clothes. Dry, warm, and bitty.

'Sand.'

I've never seen the stuff, but I know all about it. I always hoped I'd see it myself someday. Dad often spoke about Rejik, where he lived in his youth. He loved the beach, where he went on holidays and fishing trips with his parents. I can't wait to share this view with Pat.

I hope they all make it through that pipe.

I push myself into a seated position and open my eyes a fraction at a time. Bird screams and the soothing swoosh of the ocean filter into my hungry ears.

Positioning myself near the pipe exit, I wait.

Pat slides through a few seconds later. I grab him and pull him close again, pointing to the ocean and ignoring the stench coming from both of us.

'Beautiful, huh?'

'Seriously amazing,' he replies.

Hiro slides through, followed by Elera, Terra and then Sorg.

'We must move quickly.' Prince Terra is already moving away from the beach.

'Where will we go?' I ask. I'm lost in this part of the world.

Terra doesn't answer, instead running to the top of the small bank overlooking the sand. We all follow him, keen to get away from the pipe that exits the Kurikon.

When we all reach the summit, the prince turns to us.

'We should split up. Travel in pairs. They'll be looking for six people. Ghondulon is the nearest big city. It will be easiest to hide us in a place like that.'

'No way,' says Hiro. 'The girl comes with Sorg and I. She's still ours. We'll take her to the Queen.'

'You will not,' says the Prince. He touches the handle of his sword. It's his go-to move, but it's effective.

Hiro turns to Sorg for support, but he shakes his head. The

faceless man no longer supports her. I might just get away from them. And the Queen. But now we have the Kurikon at our backs.

'I'll take Pat. I've become very fond of him.' The prince smiles to my brother.

'No, he should stay with me.' I put my arm on his shoulder. 'I'm not letting him go again.'

'Corena, I understand. But you both have white hair. You will stand out, travelling together. I can take him and pretend he's my squire. People will not question me in the same way they would if you travelled with him. It is best.'

His gaze is unrelenting. I trust him but I don't know if I can let Pat go, again. I've only just got him back.

'It will be okay, Corena. I promise.' Pat gives me a small punch on the arm.

He's grown up so much in just a few days. Looking more like Gullan every day. Maybe he is better without me. I've already got one brother killed.

'I'll travel with the girl,' says Elera. 'I'll keep her safe.' The assassin turns back to the pipe, searching for pursuing Enforcers.

'I'm really not sure—'

'Sorry, time is not our ally. Ghondulon is two days travel from here. I will travel with Pat over the hills and so will arrive into the city from the north. Hiro and Sorg will travel the main road. You still wear the blue cloaks of Enforcers, even if they are not quite as blue as they once were. You should not face trouble. Corena and... Elera...you'll travel along the coast for a time, then cut inland and make a straight line for the city. Elera, do you know the way?'

'This is my land, *prince*. I know it better than you.'

'Good, then we're agreed. We must hurry.'

'We are not agreed.' Hiro moves close to Prince Terra. It's a comical site. She is tiny compared to the foreign prince. 'I must get this girl to the Queen. It is the only way that I can restore my reputation. It is the only way for Sorg to have his face restored.'

Prince Terra is unmoved.

Hiro steps towards me, reaching out to grab my wrist.

But Sorg stops her. 'No. Corena shall go. And go now, girl. Hiro will come with me.'

Before Hiro can argue again, I step forward. 'Let's just all move together. Get away from here. We can argue about this when we are further from the Kurikon.'

Nobody argues with that, and we start at a fast walk along the beach, heading south. We walk at the tideline, to ensure our footprints are swept away after us. And the water gives me a large store of ammunition, should we need it.

Pat walks alongside me and he grabs my hand. It's very warm against my cold palm. 'So, what's next Corena? What's our next adventure?'

I study him for a moment. He seems much older, much more mature than he did a couple of weeks ago. Yet, he's still a child. The word adventure melts me.

'No more adventures, Pat. At least not for now. All that matters is getting you somewhere safe and very far away from here.'

'Getting *us* somewhere safe,' he replies.

I squeeze his hand. 'Us.'

As we move further away from the sewage pipe, I start to relax and only glance back every ten seconds or so.

Hiro stays close to me, worried her prize catch might run off. Terra stays even closer. Sorg ploughs along at the very back, shoulders slumped and silent. Elera walks beside him, struggling to keep up with us.

'We should take a quick break,' I say to Terra, who is nearest me. 'Let Elera rest. She's not done this much walking in a long time.'

His eyes are wide and it's obvious he wants to disagree, but instead he simply walks to the top of the closest dune, staring back at the Kurikon.

'We can stop for a moment,' I say to Elera and Sorg once they catch up.

Neither speaks, but they immediately slump to the sand.

'Let's clean you up a little.' I pull my brother towards the sea. 'You're dirtier than the Arctic pigs after a thaw.'

We wash the worst of the sewage from our skin and our ragged clothes. Pat's are just as bad as mine; torn, sun-bleached and frayed. When I scrub his neck, he punches me.

'Oi, I'm just trying to stop you smelling like a bog.'

'Rena, that's exactly what Mum used to do. I don't want anything to remind me of that old scutter.'

'PATRICK!' I totally agree with him, but he's never cursed Mum before. 'Have a bit more respect.'

'You don't. You call her all sorts.'

'Yes, that's different...'

'How?' He put his hands on his hips. In the adorable way he always has, when I fail to live up to his moral standards.

'It just is. Mum and I never got along. She never loved me like she loves you. She'd have done anything for you.'

'Even send you away?'

I'm not sure it's a question. He just wants confirmation. I nod.

'That's why I came. You let yourself be taken. For me.'

I give him a long hug, his soaked clothes sticking to mine.

'And now we get to stick together. Like Ha and Ra.'

I frown at him. 'Not sure we can be compared to Gods.'

'Why not?' He shrugs. 'You have their power.'

'Pat, you know it's just made up. All that stuff about stealing from the Gods. It's not real. Just a way to justify killing people who have powers that the Kurikon are afraid of. Our powers are ours. Not stolen. And we are humans.'

He puts his head down. I'm not sure he's ready to give up his faith.

'Do you wish you didn't have them?' he asks.

'Sometimes. But it doesn't matter what I want. This is how it is. But from now on, keep it quiet, until we escape to somewhere far, far away.'

'Where will we escape to?'

'I've never thought about it...'

'I'd love to live on a farm, with animals and chickens and tall rows of corn. I love corn.'

I pull him down onto some dry sand. We sit, side by side, starting out across the Cruel Sea at the sun, lowering towards the horizon.

'I'd like that, too.'

'Do you promise? That we can live on a farm and have chickens?'

'I promise. If you promise not to tell anyone about my powers?'

He picks up a stone and chucks it into the sea. 'I will.'

I sit for a silent minute with him. He stares out, I stare at him. I'm so happy he came for me, in the most selfish of ways. He'd have been safe at home with Mum and Dad. But him being here with me, helping me through this, is making me as happy as I've been in years.

He stands up and helps me to my feet. 'But you do have pretty cool powers, huh?'

I laugh. 'I do. Sometimes. If I use them in the right way.'

Pat has run up the hill to get Terra.

I turn to Hiro. 'Pat and I will be going our own way after Ghondulon. You will not follow us.'

She tenses and moves close. 'Really? So, what about Sorg and I? We're disgraced Enforcers, twice over. Unless we present you to the Queen, we'll have nothing. We have nothing.'

'Not my problem.'

Before she can respond, a shout comes from Terra.

Several Enforcers charge down the beach on foot. Others come straight from the direction of Kurikon, atop horses.

'Run now. Split up like we agreed, or we'll all be taken.' Prince

Terra pulls Pat alongside and they begin to scramble up the hillside.

Elera grabs me and we sprint along the bank beside the beach. I want to go to Pat, but he's too far away. I'd get caught in the middle.

'We shouldn't split up,' I say, hesitating. Pat gets further and further from us.

'I know a short cut. Just keep up.'

I tear my gaze away from Pat, though it breaks my heart, and continue running after the assassin. I can't believe I've had to leave him again, but if Terra helped him before, he will do it again. They fought through the whole Kurikon prison to get to us, so they will also get to Ghondulon. I'll see him again. I will.

When I glance around, I notice Hiro and Sorg have not run and are currently

being taken by the Enforcers. And they've done us a big favour as very few now chase us. But no doubt Hiro will talk. She'll tell them where we've gone.

I search the hillside again, but Terra and Pat have gone. My brother's fate is in the hands of the prince. For now, I just need to keep myself alive and free of the Kurikon.

The beach becomes rocky, and the bank starts to climb, the fall steeper as the cliffs rise alongside the ocean. We take the low road and stumble across rocks, pebbles, and large stones.

The Enforcers are gaining, but slowly. My legs are tiring, but when I look at Elera, she's almost done. She stumbles twice, before finally falling on her face.

Blood streams from her forehead where she's hit a rock. 'Cave.'

I search the cliff face and see a small, dark opening. I lift her. It's fortunate she's worn away to almost nothing in that prison, otherwise I'd never be able to carry her. But I manage and we reach the cave mouth.

I take her a short way inside, but I can't see an exit. After lying her on the rocks, I move back to the mouth. The Enforcers have reached the point where she fell, they've seen the blood and they are spreading out, scouring the stony beach for where we went. Two come towards us.

I step back.

I'm trapped, just like in the pipe.

In the pipe, where I made the ice-helmet. Maybe I can make something similar to seal the cave, to keep them out. But I need emotion to power my ice. I touch the wet stone wall and think about the most powerful emotional experiences I've had.

When the village people attacked Pat and I...

The surge tickles my arms.

When I was whipped on the stone table by the Kurikon...

The surge flows from shoulder to fingertip.

When I was trapped and thought I was about to die in the shit-pipe...

The surge floods my arms and gushes from my hands.

When my parents gave me up...

The surge tsunamis from every part of me.

When I sent a stake of ice through my brother's heart...

I fall.

When I wake, with Elera shaking me, I can only shiver.

The entire cave is layered in ice. The doorway is completely sealed, the ice so thick, very little light still comes in.

'What happened?' I ask, sitting up properly.

'You saved us, darling.' Elera helps me up. 'But they will get through the ice eventually. They've been chiselling at it for a while now.'

I hear a regular, quite thump. 'I've not saved us. I've just delayed them.'

'No, there is another way out. A tunnel through the back. It's narrow but you're slim enough to get through. That's why I brought us here, darling. You didn't think I'd bring us to a dead-end?'

I shrug. My head still hurts. I think I overloaded it with emotion when I used my powers.

'Come on. If you're able?'

She helps me climb up and we enter the tunnel at the back of the cave. She was right, it's so tight, Sorg and Terra would never have made it through, but we're okay.

The darkness becomes absolute after a short time, and I become reliant on following Elera's breathing and the sounds of her hands and knees on loose rock. The tunnel climbs, that much I can sense, but little else. We continue for a long time, Elera occasionally stopping to rest, and I don't disagree when she does.

One time we stop; we can hear the echoed voices of the Enforcers below.

'They sound annoyed,' I whisper.

'They do, darling. A sweet sound to this assassin who spent a long time listening to them abuse me.'

We speak no more and move on a short while later, no signs of further pursuit. I hope Pat had the same luck as us. I hope Terra keeps his word and protects him. If he doesn't, I could never forgive myself.

CHAPTER 11

The scorching afternoon sun has burnt my exposed, pale, northern skin.

'How far to Ghondulon?' I ask Elera, who now shows no signs of slowing her fast pace. She seems to strengthen with every breath of free air she takes.

'A day, maybe less if we don't stop and walk through the night.'

'Is this the way that Terra would have taken Pat?'

'Probably. But we won't catch them, darling. The cave and then the crawl really slowed us.'

'We can try,' I say, catching up with her and walking alongside.

'I've been cooped up in a cell for three years, Corena. I'm just glad I'm still upright after what we've gone through. I trust Terra. He seems solid. He'll make sure Pat is okay. Sorg and Hiro on the other hand...'

'So, you don't trust *her*, either?' I can't help but be scuttery after all she's done.

Elera laughs. 'Of course not. She is only after one thing and she'll do anything to get it, darling.'

'What's that?'

'Status. She reeks of a fallen Enforcer, once in a position of power, and she sees you as ticket to get that power back.'

'But how can I do that?'

'You are Wiccan. She thinks that taking you to the Queen will somehow regain favour.'

We walk on, picturing Hiro presenting me to the Queen. I won't let her. She will never have any hold or claim over me again.

'The only way she can get what she desires is to give the Queen something she desires. Most of the Wiccan were executed a decade ago. It's that act that makes the people love the Queen.'

'Were the Wiccan that bad?' I ask.

'They can be good or bad just like anyone else. And with their power, many went bad. Eventually. There was war.'

'Yeah, my father once told me about that. He said that a bunch of Wiccan tried to take the crown.'

'They did. But what he probably didn't tell you was that many Wiccans fought on the side of the Queen. They fought off and defeated the evil Wiccans. At a cost. Very few survived.'

'And what happened to them?'

'They were executed, darling.'

'Even though they helped the Queen? Surely not.'

'Corena, do not mistake the effect that power has on people. When they have a taste, they will do almost anything to keep it. Even things they would never have done before. She killed them all. And publicly. And then scoured the land to capture the remainder. And publicly killed those, too. She put up big rewards for information on Wiccan. She was obsessed. I remember.'

I stare at Elera, quite unable to believe that she could be that old. She doesn't look much older than me.

'So, I'll be killed if I'm taken to the Queen, right?'

'Probably not at first. She'll want to know how you evaded capture for so long. Probably torture you. But yes, then she will kill you. Publicly.'

'Then you must help me get Pat back and escape.' I've been responsible for the death of one brother. I've spent years torturing myself about Gullan. I'll not let Pat be taken from me, too. That would be too much. That would end me.

'There's no point. Hiro knows what you are. Even if you escape her, she will inform the Queen and you'll be hunted.'

'So, I've no hope.' My shoulders slump and I want to fall right where I stand.

'I didn't say that...at the moment, only a few people know about you. Keep that number low. Aside from Sorg and Hiro. We may be able to convince the big man not to speak, but it will be a task with her. And we know Pat and Terra won't say a word. The Kurikon will want to keep your existence quiet, too. They teach that no mortal person can steal the God's power and not face execution. You've escaped them, twice. They won't want people to know this. But be assured they will continue to chase us. I'll bet they've got a ton of spies waiting for us in Ghondulon.'

'But I thought Terra said it was safe there.'

'Safest doesn't mean safe. You can hide in a large city better than out here in the open, but that doesn't make you safe.'

'So, what do you suggest we do.'

She stops walking, places her hands on both my cheeks and kisses me.

She holds for a second before pulling away. 'Kill anyone who tries to take you, darling.'

We stumble upon a farm, late into the night.

'We should rest for a few hours,' says Elera. 'You can't walk all night and neither can I.'

'But Terra and Pat might be in Ghondulon already.'

'And if they are, they will still be there tomorrow. You must rest; you may need your energy if we bump into any more Kurikon Enforcers.'

She's right, of course she's right. But I don't want to stop. Moving makes me feel like I'm doing something to get back to Pat. Stopping feeling likes defeat. And I don't like to lose.

Elera uses a small harvesting scythe, like one I used to farm the ice, to break the small lock on the barn located farthest from the farmer's house.

'We can rest in here for a few hours, then get going before the farmer wakes up and realises.' She takes the scythe with her, swinging it through the night air with skill and agility. 'It's been so long since I swung a blade. It's like the first drink after a long drought.'

We settle into a corner stacked with bundled hay. It's not too cold, especially for a northerner like me. And Elera spent years sleeping in sewage. Neither of us complains.

My stomach growls.

'Here, have this?' Elera hands me the leftover capybara meat we roasted earlier.

I hold my hands up. 'No, you were saving that. And you need it more than me.' And she does. Those years rotting in the Kurikon prison have taken away most of her muscle. Her black skin is so tight to her body.

'Have it. And say no more, darling.' She gives me a scary, warning look. Then laughs.

I take the meat and tear the small portion in half, giving her something to gnaw on. We munch silently. This late in the night, it's so silent outside. Not even bird chirrups. It makes me conscious of how loud I eat. Mum used to always frown at me, so I chew slow.

We finish and I try think of anything but Pat and how I should be marching towards Ghondulon right now.

Elera moves close to me, putting one arm around my shoulders. 'For warmth,' she whispers, tickling my ear.

Before I have a chance to think about it, we've kissed. Different from Asta, but just as nice. I need some comfort tonight, some human closeness. But I don't let it go too far. I can never let it go too far. Nobody could ever truly love me.

Eventually, we both drift off, arms wrapped over each other.

CHAPTER 12

The approach to Ghondulon is laden with steaming, volcanic springs. Built at the base of an active volcano; the hillside and valley beneath are laden with houses, farmland and a hub of activity in the centre. They look like ants from this distance.

'Ghondulon is big,' I say.

'Yes,' replies Elera.

'How are we supposed to find Pat? Where would Terra take him?' I hadn't expected it to be so large, despite what Elera had told me. This must be a million times the size of our village.

'It's pointless looking for him.'

'Then how will we get to Pat.'

'We don't. He'll come to us. You are worth much more to Terra than you think, and he seems to like your brother. He'll seek you out, I assure you. Come, let us get some food and rest. We have earned it.'

'I'm not eating until I find Pat.'

'Oh, don't be so melodramatic, darling. Trust me.'

We approach the spiralling gates, manned by two Royal Enforcers, blue cloaks flowing in the wind as they stand to inspect us.

'Any weapons?' the one on the left asks.

Elera hands them her stolen scythe. The Enforcer stashes it away in a large side house. She just took it for trouble on the road here. Luckily, there was none. But she doesn't give them the hay bale hook. I don't want to think why she's keeping that.

'What is your business in Ghondulon?' asks the other one.

'Pleasure, darling,' says Elera, winking at him.

'Be specific,' he says, looking at me. His eyes take in my white hair.

'We are visiting an old friend. Orochi.' Elera answers for me.

He turns away from me. 'She is known. You may pass. Will you be leaving by this gate or the south gate?'

'The south.'

'We'll arrange for your weapon to be transported there. Enjoy your stay.'

'Don't you need my name, darling?'

'I won't forget you.'

The large iron gates squeak open, the hinges ancient and rusted. It's all very dramatic.

'Why the gates and the Enforcers?' I ask.

'Things are much less peaceful in this part of the world, Corena. You'll soon learn that there is very little trust amongst the people of the Farmlands and the South. The capital is a viper pit of lies and deceit. Ghondulon is only slightly milder.'

'And who is Orochi. You never mentioned them before?'

'Orochi is my old mentor. She trained me.'

'As an assassin?'

'Yes. Amongst other things. I was trained to kill very well, but she taught me a great many other things.'

'And can she help us?'

'She can. I don't know if she will. She juggles a lot of things. Or she did. We shall see how she is now.'

We pass the outlying houses, mostly farms, the lands beyond stretching with corns and wheats, alongside southern, warm weather crops I've never seen. I drink in the newness of it all, the nods we get from the friendly farmers and the smell of saltless air. At last, we're far enough away from the coast that it's gone.

'So have you decided how we kill Hiro?' I ask it because it has consumed my mind these last 24 hours as we walked. We've been joking about it. She has been despicable and would happily sell me out at any moment. She'd kill me if she thought she would gain. We've both got no doubt she told the Kurikon Enforcers where we were going. So, Elera and I have had a laugh about the different ways we'd kill her.

We then went onto how we'd kill the High Klerik and the Queen. It got a bit out of hand. Even Susanoo-no-Mikoto would think our plotting too mischievous.

But killing in self-defence or by accident is one thing. I can live with it, even if it rips at my heart every time I think about it. But murder is entering a new, darker world, more likely to confirm my descension through Ka-Ferno's Gate than my ascension to the Haven.

Elera on the other hand...well, that's a different story.

'Well, the tricky part will not be Hiro. It will be Sorg. We need to get him out of the equation.'

'And how would we do that? They are inseparable.'

'Don't worry, I know men and their weaknesses. I'll quickly establish his and exploit it. I'll give you the chance to kill her without interference.'

'I've been thinking...' I say, wondering how Elera will react. 'What if we don't kill her. What if we just tie her up, or... something?'

Elera stops and turns to me. 'Do you think Hiro would just give you up? If you tie her up, she will escape and pursue you. The only way to truly rid yourself of her and what she might say is to kill her. There is no other option. But you can do it, darling. I've seen you in action.'

'What if it's not that I *can't* do it, but that I don't *want* to do it.'

'Well, then that could be a problem. One thing I know a lot

about is killing. And if your heart is not in the kill, you won't be able to do it. And the weak-hearted are always the first to die.'

'Well, that's reassuring.'

'It's the truth, darling. Deal with it or allow yourself to be taken to the Queen and executed.'

Elera has an ability to terminate a conversation like nobody I've ever met. But she's right. I know it. If I see Hiro again, one of us must die.

∽

As we descend into the valley, the shadow of the volcano blocks the sun, and the fresh air of the fields is replaced by the stinking smog of smoking structures and too many people.

The houses and buildings here are too close together so the streets are just the gaps between the tall concrete. It's like a maze and I'd be lost if I wasn't with Elera, who navigates the streets like she's never been away.

'Why is there so much smoke?' I ask. 'It is a warm day.'

'These are not the fires of people seeking warmth. Ghondulon is an industry town.'

'Industry?' The word sounds horrible and alien.

'Yes, they use fire and turbines and machines to make products. For the capital mostly, but they sell across the south and even trade with ships of the Cruel Sea.'

'What kind of products?'

'Expensive clothes made of all different materials, lavish furniture made from other materials than just wood, and the mills produce food on a vast scale. The capital becomes greedier, and the last decade has seen a boom in industry in big places like Ghondulon. It does not appear to have slowed in my absence.'

My eyes don't leave her lips while she speaks. 'Why is all this needed?'

'It is not *needed*. Merely desired and such is the world: the rich

81

get richer and more lavish in their wants and the poor become poorer and less demanding with their needs.'

I shake my head at the scale of everything. Back home it was trade wood and fur for seed. Trade ice and water for fruit. But this part of the world values items of worth, rather than survival.

'Of course, very few complain. And why would they? This industry brings work and work means coin. Coin means fed and sheltered families. Humans are a simple beast, offer it a chance to survive and it will do almost anything you ask.'

We walk along a long, thin alley between two large buildings, both belting out buckets of black smoke. I have to put my sleeve over my mouth to stop choking.

'You'll get used to it, darling,' says Elera. 'You're too used to the fresh stuff. Anyway, we're not far away from our destination.'

We move out of the alley into a slightly wider street with lower houses, these ones absent of smoke. I stand in the middle of the muddy road and take in the wide variety of people moving back and forth.

A lady taller than Sorg walks past, her hair a large bush, alongside a red-haired dwarf, the small man shouting up to her about 'taxes'.

I watch them pass, fascinated, but I turn quickly to the sound of hooves thumping on the dry mud, and I have to leap away to avoid being trampled by them and the carriage they pull. The man driving it, sitting atop the carriage, lifts his hat and nods to me as he speeds past. The carriage is plush, the wood painted and varnished, the windows curtained to hide the passengers inside.

We cross the road now; this time I look both ways as I absorb the array of mixed cultures and differing people.

A short dark-skinned man stands in front of a door, hand resting on his belt. His belt has two curved swords, sheathed on his left and right. Beside him, a tall, pale girl sits with a half-blade on her legs, sharpening its edges with a whetstone.

This is the door we stop at. Great.

'We're here to see Orochi,' says Elera.

'She's busy today. Come back tomorrow,' says the girl.

'I need to see her today, darling. Tell her it's Elera.'

'Elera, huh? You don't look much like the stories,' says the man. 'Too short and you're nought but bones.'

'I've been in...an *unfortunate* place for a while. But now I'm back, and if you've heard the stories, you'll let us in.'

'I've heard the stories, but you do not match them. How do I know it's you?' he asks, smiling. The girl watches from behind, tapping her blade on her leg.

'Deny me access and you'll know it's me as you look up from the ground, your own blades through your chest...darling.'

The man tenses, his hands move to the handles of his blades. The girl also rises, holding her blade, ready to battle.

'We haven't come here for a fight,' I say, grabbing Elera on her arm to stop her whipping out the hay bale hook. 'We can come back.'

'Do you want to wait around out here, with no plan or means of escape when you do finally find your brother?'

'No.'

'Then let me do things my way.'

In an instant, faster than I've ever seen anyone move, Elera has both the man and girl on the ground, the twin curved blades held to both their necks. They look terrified. I don't blame them.

'Enough, Elera. Leave my students and come inside.' The voice freezes Elera. She drops the blades and bows to the lady.

'Orochi, it's a pleasure to see you after so long.'

'Perhaps.' She has sprouts of grey hair and a long green, patterned silk dress which covers her tanned, leathery skin. Her green eyes move to me as I follow Elera into her house.

The two students retrieve their weapons and resume their position in front of the door as it closes after us.

Inside, we stand in a large living area, a stone fire, unlit, in the centre surrounded by carved stone seats. Ten of them. Three are occupied. The people in them ignore me but look at Elera with silence and reverence.

To our left, a small kitchen area produces a wonderful smell of a vegetable stew. And something else. Something meaty.

'Are you hungry?' asks Orochi. The lady hands a bowl to both Elera and I.

The warm meal is delicious and filling. We follow Orochi to sit on the stone seats. The others stare at us, but don't speak, allowing us to finish our meal. Mine is done in less than a minute.

'You are hungry,' says Orochi, looking at my empty bowl. 'You been on the road long?'

Elera responds. 'Yes, a few days for me. Much longer for my companion. But it's not the journey that wearies us.' She takes more of her stew before continuing. 'I've been imprisoned for a long time, Orochi. And Corena here has, too.'

'Corena? What a lovely name. And you, Elera, appear to be free once more. I'm glad. But how can I help you both.' She looks at me as she speaks, even though she addresses Elera, like she recognises me.

'We need weapons. And safe passage away from Kurikon ears and whisperers.'

'You have coin?'

Elera shakes her head.

'Then how do you propose to pay for my weapons? I'm no charity.' Orochi looks at her guests, who are also amused.

'The old arrangement. We'll do a job for you. The payment can be the weapons that we need, plus some other supplies. Food, clothes and other basics. But most importantly, a silent getaway. Abroad, away from the Queen and the Kurikon.'

'Well, well. The famous Elera has returned. And she wants her old job back. I never expected to see this day. It also seems you're in a lot of trouble. Royal and religious trouble.'

Elera nods but says no more.

'And you want to disappear? When you already have the

Kurikon and Enforcers on your trail – not to mention a reward from the Queen hanging over your head, no doubt?' She smiles at me when she says that, like she knows more than she's telling.

'The price will be very high indeed...we could just turn you in, so this job you do, it will have to be very big. The biggest...'

'We'll do it,' I blurt out, before Elera can respond.

She turns to her guests and raises her eyebrows. 'And the timing could not be better. These are three representatives of the Order of Mutare. They have asked me to provide my best assassin to their cause. And if you want it, their job is yours.'

'What's the job?' asks Elera, looking suspiciously at the other guests.

One of the representatives sits forward. She pulls back her hood, revealing white hair, just like mine would be if it were not layered in dirt.

'Regicide.'

CHAPTER 13

'You're not actually thinking about doing this?' I ask. 'We don't know these people; we can't trust them. And regicide? More like suicide!'

'I'm not *thinking* about it,' replies Elera.

'Good.'

'I'm *going* to do it.'

'That's crazy. We don't need weapons. We don't need to get involved with these people and their assassination. We need to find my brother and leave this place.' I stand in front of Elera, making sure she sees me, that she understands me.

'And I told you that we don't need to find Pat, darling. They will find us.'

I shake my head at her. She is so frustrating. I truly cannot understand what she wants or thinks.

'But first,' she says. 'We must find some accommodation for the night and celebrate our freedom. I know a nice, wee inn.'

'Celebrate? I won't celebrate until we have Pat back.'

'And when we do, *Prince Terra* takes you to his far-off land and marries you? Is that the deal?'

'Yes.' I've accepted my fate, if it keeps Pat and I free and alive. 'Or I thought we could travel with him for a bit, maybe.'

'And what will happen to Pat? He can't marry a prince.'

'Then what should we do.'

'Come with me, darling. I'll take care of you both.'

'But you're an assassin.'

'Doesn't make me a bad person, does it? It's just a job. Not like I enjoy it.'

'I know, but I don't know if I can expose him to that kind of world. He's still innocent and has so much good in him. It's too late for me, but he has every chance.'

'And I'll make sure he gets that chance.'

'Education?' I ask, looking into her brown eyes, searching for honesty.

'Yes, if that's what you want.'

'But why? Why would you do this for a stranger?'

'*You* are not a stranger. You got me out of that prison. I owe you. And it will be nice, like having a second chance that I never got with my own brother.' She lowers her head. It's strange seeing her so honest. So vulnerable.

'What happened?'

'Our parents had died the year before. Killed by some kind of sickness, but it spared me and Efren. I was the elder, about your age actually, and was out scavenging the fields of Ghondulon for food. When I returned home, he was gone.'

'Where did he go?'

'I searched for weeks and weeks. Eventually, I found his body near the Sulphur mines, next to the volcano.' She points up to the hills and mountains which overlook Ghondulon. 'He was naked. Dead. And it broke me. I ended up thieving and would have ended up losing my hand when Orochi caught me one day. And instead of taking my hand, she took me into her home. She looked after me, fed me, trained me. Until I was strong enough and skilled enough to become an assassin in her pay. And I stayed with her until I was caught three years ago.

'I've been asked how I can kill. I think of my brother, of the people who took him away to work in those mines. The same people who killed them. I picture their faces as my targets faces. Makes slitting their throats much easier.' She becomes silent, her eyes remaining fixed upon the volcanic mountains.

And then it clicks. There was good in her. But she lost it when she lost her brother. Every bit of goodness in me, everything that's worth living for, is encapsulated in my younger brother. He is the best of me. And if I lost him, I'd probably be every bit as cold as Elera. At that moment, I know she'd look after him. And me.

'Okay, I'll think about it. But I'd need to speak to Pat, too.' As I say it, the weight lifts. My shoulders relax, my frown unfurls, my strides lengthen. 'So, where is this inn, then?'

We enter the *Igneous Rock* just before nightfall. The small gas lamps hanging outside have just been lit, the stable, which is just closing, full of horses. The wooden sign swings in the gentle breeze, creaking on rusted hinges, an erupting volcano painted upon it, the name in red paint below.

Music floats out onto the cobbled street, the sounds of string instruments plucked in tune and the rhythmic beating of a drum.

'My favourite,' smiles Elera, flashing me one of her beautiful smiles. One that I know means she is truly happy because her dimples become clear on her cheeks and her eyes widen despite the lamp light. '*Fair Auld Ghondulon.*'

'We don't have many musicians where I'm from,' I say, drinking in the sweet, harmonious melody.

'Well, darling, you're in for a treat tonight. Come on.' She places her arm around my shoulders and pulls me to the door of the inn.

As we enter, an eruption of music, chat and an array of coloured light startle me. Each of the gas lamps in the *Igneous Rock* are covered in coloured glass, creating the illusion of rainbow-like lighting. The musicians sit upon a large, raised stage at the left side of the inn, several rows of people standing beneath them, singing, dancing and drinking large mugs of beer.

Straight ahead are an arrangement of large circular tables and long bar against the back wall. The right side must be for the quieter patrons. The lights are plain and dimmed in this section, with small booths. Very few people sit there. At that side, a spiralling set of stairs lead up to the second-floor bedrooms which overlook the bar.

'I hope we can get a room which isn't directly above that stage,' I shout into Elera's ear.

'Don't worry, darling. I'm not planning to go to sleep until well after the music has stopped.'

She strides towards the bar, and I follow behind, noticing that we're pulling in stares from the people seated in this middle section. Mostly leering old men, but now that I look properly, there are several nice-looking younger men also staring our way. I'm used to it, but usually the looks are frightened frowns. It's nice to be looked at in a different way.

I turn away, joining Elera at the bar. She takes her place on a tall stool, throwing down some of Orochi's coin onto the wooden bar top.

'Two large beers, Tum,' she shouts to the barman. Despite the noise he hears her easily and returns with two large metal tankards, foam overflowing and dripping down the side.

He smiles. 'Elera, long time no see.'

'Yes, I've been...*detained* on other business.'

'Well, it's great to see another of the old crew. Mostly the young, rich ones,' he nods to the people dancing at the stage. 'Or the passers-through we get in here now.' He points to the dark booths. 'Times are tight, so people are spending their coin elsewhere.'

'I'll be here for a night or two, Tum. Can I get a room? Two beds,' she says, nodding to me.

'Sure thing, Elera. Anything for you.' They exchange familiar, deep-rooted expressions. 'Enjoy your drink. I'll speak to you later. As you can see it's busy tonight.' He nods and moves down the bar to serve a group of boys and girls, about my age, all lavishly dressed.

I watch them for a few moments, thinking about how different my life would have been, brought up in a large town like this, with a family that had money. Perhaps I would have grown up, just like those boys and girls, and be enjoying a night listening to music with my friends. But I didn't and I'm not. Instead, I've lost my parents, my brother, and I'm sharing a room with an assassin tonight.

That thought brings a smile to my face.

'What's making you happy?' asks Elera, looking from me to the group along the bar.

'Oh, just thinking...about how different the world is, how different people can turn out just because of who your parents are or where you are born.'

'That's very true, Corena. And deep. But people also make their own choices. You can accept what you've been given, continue on the same trajectory that your life started on. Or you can change it. Divert your destiny.' She takes a large gulp of her beer. 'You always have a choice, darling. It's up to you what you choose to do. Always.'

I look at her, differently from before. She is an assassin, but that's only what she does. Not what she is. Inside, she's good and she's wise. And there's lots of her own light still left in there, despite what she said about her brother earlier. Maybe that's true of me, too.

Or maybe it's the beer talking.

I take a long swig and belch dramatically.

Elera gives me a look.

'I've always wanted to do that,' I say. 'My dad used to do it all the time.'

She smiles and shakes her head.

'Why don't you go join the young ones?' she says, pointing her tankard at the group just leaving the bar to return to the stage.

'Nah, not my kind of thing.'

'Have you ever tried?'

I shrug.

'Well, perhaps you should reign in your burps and chat to one of these nice gentlemen over here.' She points to the tables behind us, and as I turn, I immediately swing back round, seeing several men staring at us.

I run my still dirty hair between my fingers, feeling the heat rising in my cheeks. 'It's not just men I like.'

'I can tell, darling,' she replies, winking at me. 'But it's best for girls like us to hide that in public places. Keep a low profile for now.'

I nod.

'Why, a beautiful young girl like you could get anything you wanted from any of these men, I'll wager.' She turns. 'Men are on this Earth for many reasons. War, work, and sex. I don't need them for two of those. Come join me if you get bored of drinking on your own, darling.' She winks, gets up from her stool and joins a table of men behind me.

As I sip my beer, I half-listen to the conversations. Well, what I can hear over the music. Elera leads the chat, as they recount old stories of Ghondulon, discussing the latest trading prices and fashions, and the current political climate. Very little of it interests me, and as the chat continues and I drink tankard after tankard, I drift away and into my own thoughts. I can't stop wondering where Pat is tonight.

I'm brought out of my funk by Tum, the barman. 'Here's your key, ma'am. I'm assuming Elera will be up for some time and thought you might want to get an early night.' He smiles kindly and I give him a nod.

I slide off my stool and walk to the stairs.

Elera is sitting on the knee of a large, muscular man who looks like a farmer. They are laughing and drinking spirits straight from the bottle. She'll be fine.

When I reach the top landing, I check my room key and follow the numbers on the doors until I'm outside.

I unlock and open, the room in darkness. I fumble, the effects of too much beer making me accidentally smash a lamp.

'Dash!' I say, feeling around for another. But I think it's the only one.

I turn to open the door and let the low light from the bar come in.

But a large shadow blocks my path.

'Sit, girl. And don't shout out.'

CHAPTER 14

'Sit on the bed.'

I still can't see anything. My eyes need a moment to adjust.

'Who are you?' I ask.

'Just listen. Orochi would like you to come with us.' The voice is smooth and slow.

'Where?'

'To her home.'

'Why?'

'Too many questions. Will you come?'

'I'd better tell...'

'No. Come alone. Do not tell Elera.'

'But she's my friend. And she'll wonder where I've gone.'

I move towards the speaker, but a hand on my shoulder tells me there are others in the room that I can't see. Already my arms are tingling, ready to strike.

It would be stupidity for me to leave with strangers who've broken into my room during the night, telling me to abandon my one friend. I won't leave, even if I have to fight. I begin thinking of ways to get Elera's attention.

'Our men will keep her occupied for a few hours. And she is nobody's friend.'

'She is my friend. And I'll not leave without telling her or until you tell me what this is about.'

'It's about you. And your brother.'

And there it is. The trigger word. The one thing they could say to make me go with them. But I'm still reluctant. They might be lying. I keep my body tense, ready to strike if I need to.

'Do you know where he is?'

'Yes.'

'And let me guess, you'll not tell me where he is unless I come with you?'

'Correct.'

'And as long as I don't tell Elera?'

This deal is getting worse all the time, but what choice do I have.

'Affirmative.'

'Well, I'd better come with you, then.'

All I can see are outlines. These people could be lying, but I can't take the chance. It would be entirely within Hiro's capability to set me up like this. 'Okay, so how do I get out of here without being seen?'

Everyone goes black as a bag is squeezed over my head and my hands tied up. I'm feeling more and more like this is a trap.

'Hey, what's that for?'

'Protection.'

'I don't need protection.'

'No. Ours. You cannot know where we're going.'

'I know where she lives. Where are you taking me, liar?'

'No, this is still her home. Just not the one you know.'

A rope is tied around my chest and my feet leave the ground as someone picks me up from behind. A breeze of cold, night air drift through my hood as the window opens.

'Hold the rope.'

I obey. Then my stomach jumps right up into my mouth. I fall the twenty feet from window to ground, being slowed just before my feet hit the ground.

A horse neighs. Two people whisper.

I'm pushed up two steps and into somewhere warm. Paint and varnish hit me as I sit on a cushioned seat. A door closes behind, wood on wood.

An image of a horse drawn cart from earlier comes back to me.

'Hello?' I ask, not sure if I'm alone.

'No speaking,' say a rough, gravelly voice. Male. Older.

'It's kind of hard to trust you folks.'

Without the hope of seeing Pat, I'd have fought my way away from these people back in the room. But that hope keeps me on my best behaviour.

'How so?'

'You know with the whole threatening me in the dark, whipping a hood over my head, throwing me out a window into a cart, and taking me to a secret location.'

'I can see your point of view.'

Weird thing to say. 'And am I wrong?'

'Yes.'

'So, I can trust you?'

'Yes.'

'We shall see.'

We proceed in silence, my thoughts only on Patrick.

He had better be safe. If anyone has harmed him...

The rage rises.

But I breathe.

Not yet.

Control.

We stop and I'm hurled out the cart, nearly falling in my blind state.

'You could be gentler,' I say, not sure who I'm speaking to.

'Gentle is back that way. The way forward is rough.' Like his voice.

'Yeah, I'm getting that impression.'

A large hand pushes the middle of my back to urge me forwards. I hate walking without seeing. I keep thinking I'm going to smack my head on a wall or door or stub my toe on something.

We enter a first door, descend sixteen stairs, then enter another door. The hand at my back then departs. I'm left. But I'm not alone.

I sense many people around me. Like they are closing in and they're going to hurt me. I start thrashing at the rope around my wrist and swinging my head, trying to get the hood off.

'Get it off me. Let me out. Don't touch me. Where's Patrick?' my voice booms around the room.

My echoed voice calms me again, just as the hood is removed.

I instantly close my eyes as the single lamp in the centre of the room attacks me. But no-one else does. The ropes are loosened from my wrists, and I bring them to my chest, rubbing each softly.

'No harm will come to you here, Ice-Wiccan.'

I'm startled by the name and their knowledge of my abilities, but perhaps I shouldn't be. They already knew about Pat and knew they could use him to get me here.

'Where am I? And who are you?'

'You are somewhere secret. We'll not tell you until we trust you. You understand that we need secrecy. Our group is not exactly approved by the Queen.'

I squint my eyes open to see a young man standing just two yards in front of me. All around me others sit, all looking at me and not the speaker. Orochi is among them, as are her three guests from earlier.

'As for my name, we do not use them here. Not real ones. It's safer for us. So, I am Cerebrum, and you are Rime. Acceptable?'

'I don't care what you call me. I'm here for my brother. I was told you knew where he was.'

'We'll get to that but first indulge me. Are you happy to accept the use of no formal names, using the name provided for you?'

'Yes, sure.'

'Good. Before we continue you must swear to never mention this meeting, nor anything discussed, outside this group of people.'

'Fine, I don't know any of you. And I don't want to. I just want to get Pat and leave this town.'

'Well, let us have a discussion first. Then you can go down whichever path you wish. Please sit.' He points to an empty chair to my right.

I sit in the circle, the eyes and faces of strangers following me. Many have their hoods up, much like the three at Orochi's earlier.

'How long have you displayed abilities?' asks Cerebrum. He looks young, his brown skin unwrinkled. Much too young to be the leader of this group. His dreadlocked hair hangs loose from beneath his hood.

His eyes penetrate me. I'm naked in his gaze and his thoughts search me, moving through my head.

'What abilities?' The moment I say it, I begin shaking.

'Really?' He knows I've lied. Somehow, he knows. He raises his eyebrows.

'Define abilities.' I try being smart. It's the same attitude I used to give my dad when I stayed out too late or hung around with the wild boys from the mountains.

'Don't waste our time, girl.' The voice snarls from my left, opposite Cerebrum. 'We all know. Just spit it out, or we'll be forced to do more than speak to you.' The girl who speaks is huge. Easily over six-foot, thick muscle in her exposed arms and legs. Her eyes seem to glow yellow beneath her hood.

'Easy, Sway. Be nice. She is one of us.' Cerebrum has the calm of a leader. And the authority. The huge girl does not argue, even though she'd dwarf him.

I look back at the leader, who holds one arm up to calm her. I try not to stare or gasp or say anything, but his wrist and hand are missing from his right arm. A sword wound by the looks of it, smooth and flat, the work of a very sharp blade.

Now that I've noticed it, I can't help but watch his stump as he speaks.

'Rime, we know about you. And we know what you can do.'

'But how do you know?'

'It's only fair we're honest, if we demand the same from you.' He looks to his left at Orochi, who nods. 'Both Psych and I are clairvoyants.'

'You can read my mind?'

'Not exactly. It doesn't work like that. But we can tell when you lie for example. Or that you are a fellow Wiccan. But we couldn't say how many tankards of ale you had tonight.'

A few laughs flutter around the room. Cerebrum is clearly popular and well liked. I can see it myself already, and it makes me feel more at ease. I think I might even be able to trust him.

'Everyone in this room has a mutation, an ability which most people would find unusual. We are called Wiccan by the Queen, and she has hunted us for more than a decade, even when she was Princess Freya. She hates us all. Everyone here. And we're unified against her. This is our union against her discrimination and the Kurikon, who changed their religion and beliefs to suite her. We are the Order of Mutare.'

Several people whoop or cheer at the speech. Chests swell and eyes focus upon Cerebrum. He has united these outsiders, these people who are different from everyone else, and they love him for it.

'Rime, I'll ask once more: how long have you known of your abilities? And how well developed are they?'

These people are like me. And Pat. They think like me, too. I swallow under the intensity of the room. Of the magnitude of the revelations. Of how important my next few words might be. So, I'll make them honest.

I'm fed up lying.

I'm sick of hiding who I am.

I want to share my abilities, even if they terrify me more than I'll ever admit.

I never wanted to be Wiccan, but being a Mutare might not be so bad.

CHAPTER 15

'I've known since I was young.' I pause, wondering if I should continue. I've not told anyone before. Not confessed the whole truth in this way. My hands shake as I continue. Can I really trust them? Can I really trust anyone?

'That was six years ago. But I did something terrible then. I killed...my brother.' I look around the room, expecting shocked faces. None are.

'And ever since I've tried to hide my abilities. I'd hoped if I hid who I was, pretended not to be different, that life would easier. But it wasn't. I lived in a small town and was never forgiven for what I did. Then I showed my powers to many people by accident. So, my parents let me go, ashamed of me and eager to restore the family's reputation with the Kurikon.' Again, no sign of shock. I wonder how familiar my story is.

Why am I telling them all this? It's like my brain has been opened all that I've kept hidden in there is spilling out. I look at Cerebrum, wondering if this is his powers making me so candid.

'I've been called Wiccan for years, thinking it terrible. But I should have realised then, as I do now, that I'm lucky. My abilities are a gift. My greatest fear has not been the dark but my own light. And now I'm ready to let it shine.'

I kept my eyes closed as I spoke, hoping that it would keep my words honest. The faces that study me now are the faces of people who understand. They nod and one by one, they approach me.

As I stand, they each hug me for a moment and whisper, 'welcome.'

Once each of them has returned to their seats, I also sit. I look back to Cerebrum.

'Well said, Rime. We are here to help your light shine. Stand in the centre of the circle.'

I obey, crossing my arms over my chest and looking to Orochi for reassurance. Her nod helps, but I'm exposed.

Everyone stands and holds their arms out towards me, eyes closed. Nobody speaks or gives me instruction.

So, I copy them, placing my hands out in front and closing my eyes. My mind relaxes: everything drops out, even my worry about Pat. Slowly it clears, and my thoughts are consumed with ice.

Icebergs, stalactites and stalagmites, icicles, and slow-falling snow. White-capped mountain tops and frozen waterfalls. Avalanches and blizzards. A whole city covered in ice. An ice-shard piercing an eye...

My mind suddenly fills again, and I open my eyes.

I'm encased in ice, completely immobile, yet with no sense of being trapped. I control the ice. It's my friend. My servant. If I want to it break, to melt, to thicken, to morph – all of these I could do in a moment. I'm the god of my own power and I like it.

With a tight squeeze of my muscles, the sheath shatters. Large lumps thump onto the ground, sliding across the floor to the feet of the other Mutare.

My head quickly spins round, taking in the variety of forms and powers; a woman with fists wreathed in flame, an old man who floats a foot off the ground, a girl, younger than me, drawing my broken clumps of ice to her, where she pools it into a cube of water.

Many of them must have abilities not visible, or perhaps they just resist the urge to show off, like I did. Like the others do. My mouth remains wide open.

'Thank you everyone. Please be at ease. Save your energies.'

Everyone sits, the abilities gone. A puddle beneath the young girl is all that remains to evidence the last few moments. She moves her hands and the water drains into the floor.

'Rime, that was impressive for a Mutare with limited experience.'

Heads nod and Orochi looks at me intensely, in a way that she didn't when we met a few hours earlier.

'It was like you all helped to clear my mind. Like your power helped me to control mine. It felt...incredible.'

'We are stronger as one. The Queen has sought to keep us divided, but we never realised why. Not until we came together and each of us realised our power is amplified by the presence of other Mutare. It's our major strength. But we worry it may also be our biggest weakness. If we were caught together like this, we could be wiped out with one Golden Ennead.'

'Golden Ennead?' I ask.

'It's the Queen's personal Mutare killing crew. They are also Mutare, but under her influence. They serve her, willing to harm their own. They are mercenaries and savages and deadly. They are our biggest threat. They are the reason we have not moved to assassinate the Queen.'

'But you plan to soon? That is what you asked of Elera today.'

'Correct.'

'But why her? Is she Mutare, too?'

'Yes.'

'Then why is she not here?'

'Elera...well, she has a mixed past.'

'I know she's an assassin. But she has a good heart. She offered to look after my brother and me.'

'She did?' asks Orochi.

'Yes. I trust her. She has saved me twice now.'

'You come from a different part of the world,' she says slowly, emphasising each word. 'Here, trust is a fragile concept. People do things and say things for their best interest. I would not freely give your trust, despite your instincts to do so. The people of the south can have a fair face and use fair words, but often you'll find venom beneath. Do not be bitten. The poison will be too much for a good soul such as yourself.'

'I'm not a good soul.'

A silence follows.

'Neither am I.' To my surprise, it's Sway that speaks. She gives me a small nod. She flexes her bulging bicep as if to show us all her strength once more.

'Or me,' says the old man who floated.

'And me.' This time it's the woman with the flames.

'I've no soul.' It's the young girl who controls water. I stare into her child-face, thinking about how someone so young can feel like that. Has she killed someone, too? Have they all? Or are they just trying to make me feel better?

Cerebrum stands.

'Thank you everyone for attending and welcoming Rime into our circle. For tonight, we shall depart and meet again next week for our more formal summit.'

The Order rise and slowly exit the room via a door in the shadows that I'd not noticed until now. I wait, staring at my hands and unsure of what to do next. Am I a guest or a captive?

'Rime, you are free to leave if you wish, but if you have the time, I'd like to talk to you about a few things.'

'Fine,' I say, not sure how true that really is. As the last person leaves the room, I become faintly aware of my own smell again, so that when Cerebrum and Orochi sit next to me, I move back a little.

'It's okay, you have nothing to fear.' Orochi gives me a kind smile.

I stay silent, preferring them to think I'm afraid rather than trying to hide my hideous stench.

'So, what do you think? We are an odd collective. Not perhaps much to look at, or with the best moral compasses at times. But we do all have something in common. And in times like these, being hunted as a pack is much better than as an individual.'

I nod. 'I agree. But before I join you, I need to get my brother first.'

'And we shall help you,' replies Cerebrum. 'I'll help you find him myself. But my loyalty is to the Order. I won't do anything that undermines us.'

'I understand,' I say, smiling through cracked lips. 'And thank you.'

Orochi turns to me, much more serious. 'And in return for our help, you'll then help us, yes?'

Her cracked, aged skin is dry from constant exposure to the sun, a tone that nobody in the north has, or could achieve, with the short days we have. The people here look so different to my own, yet I've a greater affinity to them, like a long-lost family. Orochi in particular.

'Yes, I'll help. As soon as Pat is safe, I'll help the Order. But why me? There were so many people who are more experienced and capable than me.'

'The problem with experience is that it leaves its mark. Those with less experience will be harder to detect and more likely to get close enough to the Queen. That is why I cannot do this. Or cerebrum or the others in the Mutare. Many are capable. I believe you are, too.' She smiles and it doesn't suite her. 'I must go, Cerebrum. I need to get back to the plans and my spies are due back any time now. I must be at home.'

He nods and places his good hand on his heart. 'I'll help Rime in the meantime. Fair journey.'

She nods, also touching her heart with her hand. 'Fair journey.'

I watch her leave, slowly, with a limp. She's old. Very old. Cerebrum appears to be the leader, but she is the one in charge. She has steel in her heart, hardened from years of some kind of hurt. I know because I have the same heart.

'So where shall we start?' Cerebrum asks.

'I don't know Ghondulon. I've no clue.'

'Well fortunately we both know someone who does. Let's go and sober Elera up.'

~

We walk back to the *Igneous Rock* in the pre-dawn light.

The streets are scattered with the early risers. Farm-boys walking out of Ghondulon to the fields back up the main road, horses pulling carts full of market goods, miners moving towards the subterranean entrances of the coal, salt, and diamond mines.

It reminds me of the sulphur mines which took the life of Elera's younger brother. I wonder how they get up and down the volcano each day. I stare up at the mountain side, but see no movement, aside from the cattle chewing the dew-covered cud.

'How do you like the south?' Cerebrum asks me.

'It's different.'

'Better or worse?'

'Just different. It's busier and warmer, as are the people. Nicer on the surface but more complex beneath. And so many statues and pictures of the Queen. It's like she's watching us all the time.'

'It does feel that way sometimes. She has spies everywhere, too, so always mind who you speak to. Even me, or other Mutare members,' he says, smiling widely.

I smile back. His face is near perfect, like he was crafted by an artist for a statue, to resemble one of the gods. Ha. He looks a little like Ha, God of the desert and the south. I wonder if he comes from farther south.

'Do you smell burning?' I ask.

Just ahead of us, black smoke spirals into the air, from directly above where we are heading.

A young boy sprints past us and barges into me by accident.

'Watch your step, boy,' shouts Cerebrum, grabbing the young boy with his good hand. 'Apologise to the lady.'

'Sorry, ma'am. But words got out that there's to be a-hangin'.'

'A hanging? There's not been one of those in years. Are you sure?' Cerebrum asks.

'Aye, sir. Auld Granny Grossit told me hersel'. There was a boy who set fire to the inn, but they overpowered and hauled him away.'

'What did they look like?' I ask. 'The boy?'

'White hair, small. He is a fire-wiccan, someone said.'

'Which inn?'

'The Igneous Rock.'

Cerebrum lets the boy go and he sprints off down a road to our left.

'Come, we want to get to the inn before the rush of people. When they hear of this, they'll all flock from their beds or work to see. We do not want to be in the way.'

'We should go,' I say.

'No, it will be too crowded, and we need to find your brother, remember?'

'I remember well enough. But what if it's him that they're hanging? What if he got caught? I need to check.'

Fear is flooding my brain. Images of the old hanging platform next to our village church amplify it.

'Is Pat a fire-wiccan?' asks Cerebrum.

'Well, no.'

'Then there's no point in us going to the hanging of a wiccan – we'll only draw attention to you. Now is a good time to search for Pat while everyone else is busy.'

'Just let me check it's not Pat. Then we'll go back.'

'Fine, but we check and then we go. We don't get close to any of the Enforcers or do anything to stop or intervene. Your mission is too important.'

We follow the road the young boy just went down and as we move along the lengthy, muddy track, people begin to emerge from the houses and side streets as Cerebrum predicted. As we get closer, Enforcers are lining the streets.

'We should go back, Rime.'

His resistance only increases my persistence. 'No.'

I push ahead, slicing through the crowds that now gather, inducing annoyed glances and harsh words from the people I push, but I don't care. I need to see who they are hanging.

Just ahead, between two tall houses, the street ends and the town square opens up. It's already packed. But a large wooden stage stands high in the centre.

'They usually use this for Royal visits and speeches or sometimes big musical concerts, or when the circus comes, but it's never this busy. Death seems to bring everyone out. Isn't there something wrong with that?' Cerebrum tells me.

I don't answer because I'm surging closer. I can't see anyone up there yet, but the hangman is getting the noose ready. I watch him checking that the trapdoor mechanism still functions. It does.

Then two Royal Enforcers bring someone up onto the stage. The crowd's volume increases, the intensity of their surge forward snowballing. I'm nearly decked twice but manage to keep my feet and get close enough to just about see.

The hangman is placing the rope around the neck of the person.

A young person.

The blood-thirsty crowd begin to cheer. They are chanting something, but I close it out. I push forward farther and climb onto someone's shoulders.

'Oi, geroff.'

I ignore the man who I'm on top of.

An Enforcer is reading something to the crowd. The rope is

around a young boy's neck. With white hair. He's covered in soot and his head sags, like he's exhausted.

'PAT!?' I scream as loud as I can. The boy's head flicks up in response.

But the man beneath throws me to the ground. 'Quit yelling, girl.'

Cerebrum arrives behind me and helps me to my feet, before shouting at the man that just dropped me.

But I ignore them both.

The words of the chant finally penetrate me.

'WICCA! WICCA! WICCA!'

'Help me up.' I climb on the shoulders of Cerebrum.

The stage is alight. Fire wreathes it, from the rope itself to the wooden frame and floor and stairs. The Enforcers are huddled together, next to the lever for the trapdoor.

They pull it.

'Nooooooooooo!' My throat hurts as I scream but the commotion from the crowd, and squeals as people run from the fire, drown it out.

I focus and try to recreate my powers, like I did with the Mutare. If I can form a shard and slice the rope, I can save him. I close my eyes.

But I'm knocked from Cerebrum's shoulders, and I crash onto the ground as the fleeing melee stamp all over me.

I fight my way back up, and there's a small gap where I can see the stage.

The trapdoor is open.

The boy on the end of the rope swings motionless.

CHAPTER 16

I barge and shove people aside, thrusting myself towards the burning stage. Enforcers are throwing water and using blankets to douse the flames.

'I need to see his face.' I shout it, but no-one listens. Their interest is waning. They are turning, moving back to their lives.

Cerebrum is far behind me, shouting for me to stop, but I won't. I need to see if it's Pat. Nothing else matters.

I jump up to see the body. It spins slowly at the base of the still-burning rope, but as I rise above the crowd, I can only see the back of his head. White hair, muddied and blood-stained.

As I land, I push forward once again, but trip on someone's foot. My face crashes to the earth, my arms forgetting to break my fall. Feet trample all down my back and legs. One foot stands on my head.

My body shakes, my fists ball. I force myself up beneath the feet of these people, knocking two on their back. They shout angrily at me, but I surge on.

Finally, the crowd thins and only a few stragglers remain. I'm within a few feet of the scorched stage. The body still faces away. As I race towards it, an Enforcer blocks my way.

'Stop. The boy is Wiccan. Nobody is to touch him. Look at what he did?'

I push the Enforcer as hard as I can. He flies through the air backwards, landing two feet away with a thud. I freeze for a second, shocked, before refocusing and moving towards the swinging body.

A second Enforcer approaches but I'm sprinting, and I'll get to the body first. I reach up, grabbing the shoe-less foot and using it to turn the boy.

Staring down at me, eyes blank and soulless, is Patrick.

I collapse. On my knees, I cry out. 'PAT!'

The second Enforcer stays her hand. She waits beside me but does not force me up. The footsteps of another Enforcer come close, and the sun is blocked by their bodies behind me.

But they are irrelevant.

Pat is gone.

My brother is dead.

'How...how, Pat?' I bubble his name out.

I punch the ground. And then again. And again, and no-one stops me. Snot pours from my nose, tears stream for my eyes, but my fist does not stop hitting the ground.

Somehow hitting the ground will help, like it will bring back Pat.

Finally, one of the Enforcers grabs my wrist to stop me.

I look up and see a kindly smile from her. She then releases my wrist, but I'm done punching. I hold Pat's bare feet close to my face. Skin to skin.

He's so cold already, despite the fire around us.

His soul will have left for the Haven, oh I hope he ascends to the Haven, but I'm not ready to let it go.

He's too young to leave this world.

He was supposed to go to school.

He was supposed to be the one who made my parents proud.

But now he is a cold corpse, hanging from a stage in the square of a strange town. How did I let all of this happen? I turn to find Cerebrum, but the Enforcers start tying rope around my wrists, their sympathies at an end.

'You'll come with us. The Paramount of Ghondulon will want to discuss your relationship to the Wiccan,' says the female Enforcer.

'He's not Wiccan! He's my little brother who's never hurt a fly in his life. Who is kind and loyal and innocent.'

'He was Wiccan. The Queen's decree states that all Wiccan must be tried and executed upon discovery. We must follow the law. Just as you must follow us now, if you are his sister.' The woman's face has lost its warmth, replaced with cold efficiency.

I spot Cerebrum in the crowd which has gathered to watch me now. Is there nothing they won't watch? Is this just another scene to brighten their dull day? I stare at them all, my eyes condemning each one.

I hope every single person watching descends and passes through Ka-Ferno's Gate. I hope all the God's curse down upon them.

But I know it's useless. The Gods have abandoned me. And Pat.

He'll never live on a farm. With chickens and animals and everything else. My promise to him is broken.

When I lock my gaze with Cerebrum, I try to transmit hatred, hurt, frustration, anger, but he only returns kindness. He is crying. And as he wipes the tears away, he turns and disappears into the crowd, abandoning me to whatever comes next. Leaving me to deal with my grief all on my own, in a strange town where nobody knows me or will miss me.

I turn back to Pat, whose body has spun to face me. The Enforcers allow me a moment. 'Bye, Pat. Fair journey. I promise I'll make you proud. I'll do something amazing, just like you would have. And I promise you this: your death will mean something.'

My muscles fail, my brain becomes blank, and my senses numb.

I'm dragged along by the Enforcers who give me an occasional kick to ensure I'm still alive. Eyes stare at me as my body is transported to the largest building overlooking the square. It's old. Really old.

I only notice because I'm dropped to the ground right outside.

Another large statue of the Queen stands over me, peering out at the city of Ghondulon, keeping her watchful eye over her kingdom.

'I'll just make sure the Paramount wants to see her. Keep her here.' The female Enforcer moves inside.

How did Terra let Pat be taken? He promised me he'd keep my brother safe. And where did his powers suddenly come from. I wonder if he knew or suspected this before. It makes sense, he's my brother, but I just figured that it might have spared him, that he was 'normal' like my parents.

I'm left on the ground, the Enforcer having no interest in me. My hands are white, blood cut off by the rope and my body in a general state of exhaustion. I can't remember the last time I slept properly.

I know I'm shutting down and despite my efforts, I can't stop it. First the light dies. Then the sound. Then everything.

'Wake her up.'

I'm already awake but I keep my eyes closed. I want to stay asleep and never wake to this nightmare. Falling water splashes.

A gentle slap on my cheek. I decide to open my eyes and see where I am and find out what the hell happened to Pat.

'Are you Wiccan, girl?' A man sitting in a tall, golden throne eats his breakfast, not looking at me as he speaks.

I refuse to respond. I won't be called girl anymore.

'Are you deaf? Answer Paramount Regus.' It's the male Enforcer from earlier, who raises his arm as he speaks. Behind him I spot a water fountain. I could take him out with one sharp shard of ice. If he touches me, I will.

'Now, now, Titus. No need for violence...yet. So, are you Wiccan? I'm told you are a sibling to the Wiccan we hanged.'

My body tenses and my teeth grind as he calls Pat Wiccan. When he says the word hanged, I can't stop myself.

'What did he do? Why are you calling him Wiccan? He did nothing to you. Nothing.' I stand as I speak, stepping towards the Paramount, but the rope on my wrists becomes taut and I remain six feet from the golden-haired man.

He tilts his head as he analyses me, taking his time to work me out most likely. I give him nothing, keeping my face impassive, save for rage.

'What lovely hair you have...it could do with a clean...perhaps you'd make a nice maid for me...you'd look good serving wine at banquets...yes, perhaps...'

'WHY DID YOU MURDER HIM?' It hurts my throat, but I must get it out.

A thump to the back of my legs makes me collapse to my knees, but I keep my eyes on him, showing no sign of hurt or acknowledgment of the punishment, even though it hurts like a prod from Ka-Ferno's trident. I need answers.

'On second thoughts, you have far too barbaric a nature to serve...I grow bored...give her the Wiccan Test.' He turns back to his breakfast.

The Enforcers take me to the side of the large chamber we're in, placing me in a large chair and strapping my arms and legs to it. I resist as they do it, but another two Enforcers join them and force me in. Large, metal cuffs lock my limbs in place. I don't care what happens to me now. I just need to know.

'Why will no-one tell me what happened? At least tell me that before you torture me.'

'Oh, we're not torturing you. Not yet. If we find you are Wiccan, then yes, you shall be tortured and executed.' He rises from his chair, wiping crumbs from his waistcoat as he approaches. 'But to answer your question and shut you up, your brother killed four Enforcers last night at the *Igneous Rock*. Him and that foreigner, who took out twenty more of my soldiers, before escaping. He is... sorry, he was...a fire-Wiccan. He had to die.'

My heart burns. He was at the Inn. He was probably there to meet me. Elera said Terra would come to me with Pat and I didn't have the patience to wait. And because I left, I wasn't there to protect him. To take him away from this place. It's my fault he died. It's my fault.

'Turn on the machine. Let the electricity test her Wiccancraft.'

Energy flows through me, tickling me inside and cracking on my skin, like the noise lightning makes. My power, the feeling I have when I'm about to use my ability surges inside me. I could draw the water from the fountain in the centre of the chamber. I change it all to the sharpest ice shards possible and project them through the air, piercing the hearts of these people.

The Paramount would fall with his breakfast undigested.

The Enforcers would not see their families tonight.

I would have my revenge.

But it would not be enough. It wouldn't bring back Pat. Nor allow the ghost of Gullan to rest.

I sense the fountain's water changing and I fight the urge. I can't show them my abilities, or they'll hang me like Pat. I can't die.

I must live, if not for my sake, then for Pat's. I won't let his end become mine. I'll take vengeance, but not on these people. They are pawns of a deeply corrupted and flawed system. A system which persecutes and discriminates against those who are different.

To kill a tree, you must remove its roots.

So, I will remove the roots of this land.

The Queen and the Kurikon.

And every blow, every wound, everyone I destroy on the way, will be for Pat.

CHAPTER 17

'Stop. She's clearly not Wiccan.'

The electricity stops passing into me. I breathe again, having held my breath for ages, trying hard not to show any sign of my powers. And I've managed it. I've tricked them.

One of the Enforcers touches me with a wooden stick. The flow of energy leaves me completely.

'Take her away. Assign her somewhere that she won't have to speak to anyone important.' The Paramount turns from me, like I've spoilt his breakfast.

How dare I interrupt him and inconvenience him with the death of my brother.

But I keep it in. He's clearly an idiot and so not worth it.

The Enforcers pull along my exhausted body through several doors and stone corridors. They stop at one, open it and toss me onto the floor, slamming the door shut after me.

'Treat us real nice, huh?' Hiro's smug voice ignites the rage in me.

I leap to my feet and dive for her throat with two arms outstretched. She easily pushes me aside, my weak, exhausted body an easy defence for a trained Enforcer like her.

Her deflection and my momentum take me onto one of four

bunks, the thin mattress taking the bulk of my lunge. I twist onto my back and try to get up, but my arm buckles. I stop forcing my body. There's so little left in me, my emotional hourglass emptying.

Sorg moves across the room, coming to sit on my bunk. I move away from him, making myself small in the corner of the bed. He moves closer and I shrink away, curling up even more.

'We'll not hurt you, Corena,' he says, in his deep, reassuring voice. His featureless face will always seem strange. Yet I'd rather look at it than Hiro's.

The tension in my muscles falls away and find myself burying my face into his shoulder, sobbing uncontrollably.

'We are sorry. We were captured. They forced us to talk. We told them about the plan to come to Ghondulon but no more. They'd have worked that out themselves.'

'Traitors.' I enjoy spitting my guilt towards someone else.

'I won't deny it. We've both been traitors for a long time. But we did not sell out Pat or Terra. The Enforcers found Pat themselves. They had us tagging along to confirm identity. But it was not needed.'

'What happened?'

'Pat and Terra were upset that you were not there and Elera did not know what had happened. Pat lost control. And so did Terra.'

I look up at him, waiting for him to finish the story. I didn't think I'd want to know the details, but now he's speaking, I don't want him to stop. I want to know and treasure every last action of my brother.

Sorg looks over to Hiro and shakes his head. 'Anyway, the Enforcers tried to take Pat and Terra away, but he suddenly produced fire. He seemed surprised. It must have been the first time because he couldn't control it. We all hid when it started. He killed four before he managed to stop himself. But by then, it was too late. A whole troop of Enforcers engulfed them. Terra killed many, but he was overrun. Both he and Elera escaped, I think. But they got Pat, eventually. Hiro and I were then taken away and locked up in here.'

'Was he with you…you know, before he was…'

'No, they had him somewhere else. When we got here, we were thrown in here, and here we have been since. One of the Enforcers questioned us about him but believed that we knew nothing about Pat's powers. I couldn't believe it when it happened. He was obviously just like you, Corena. But with fire.'

I nod and sit back on the bunk, leaning my back against the wall. Sorg gets up to give me some space. I smile at him as he walks back to his bunk. Hiro sits on her own, directly across from me. For once, she doesn't have a smirk or a wise word to give me. There is almost sympathy in the frown she gives me.

But they say nothing else to me. And I've nothing to say to them.

I picture the scene of Pat's last stand. I imagine how he must have felt, to arrive at the inn, thinking he'd finally got back to me. But then to find I'd gone, Elera with no clue where to.

And now he's gone. Never reunited with me. Dying on his own, in front of a crowd of horrible people he didn't know for powers he never knew he had until right at the end.

I failed my brother.

Slowly, exhaustion cripples me and I slide onto my side and fall fast asleep, my dreams full of a tight rope squeezing my neck.

When I wake, the first thing in my head is the image.

Pat swinging.

I force my eyes open to see anything, anyone that isn't that.

'How are you?' Sorg asks. He's pacing up and down the room.

'Fine.' I fight away the urge to bang my head off the floor, to punch the walls, to launch a thousand ice-shards at the ceiling.

'If you want to talk…I'm here.' He nods and continues to pace.

I study his long strides, moving quickly from one end of the cell to the other. He's a man with no face and I've never even asked him why...anything to distract me.

'Sorg, what happened to your face?'

He stops. 'It was taken from me.'

'Why? What did you do to earn...this?'

He slumps back onto his bed. 'I failed to protect the King and Queen.'

Hiro pops her head out from beneath her blanket, listening.

'Hiro and I were part of the Royal Guard. Ten Enforcers chosen to protect the monarchs. One day an assassin got past us, killed the King and Queen, and got away. We were all disgraced and sent off to the far parts of the land. We were sent north, assigned to the district of your village.'

He shifts on his bed, pushing himself up to a seated position. 'Queen Freya held me personally responsible. She hated me as a child, and wanted someone to pay, so she had an old Wiccan lady cast a spell to remove all my features. That way she would never have to look at the face of the man who failed to stop her parent's deaths.'

'So, you both knew Queen Freya? Is that why you were so desperate to give me to her?'

He nods and slumps back down.

'And if we get the chance to, we'll do it again,' adds Hiro. She leaps off her bed and moves closer. 'But Sorg doesn't tell it all. It was a Wiccan who killed her parents. That's why she ordered you all hunted and hanged. That's why we will never, ever like you or your kind. It's you and people like you that got us sent away. That has us here, right now.'

She returns to her bed.

I bury myself beneath my blanket, feeling even worse than before, not better.

'But you have shown me a different side to the Wiccan, Corena.' Sorg's voice is thick with emotion. 'You could have killed us a hundred times over, but you've stayed your hand, despite how cruel both Hiro and I have been to you. I've spent too many years hating the Wiccan and thinking of revenge and it's only made my life worse. I've lost Graf and I'm now in prison. My blue cloak has been taken permanently. I have no face. Hate has got me nowhere.

'I forgive you and all your kind. From now on, I will direct my anger at the right people. At the person I should really hate.'

'Who's that then?' asks Hiro.

'Queen Freya. She did this to us, Hiro. Not some girl who was barely born.'

The room descends into a silent torpor.

We each have our own dark thoughts and griefs to deal with.

Hiro lost her family and her position in the Royal Guard.

Sorg lost his husband and his face.

They were both exiled and sent to the north.

I've lost both my brothers, both my fault, directly and indirectly. But both make me feel equally hollow. It matters not the hand that holds the blade but the person whose inaction allows it to plunge into the innocent's heart.

Rough hands haul me from my bed.

'We are Royal Enforcers, like you. Have a bit of respect,' says Hiro, being pushed out the door of our cell.

'When you accompany Wiccan, you lose the Queen's respect,' responds one of the Enforcers. 'And your fellow Enforcer's.' The Royal emblem, stitched onto her shoulder, is ripped off and tossed on the floor. Sorg's is also removed as they push the big man, unresisting, out of the room.

Fortunately, they have nothing to tear from me. I've lost everything that I ever valued. They can't hurt me.

We are marched back through the corridors, but we don't arrive in the fancy surroundings of the Paramount's chamber, instead lined up in a cobbled square in the centre of the building, four walls surrounding us. Small drops of rain fall. I open my mouth to quench my thirst. As I do it, my stomach rumbles. I must have been asleep for quite a while. It might even be the next day.

I look along the line, and beyond Hiro and Sorg are a sorry looking collection of people, most dressed in rags, covered in dirt. Grubby beggars or criminals I'd say, but the moment that sympathy stirs in me, I look down at myself. Stinking, unwashed, hungry and homeless.

I am one of these people.

But unlike most of them, I will rise.

I will make the world better for those who are marginalised.

I will fight for people like this.

'Stand straight and look respectable. Sell yourself, if that's possible, to the Masters who come. The better you look, the better your new job will be.' The Enforcer who ripped the emblems speaks to us, before disappearing through a door in front of us.

We wait in silence.

'Look strong when the Masters come out and we may yet stay together. The fit and strong get picked first.' Sorg whispers, but his voice carries. An Enforcer spots him talking and marches over, striking him on the jaw with his long, wooden staff.

Sorg hardly moves, but a harsh red mark quickly appears on his otherwise featureless face.

'Keep it quiet. You're a disgrace to us all. If it were up to me, I'd kill you, Necro-friend!'

The Enforcer moves away as the Masters begin to file out of the door. Seven of them walk back and forth inspecting us. Several run their fingers through my hair. One of them jabs my stomach. Fortunately, I saw her do it to someone else further up the line and contract my stomach muscles at the last second. She nods and moves on.

I could kill these Masters right here, right now. But I'd have to fight my way through the city and would be chased. Better to bide my time and take the punishment for now.

'Master Magma, you have first choices for your sulphur mines.'

The woman who punched me moves forward. She begins pointing to people down the line. She takes three, each of them removed by an Enforcer the moment she picks them.

She reaches Hiro and places her hand on her chin. She frowns. Then points. Sorg is also picked immediately after. Both are taken away.

She comes to me. Again, she moves forward.

'Not much to you, but you look determined and healthy enough that you won't die on me. And your hair...it intrigues me.' She fingers her own hair. 'Perhaps I'll chop it and make myself a white-hair wig. It's one colour that I'm missing from my collection.'

'And her,' Magma says, as she turns and exits the square through the door.

An Enforcer pulls me after her and when I pass through the door, there are several wagons all waiting, horses champing at the front.

I'm pushed onto the same wagon as the others who were picked. Six of us in total. My two companions and three strangers. One tall girl, extremely well-built, and two very small, skinny boys. All of us chained onto the floor of the cart.

I spot Master Magma entering her luxurious-looking horse drawn carriage ahead of us. That scutter will not get even a strand of my hair. When the time comes, I'll make sure of that.

'Well, well. Together again, huh?' Hiro smiles at me, in the way she always does, but this time there is something else. What is it? Friendship? No, that's way too much for her. Respect? Perhaps. Or sympathy? Unlikely.

Whatever it is, our old relationship of Enforcer and slave is dead. We are both something different now. Neither of us will go back to what we were. While she has fallen, I know I will rise. Her identity taken, mine only just being discovered. Perhaps we can work together to get out of this situation. Perhaps she could be an ally.

'Yes,' I reply.

'Things are different now, though.'

'They are.'

She holds out her hand and I take it. 'I've been...well, what I am. What I was. But what happened to your brother. I didn't want that. And I want you to see a better side to me. I don't ask forgiveness, nor do I want it. But can we move on...as equals.'

I nod slowly, waiting to see if she smirks or laughs, but her face is fixed, intense, and sincere.

'Well, heck. Of all the people in the world, who'd have thought you two would become friends after all.' Sorg laughs as he finishes speaking.

I look back to Hiro and together we share a smile.

Her debt is cleared.

And I have a new target in mind.

But it will have to wait. I've bigger problems right now.

'Elera said her brother died in these mines,' I say.

'Most people die in these mines. We'll likely be no different,' says Hiro, her old smirk returning.

'I won't die there.'

'What, your lungs made of steel? Give it a few months and you'll see.'

'I'm not going to be there for a few months. I plan to escape. Are you in?'

CHAPTER 18

'Anything's better than slowly dying in the mines. What you got in mind?' Hiro asks, leaning close.

I notice the other three in the cart are listening intently, the boys leaning forward, the tall woman pretending to look behind me towards the town as we begin to leave.

'Later,' I say to her, nodding at our unknown companions.

Our cart is pulled toward the mountain that leans over Ghondulon, it's immense shadow both a volcanic threat and the heart of the town's mining industry.

But I look back at the town, focussing on the sunken centre, where Pat drew his last breath, alone and probably confused. He would have regretted it all. He would have been consumed with guilt about the killings. He would have selflessly worried about me, having found me missing from the inn.

I close my eyes, trying to imagine his face, to re-run some of my memories of us together, to keep them fresh as no more new ones will be made. I swallow several times. First, I kill one brother, then the other is taken from me, and I can't help but feel responsible for Pat's death, too.

I should have chased after him on the beach. I should never have let him leave my side.

'You okay?' asks Sorg, placing a thick hand on my shoulder, his chains rattling.

'No,' I reply. 'But I will be. Or at least, I'll be better. He was the only good thing in my life, really.'

'Losing family is hard.' He stares up at the clouds. The Haven.

'Who's up there?'

'All of them. Mum and Dad. Brother and Sister. Husband.' He turns to me. 'We have all lost, Hiro especially.'

I turn to Hiro. She shakes her head at Sorg.

'You lost family, too?' I ask.

But she does not answer. She looks up at the mountain we're climbing and chews on her nails.

It's Sorg who answers. 'Her whole family. Husband. Three children. The Great Plague took so many of us.'

I'd heard of the Great Plague from Dad and the little schooling I had. But it didn't affect us in the north. We were too spread out for it to reach very far. My small taste of grief is nothing compared to what both of them have gone through. It makes my sorrow seem shallow. It also explains why Hiro is such a scutter. I'd be cold and I'd hate the world if I'd lost my own family, too.

'I'm sorry.' My hollow words end our chat. We all drift off into our own uncomfortable memories of loss and grief.

The air temperature increases as we ascend closer to the summit, the town becoming smaller and smaller beneath us, occasionally being lost to view when the track turns around the side of the mountain.

A strong, toxic smell also begins to drift to us in small gusts. Chokingly strong. After the third one hits my throat and I cough up more mucus, I know I can't do this. I can't stay up here.

'We are doing this soon.' I speak quietly to Sorg and Hiro.

'How soon? We're not even there yet.'

'Days. Just enough time to work out how we'll do it. I assume there won't be much water up here.'

'You kidding? The only water up here is the sweat that constantly pours from your skin.' Hiro smirks and wipes her brow.

Sweat? I'd never even considered it before, but perhaps I can use it. And I'm sure Dad once told me that we're mostly water. It's a long shot, but I stop wiping my skin and let the perspiration build up.

The cart begins to level off, and I turn to see we're now moving downhill towards a dark opening in the side of the mountain. A painted wooden sign above it reads *Station Eleven*.

'I'm Davin.' The tallest of our three new companions speaks. 'These are Kei and Kin, my two annoying brothers.'

'Sorg, Hiro and I'm Corena.'

She nods to us all in turn. 'Corena, it's time to go.' Davin lifts her wrists, and the cuffs fall to the floor.

She disappears.

I gasp. Sorg stands, searching for where she went.

Within two seconds, she re-appears, and the cart has stopped.

'It is time to part ways,' says Davin.

'Fine by me,' says Hiro.

One of the twins, Kei I think, moves over to me and melts my cuffs, his own long since melted.

'We are part of the Order, Corena. Cerebrum sent us. You need to come now.' Davin looks from me to Hiro as she speaks.

'Sorg. Hiro. I must go with them,' I say.

'What?' says Hiro, narrowing her eyes at me.

Sorg stands behind, nodding. 'Yes, you should.'

'What? She's with us, Sorg.'

Sorg starts shaking his head. 'No, she must go with others like her. And she is no longer ours to use, Hiro. If she ever was. We owe her freedom after what has happened. I'm done being an Enforcer anyway.' He looks off into the distance as he says the last part.

'We really must go,' says Davin, looking at me.

I'm suddenly torn. Sorg and even Hiro are hardly friends, but I don't have many allies in this world. I can't just leave them, despite how rotten Hiro can be at times.

'They are coming,' I say.

'No. They are not,' she replies, shaking her head.

'Then I am not.'

'Corena, don't be a fool. She'd turn you over to the Queen for her own gain. Come with us. You can make a difference with us. They are not like us. They can't come.'

Shouts from the opening. The footsteps of many Enforcers echo to us.

'Time to go,' I say. 'They are coming.'

Davin turns to Kin. 'Slow them down.'

The twin faces the tunnel, hands aloft, and the entire roof collapses, sealing us off from the Enforcers.

'That won't hold them long. And others will come via the path.'

'So how do we escape? If we go down, they'll be waiting for us. If we go up, magma and sulphur fumes.' I really hope I haven't made a bad choice by trusting them.

Davin turns to me. 'Take my hand.' She holds it out to me.

I look at Sorg, who shrugs.

My hand clasps inside hers.

'Now what?' I ask her.

'Hold your breath,' she replies, looking at Kei and Kin, and nodding.

With a pop, everything disappears.

Every second the landscape changes. Pop after pop. The only constant is Davin. And Kei and Kin, holding her other hand.

My head is spinning, and I eventually close my eyes, trying to stop myself from vomiting. Then it stops.

A bird chirps. The poisonous fumes have gone. The heat from volcano replaced with a chill wind.

I open my eyes.

I'm surrounded by trees, pines and palms. That's the first thing that confuses me. Those two trees don't go together.

Cerebrum smiles at me. Orochi stands at his shoulder, a much sterner expression on her aged face. That's the second confusion.

'How did I get here?' I ask.

I spin and see Davin, Kei and Kin.

'I jumped us,' responds the tall girl. We are now five miles away from Ghondulon. Free and safe.' She turns away with Kei and Kin.

'Where are Sorg and Hiro?'

She doesn't turn. 'I told you they weren't coming.'

CHAPTER 19

A small stream provides me with the raw materials I need.

The ice shards quickly form in my hand, and I launch them at Davin's back in a matter of seconds.

But at the moment of impact, she disappears, reappearing five feet to the right, facing me and smiling.

'Nice try, Icicle. But I'm too fast for you.' She disappears again. A hand slaps the back of my head.

Control your emotions, Rime.

I whirl round, a blade of ice formed in my hand, ready to slice her, but I hit air and nothing else. When I turn back round, she is back in the spot she started in. 'They'll be recaptured and killed. Or worse, they'll keep working in that poison factory.'

Stop this. Davin saved your life.

'I do feel for the big, faceless one. He seemed decent, but that other scutter...well, she got what she deserved.'

As she speaks, I grow a series of tiny, sharp shards. When she finishes, I hurl them all at her face. This time she doesn't move.

Instead, a blanket of fire erupts in front of her and melts my weapons. Kei holds his arms out, instinctively protecting her with his power. My ice is nothing compared to their powers.

Enough? We are your friends. Even if it doesn't seem like it.

I slump down onto the ground, next to the small fire that burns. The canopy of trees has kept the smoke from wholly escaping, so it's stuffy but it's also warmer than it would be otherwise.

From the trees to my right, Cerebrum and Orochi approach, taking a seat at the fire, also.

'Is that any way to thank someone who just saved you from the hell you were in?' Orochi's eyes pierce me as she speaks, searching around in my head and my soul. She'll find the latter empty.

'They could have brought Sorg and Hiro,' I say, picking up a branch and chucking it into the fire.

'No. They were instructed not to. We have been betrayed by outsiders before. We can't risk trusting anyone but our own kind.'

'They didn't have to bring them here. They could just have taken them somewhere safe.'

'They can look after themselves. For now, our priority is to look after you. We heard what happened in Ghondulon with your brother.' Her eyes turn kind and wide for a moment.

'I'm sorry,' says Cerebrum, speaking aloud.

My words die. The hateful thoughts die. I just want to crawl up and sleep, to hopefully dream of the times that Pat and I spent climbing trees, fishing and finding new and unique ways to annoy our parents. He was the best of us. But I'll never know how powerful he could have become.

It should have been him who met the Order. It should have been him. Not me.

But it's me. So, I break out of the slump, putting the grief on ice and begin the process of ending the hunt of the Wiccan.

'So, you got me out. What's the next move?'

Orochi gives a one-sided smile and nods to Cerebrum.

'There are too few of us to take out the Queen with an upfront battle. And even if we did, the people would just see us the way the Queen has painted us. Barbaric, evil Wiccan. It's important that the way we do this, reflects who we are and so must influence change from the inside, rather than battering down the door from the outside.'

'I understand. But how do you plan to do that? The people call us Wiccan. They are afraid of us. How do you change the mind of a whole kingdom while murdering their Queen?'

'We hope you can do that,' Cerebrum says, like it's the most obvious thing in the world.

I stare at the edges of his mouth, hoping they'll turn up. But they don't.

'You're being serious?' I ask. Still I hope for a smile, a laugh, anything.

'Absolutely. Why do you think we rescued you?'

'Because you're nice and want to help people like you.'

At that comment, Orochi does laugh, but Cerebrum remains stern.

'Well, we're nice. But our agenda comes before any individual. Since you were sworn into the order, we have had in our minds an idea. One which you'll be central to.'

'So, you saved me, so you could use me?'

'Precisely,' says Orochi, the smile now extinct.

The fire continues to crackle merrily, but I put another branch in anyway, just to do something. I'm feeling cold and exhausted, and my lungs still burn, but they've got me intrigued. And I suppose I do owe them.

'So, what do I have to do?'

'You are going to kill one of the Order. You are going to do it in a public place, where your full powers will be displayed to all. In Rejik. And when you come before the Queen, you'll pledge your allegiance to her and plead to serve as one of her Golden Enneads.'

I frown at Orochi as she speaks. They want me to kill one of them, then sign up with my and their sworn enemy?

Trust us. We trust you.

I search for trust in Cerebrum's eyes. But instead of clarity, there is cloudiness. Like he's not letting me fully in. I don't trust him. Or Orochi. Or any of them. Not yet. They need to earn it. The way Davin is, it will be hard. I won't forgive her for leaving Sorg and Hiro behind.

'So, what do you say?' asks Orochi.

'I'll think about it,' I say.

'Take your time,' says Cerebrum.

'But not too long,' adds Orochi. 'And remember you owe us, for the rescue. And you said you'd help once you'd found your brother. Remember?'

'I remember.' I whisper the words. The reminder of Pat stings.

'But right now, you must rest. We have a tent over here for you.' Cerebrum helps me up and takes me to a small cluster of green tents, situated beneath low-branched trees. Invisible, except if you knew they are here.

'Thanks,' I say, as he leaves me at the entrance to an empty one.

'Sleep well.'

And I do.

I wake up coughing. My throat scalds, like I poured lava down it.

When I swallow, it hurts. When I breathe, it hurts. And when I move, it hurts worst of all.

Despite this, my sleep is the best I've had since I left home, but sleeping on the ground is always bad for my back. My muscles ache as I zip open the tent and amble back towards the fire.

It smokes, but little burns. The morning is well underway and most of the other Order members packing up and readying to leave.

Davin spots me.

'Morning, Rime. Going to throw anything at me this morning? What a nice reward that was for rescuing you, huh?' She turns to her brothers, who sit in silence eating some fruit. They don't have the same twisted nature that their elder sister has. They live in her shadow, silent and still. But quiet doesn't always mean good.

I decide to ignore her and approach Cerebrum instead. He is talking to the muscular Mutare, Sway. She flicks her hair as I approach, ensuring Cerebrum's attention remains upon her and not me. I wait patiently as they finish their chat.

'We need this done today. Can you get the message to her?'

'Of course, Brum. But I don't see why Davin couldn't do it. She'd do it in a fraction of the time.'

'She is needed for something else,' he says.

I'll be with you in a moment, Rime.

'Fine, but I do hope you and Orochi appreciate everything I do. It could be dangerous.'

'We do, Sway. And I know it will be, that's why we're sending you.' He places his hand on her shoulder and gives it a squeeze, before turning to me.

Sway scowls at me but doesn't linger. Before I can start speaking, she has sprinted off into the trees and out of sight.

'Seems like you are doing a lot of plotting at the moment.' I smile as I say it. In the morning, after a good sleep, everything seems better.

'Yes, overthrowing a monarch takes a lot of organising. But in every good team, each person must do their job. And do it well. Have you decided upon our proposal?'

'I wasn't certain Orochi was giving me a choice, but I did give my word. I owe you. I'll do it. But I do it for Pat, not for the Order.'

'Whoever you do it for, if it keeps you from straying from the task, then I am content. It's decided then. The only thing left to do is to work out the details.'

I think about the first part of the mission. I must kill someone. I guess I've done that before, but I've never *murdered* someone. And that's what this would be, whatever the nobility of the end result, or the greater good or whatever. I'll be a murderer. But I know to fully avenge Pat, that is what it will eventually take. So, if it must end in murder, it may as well start with it.

'Okay, so am I to kill?' I try to say it light-heartedly, but the words are heavy in my mouth. My burning throat making it doubly tough to say.

We'll not speak of it openly. Only Orochi and I know the plan. You'll travel with Davin: she will jump you to the capital, to the main marketplace in the centre of the city. It's close to the Palace. There you'll kill someone, using your Ice abilities to their full extent. Show off. Make them notice you. Make the Queen notice you. Trust me when I say that she will desire you for her Golden Ennead even more if you do.

'Okay, got it. So, who?'

Orochi.

'What? I can't do that.'

She has volunteered. She does it willingly. For the Order. She knows that her small sacrifice will benefit our kind.

'Small sacrifice? Why don't I just injure or wound her? Or someone else I don't know?'

It was her idea. And it can't be anyone else, because we do not kill innocent people. The moment we do that, we become no better than the tyrant we aim to overthrow. And it needs to be a kill. The Queen needs to see that you are willing to kill one of us. She needs to be convinced of your loyalty and what better way to do that, than to kill one of the Order's leaders.

'I'll be hated by the Order. They'll think I am against all of you, not with you.'

They will. And we must maintain that pretence. Orochi and I believe we have a spy in the Order. Someone reporting to the Queen. She must not know your true intentions.

'And what if she sees my intentions? What if I'm found out?'

Then you had better put on a great show or you'll be terminated immediately.

CHAPTER 20

I can't believe what I'm being asked to do. I agreed to help them, but if I'd known this is what they wanted, I'd have run for my life.

But I can't turn my back on them now.

Because it wouldn't just be them I'd let down, it would be Pat's legacy, too.

The only conclusion that I can accept is the death of the Queen and the Paramount that ordered his hanging. When I scour them both from this world and send them flying through Ka-Ferno's Gate, I will rest knowing Pat looks down upon them from the Haven.

Rime, we're about to eat. Come join us.

As cool as Cerebrum's ability is, and convenient, I just wish he'd speak to me normally. I feel so vulnerable when he gets into my head. I know he said he can't read my thoughts, but it puts me on edge, and I try to avoid thinking about anything I wouldn't want him to know. Stupid stuff, mostly, like the boys I've kissed, like the stupid pranks Pat and I used to pull, or the abuse and attacks I was subjected to on the way to Ghondulon. But I also can't get the image of Sorg and Hiro being tortured or punished out of my head. Or being sent out to mine Sulphur.

Worst of all, if Cerebrum finds out my biggest secret.

I push myself up from my sleeping bag and unzip the tent, crawling out into the dusk air. As I walk towards the fire, my fingers twitch and strain towards the streams that run throughout the forest. They are particularly drawn towards a large body of water which lies beyond the forest. It's like a beacon calling me to it, but I manage to force it out of my head and hands.

I need to learn to control my powers if I'm to convince the Queen of my worth.

To gain her trust.

To eventually kill her.

'Rime, come quick or nothing will be left,' shouts Davin, from the fireside. 'I didn't want to leave you anything, but the others insisted.'

I see her in the reflection of the firelight, smirking and looking to her twin brothers for gratification. To my immense delight, neither of them cracks a smile. Not that they ever seem to, but it still warms me as I approach the small group.

Cerebrum, Orochi and two other Mutare sit with my three rescuers, all of them finishing their meals. Mine sits in a wooden bowl next to Cerebrum.

I take my place and nod at all the others, before tearing into my meat. I've eaten so little over the last week or so and put my body through so much that I know I need to get good food into me. Especially, if I'm going to do what I need to.

I glance at Orochi, who is nibbling at her bone, removing the last of the meat. She throws the bone into the fire and takes a drink of her water. I think about the water entering her mouth and how I could change it into a hundred tiny little blades, to let her die tonight and it would look like an accident.

Or I could make the water turn into a large chunk of ice and block her throat, so she can't breathe. It would look like an accident, also.

But I know what I've been asked to do. So, does she and that's what unnerves me the most. When she turns to me and notices I've been staring, I turn my head downwards and chew in silence, watching the base of the fire and not daring to look back up at her.

I finish my meal without talking and I'm glad that no-one tries to speak to me either. Particularly Orochi. The rest of them chat merrily, recalling past missions together or funny moments involving members of the Order. It seems they have been a royal nuisance for several years now, destroying goods vehicles, factories and transport ships, all of which provided to the Queen.

It seems their favourite story, the one where they all laughed, even Cerebrum, was when they destroyed the Queen's favourite country home, which is close to Tantuyen, a large city located inland.

'And after Kei had lifted the place up, Davin grabbed us all and was about to jump out of there, when a huge burst of fire came from behind. Now, at the time it was scary, but when we were safely out of there, and she was running around with a burnt hole at the back of her trousers, she howled so loud that all the sheep in the field ran for their lives.' As the boy telling the story finishes, everyone round the fire howls with laughter. Even I produce a smile.

'Think it's funny, Corena!' shouts Davin, throwing a bone at me.

I stand to say something back, but Cerebrum put his good hand up. 'Davin, behave.' He holds her gaze until she nods and settles back down. 'And don't use real names. We have a code, remember. She is Rime.'

'Whatever. Once she has earned the right, she can laugh at me. But she has done nothing for us and yet she sits there and laughs at me. After all I've done.'

'Davin, we appreciate everything you do for us. You are a valuable member of our Order, but you'll not harass Rime any longer.

She is one of us now and she will prove her worth to you in time. In fact, you'll be working together on the next mission, so drop whatever feud you have right now. For the greater good.'

She opens her mouth to protest but thinks better of it. Instead, she gets up and storms off towards the tents. Kei and Kin follow.

Silence falls on the remainder of the group. I glance up at the two people I don't know. The boy who told the story is looking at me. The other girl gazes into the fire.

'You'll need to work with her, Rime. And you'll need to be the one to forgive and extend the olive branch.' Cerebrum sounds serious as he speaks. I know he's right, but I won't forgive her. I don't think I could, even if she was nice.

'I'll work with her.' I say, knowing that he knows I've worded it deliberately.

But it seems to appease him. For now.

Cerebrum looks over the fire. 'Rime, this is Sense and Marina.'

The boy smiles and the girl nods briefly.

'And what are their powers?'

'Why don't you show her?' Cerebrum suggests.

The boy's face lights up, then screws up in concentration. 'The air temperature is sixteen degrees; the wind speed is seven miles per hour, and you haven't washed in over a week. In fact, you've been through a sewer, in the ocean, at a fish port, in a Sulphur mine and you have three people's blood on you.' As he speaks his face gradually darkens, like his words tell a sad, sad story.

He must be Sense.

'That's incredible. So, you can sense anything?' I ask him.

'Not quite. I have to be able to see it usually or be near it. I'm getting better, but I'm not quite good enough to sense stuff which is farther away.'

'You'll get there,' says Orochi, patting him on the shoulder. 'Sense is one of our best students. He works so hard to improve his powers every day.'

At that, his smile returns. I momentarily catch Orochi's eye, but I look away to the girl. She must be Marina.

'What about you Marina?' I ask.

She looks up at me, her dark hair falling over her face. She doesn't look happy. Well, what I can see of her doesn't.

'Water.'

'So, you can manipulate it, like Kei with fire?'

'Similar. Not the same.'

'I use water for my ice...'

'I know.' She gets up and leaves, following Davin and the twins.

'What did I say?' I ask, looking around.

'Nothing,' says Sense. 'She's just a little put out because your power also involves water. She's not really annoyed, but she thought she was unique, and she doesn't realise that she still is.' He huffs and watches her disappear into the trees. 'Anyway, I'd better get to bed, too. Nice meeting you, Rime.'

'Nice meeting you, too.' And I mean it.

I watch him leave the fire and disappear, wondering if he can sense my feelings right now. My hate for Davin, my guilt about Orochi, or my grief over Pat.

I can't stop thinking about Pat and those bloody chickens. Images of him running through fields of corn and laughing as loud as he used to. Probably picking whole cobs and chucking them at me when I wasn't looking.

'Now we're alone, we should discuss your training,' says Cerebrum.

'Training?' Thumped to reality.

'Yes, you are very capable for a newly-developed, but if we're to convince the Queen of your worth and to make Orochi's execution look convincing, then you must become excellent. You must train as hard as Sense and be as ruthless and cold as Davin. Are you up for that?'

'Yes.' I don't hesitate. 'Who will be training me?'

'I will,' says Orochi, a smile curling from one side of her

mouth. 'I'll train you to kill me. And I'll make you so good, everyone will be convinced of your worth.'

I finally hold her gaze, meeting her eyes and forcing myself not to look away. I stare deep into the eyes of my trainer, wondering just how I'll be able to kill her, when the time comes.

139

CHAPTER 21

It's dark. My tent shakes.

Rise, Rime. It's time to wake, before the sun comes up.

Today we need to make an assassin out of you.

Meet me at the lake.

Then she leaves my head. I can actually feel her leaving. It's the weirdest thing and I'm sure I'll never get used to it. At least when Cerebrum does it, he is nice and gentle. Orochi had made my brain feel like a thousand tiny feet just trampled on it.

I hope she doesn't have to do that too often.

Then I remember what I've to do and wonder if she'll ever do it again, before I...well...before I do what I've to do.

I scramble through the trees in the dark, tripping over surface roots and fallen branches. Someone curses from inside a tent, and I hope it's Davin I've woken.

When I reach the opening where our fire still glows red beneath a layer of dark ash, I realise I've no idea where the lake is.

Yesterday I remember being drawn to a large body of water. That must be it. I relax and let my mind and body fall into ice-trance. Like a lamp being lit, every drop of water for miles around is suddenly drawn to me, and I to it.

I search for the strongest pull and move in that direction,

simply following the tug of longing. It's become a relationship – I thirst for it, like it yearns for me. The feeling makes me more alive, packs me with purpose and gives me a sense of power that has for so long been hidden in my darkest fissures. Cracks born of abuse and longing to be normal.

But today I embrace my abnormality. The ice has healed them. Or at least filled them. And as I descend the hill into the valley with the large lake, I run towards the water.

As I reach Orochi, standing ten feet from the edge of the lake holding a bright lamp, I'm tempted to run right past her and dive into the water.

But as I slow to a stop, the urge overtakes my own conscious decision making and I hurl myself forward and into the lake, leaping headfirst into the dark pool.

Beneath the surface, I swim forward, eager to drive down into the depths, where the water is almost ice-cold. It calls to me. It pulls me in like a magnet. I can't stop. This is the strongest urge I've ever experienced, and I know as I get deeper that something is wrong.

Rime, your power is taking over.

Regain control.

Focus.

As soon as Orochi gets into my brain, I regain my senses.

My body is impervious to the low temperature, but my oxygen is running out and it's so dark, I can't navigate beyond my inner primordial instinct to find icy water.

As my brain clears, I can still feel Orochi in there, like a little supervisor, making sure I do the right thing. And I do.

I kick upwards, deciding to just get to the surface and swim back from there. As I crash through the surface, the pressure in my head disappears and I know she's out of there.

I swim back to the edge of the lake, the moon's light reflecting beautifully on the ripples I create. I frost the tips of the waves and make beautiful little patterns to amuse myself.

'Are you ready to begin?' Orochi asks, her hands on her hips and her frown so low, I can barely see her eyes.

'Yes.' I'm glad it's dark to hide my red cheeks, which fill with heat, thawing my frozen skin.

I'm like a little girl, when my parents used to chide me for doing silly things, like climbing tall trees and swimming naked in the river. My clothes drip all over the small pebbles which border the lake.

'As you are wet already, let's start with defence.' She turns to face me now. 'Using only the water in your clothes, form an impenetrable ice-shield around your body. And make it strong, because I'll test it.'

I nod, thinking back to my induction to the Order. I let my arms relax and focus, my eyes closed.

A film of ice starts to crack into place around me as it morphs and binds, the layer becoming gradually thicker and thicker. My arms become heavy and my feet immovable. Even my head feels clamped in place.

When all the water has been transformed, I open my eyes but see little except the solid block of ice in front of my eyes. I realise I can't bring in new air, so I form a small, narrow breathing hole in front of my mouth. I can also use it to talk.

'Okay, that's me fin...'

A loud thud and a crack come from the ice at my chest.

Then another at my back. But the ice-shield holds.

Then silence. No attack. No thud. No noise at all.

'Orochi?' I shout through the breathing hole.

No response.

I'm just considering melting the shield, when bright, angry flames engulf me. As they fly in the breathing hole, I've to react quickly to seal it up with ice. Then I've to work hard to keep my shield from melting.

The flames endure and as each part of the shield melts and I seal it again, it becomes less and less thick.

After several seconds of this, gaps appear all over in the shield and my clothes and skin begin to scorch. I use my ice to extinguish them as quick as they catch, but by the time the flames die, I'm covered in burns from hair to foot.

My white hair is singed and missing in clumps. My pale skin is blackened and blistered. I tumble to the ground, my whole body shaking from the exertion. Orochi approaches me slowly, shuffling across the pebbles, her limp making quick movement impossible.

Not bad, Rime. But you need to be stronger than that to kill the Queen. In fact, you'll need to be stronger than that to beat me.

To kill you, you mean.

It all becomes too much; the pain, the grief, the thought of murder, the expectations. I can't do it. Sorry, Pat, but I can't.

She limps closer and kneels slowly, her joints popping loudly. 'Rime, I'm staying out of your head until you recover. But once you do, you'll keep those negative thoughts away from the surface. I wasn't even trying, and I could hear them.'

'How could you know what I was thinking? Cerebrum said you couldn't do that?'

'Cerebrum can't. Or won't. He's very noble and idealistic. It's his main weakness. As well as his trust and faith in people. But I'm much older and therefore wiser. This world is not noble. It's not fair and it never will be. You cannot trust anyone. To survive, you must become ruthless and tougher. Bury your feelings deep inside. Encase them in ice. Do what you must but keep them from the surface where people can use them against you.'

As she speaks, her hands move over my skin, touching the burns. A warmth is exchanged and when her hands move away, the skin is healed, good as new.

'You are a healer? You have two abilities?'

She nods, continuing her work, healing my cooked skin quickly. Her touch even regrows my hair, coming back in softer and sleeker.

'I am an Absorber. That's my ability. Everything I can do, I took from another Mutare. My psychic abilities all come from Cerebrum. My healing abilities come from Darn. You've not met him yet, but he's the Orders doctor.'

'What else can you do?' I ask, my injuries forgotten.

'I've now absorbed many abilities. I can manipulate fire, like Kei, and I can manipulate the water like Marina. Though, not as well as any of the people I took the abilities from. That's the drawback of being an Absorber: become the Princess of all powers, Queen of none.'

'Could you take my Ice?'

'Yes.'

'But you don't want to?'

'With what is coming, there is little point. It would only assist me, and we don't want that. You must kill me and if I had your abilities, I'd be able to defend myself. As you now know, sometimes the abilities have a mind of their own and they would probably defend me. No, it's best that I don't absorb your ability.'

She gets back to her feet with difficulty, her knees popping again.

'So, you are really okay with the plan? With me doing...you know?'

'Yes, it was my idea. I'm too old for all of this. My time has come; I'll either ascend to the Haven, or descend to Ka-Ferno's Gate, but either way, my physical pain will go. I'm wearied of the world and its injustices. And revolutions are for young ones. If this is the best way for me to contribute, then so be it.'

I stare at her as she hobbles away. She has so much power and ability. She could be so useful to the cause. I can't kill her. It would be such a waste.

'Okay, back to training. Your shield needs to be stronger than that. Any old Fire-Wielder would get through that defence, and much quicker than me.'

I don't move, wondering what's coming next.

'Well get in the water, then. Get yourself wet so you can defend yourself. Water is your ally, Rime. Make sure you're always near it.'

I splash into the cold lake again, soaking what's left of my burnt clothes. Orochi's healing ability can't mend fabric.

We train all day, every day for a week. We skip breakfast and lunch. Fortunately, Sense pops down with a snack mid-morning. He stays to watch for a while, but all he sees is me failing time-after-time to stop Orochi's flames. I don't like people watching.

When he leaves on the seventh day, I start to fare better, finally producing a shield that Orochi takes half an hour to melt.

'Good, Rime. That is better. You are unlikely to have to hold out for longer than that, so we can move on.'

'Attack now?' I ask, hopefully. Defending is boring and involves taking a lot of hits. I'd much rather be dishing them out. Especially if Davin were on the other end.

'No. More defence.'

'More defence? I thought you said I did well?'

'You did. But that was a static defence. One to use in a situation where you can't attack or are outmatched and need to wait for reinforcements. Now, we will look at how to use a more mobile defence.'

She moves towards the lake.

Someone approaches from the trees. I turn to see Kei and Kin. And Davin. Cerebrum follows them.

Great, the last thing I need is a crowd.

I'm thumped from my blind side, and I fly across the pebbles, a water jet driving into me from the lake. Orochi must be using her absorbed water ability.

But water is my ally, not hers.

I concentrate and change the stream that strikes me into a solid ice shield, and gradually I transform the water into ice.

Chunks fall on the pebbles as I walk back towards the lake. Towards Orochi, who is beginning to tire from directing the water at me. The water which isn't hitting me anymore.

When I'm ten feet from her, she stops and the water stream dies.

Using my power, I make the water at her feet morph into ice and quickly encase her in it, thickening it as quickly as I can.

Laughing, I stop. Happy that I've disabled my opponent. A high-pitched cackle emerges from inside. I create a gap at her mouth to let her breathe and speak.

'Nice one, Rime. Very good. That was a great counter. But you're forgetting one thing.'

'What's that?' I ask, suddenly wary.

'Don't ever be merciful to an enemy.'

As she speaks a tsunami of water cascades down upon us, crushing us both beneath the crashing wave.

For several seconds, I'm disoriented, the world becoming black, but then I regain my bearings. I know which way is up and I swim for it. But I don't need to.

The moment I kick up, the water comes down, disappearing back down the pebbles towards the lake, leaving only small puddles. One of which I lie in, bruised and soaked, but otherwise uninjured.

I look round wildly for Orochi, but she remains exactly where she was, the ice melting slowly around her.

'Never be merciful, Rime. The Queen will spot it straight away and you'll be hanged. If you are not a ruthless killer, she will execute you. A member of the Golden Ennead with a weak heart is no good to her. It must be stone. Or ice!'

As she says the final word, she disappears. Gone. Like Davin must look when she jumps. Another absorbed ability.

I turn to the crowd that gathered just before the show.

Davin is on her back, laughing. Kei and Kin both share a tiny grin. Even Cerebrum is smiling, but his is warm and friendly. He walks over to me.

'Training going well I see?'

'She pushes you hard.'

'Orochi is the best. That's why. So, are you feeling ready to kill her tomorrow?'

'I don't know. I just don't know if I can do it.'

'I thought that might be the case. So, Orochi thought that we should take out an insurance policy.'

'Insurance policy?'

'Yes, just in case you decide not to kill her tomorrow.'

My heart begins to beat fast. My brain whirls as I try to figure out what he means.

'I don't understand...what have you done?'

'Davin, bring them here.'

Davin disappears, still laughing.

I stare at Cerebrum, in silence, for several seconds. Suddenly that warmth and trust have gone. He looks guilty, like he's hurt me and feels terrible for it. They've done something bad. I can feel it. Orochi was right, I shouldn't have trusted them.

Davin reappears.

But she is not alone.

'Just in case you change your mind,' she shouts.

Suddenly, my heart and my head are frozen.

And it's then I know I will kill Orochi tomorrow.

Because she is standing ten feet from me, holding the arms of my parents. Dad stares at her like she's a monster from all his worst nightmares.

And maybe she is a monster.

CHAPTER 22

I sit beside the fire for the last time. Tomorrow, I leave here. I leave the Order. I leave behind my parents in their *care.*

I watch my mum and dad, who huddle across from me. Mum's eyes dart from one Mutare to another, clearly frightened half to death. Dad puts on a braver exterior, having witnessed my powers first-hand. He suspected I was Wiccan. Heck, I thought I was Wiccan.

But that was before I knew about Mutare and the Order. Now, I know what I am and even though I will never forgive them, I won't let anything happen to them.

That's why I will kill Orochi tomorrow. That's why I will help the Order. They don't trust me, and I don't trust some of them, but I'm not doing it for them. They've betrayed me twice now. This is now for Pat and now for my parents.

I am sorry.

I refuse to turn my face towards his. I won't allow him forgiveness. He won my trust, then he betrayed it. He's just like everyone I've met; fair-intentioned, foul-hearted.

You must believe me. It was not my idea. Can we talk when the others have gone to bed?

Again, I don't acknowledge his message. I hate that he has a direct line into my brain. I want him out, so I nod, only slightly moving my head. Nobody else knows why my parents are here, except from Cerebrum and Orochi. We've both been warned not to communicate or show any sign that we know each other. It's easy for me, I'd be ignoring them anyway.

Thanks.

I finish my roasted rabbit and walk away from the group. There's no-one there I want to talk to. I wish Pat were here. We could climb the tallest trees and spy on people, scare the birds off or just sit and watch the stars, like we once did. Before this nightmare began.

I scrunch my eyes closed as tight as I can. Hold for ten seconds, then I open, hoping to wake up. But I'm still in this forest, somewhere in the country, well away from home, my parents' hostage and my best friend is dead. Poor Pat. I can't get his small, swinging body out of my head.

I walk down to the smoothed pebbled shore of the lake. It's silent and reassuring. But someone has followed me.

'Rime.' Sense's voice is soothing, like he can alter his tone depending on mood. Maybe he can.

'I want to be alone for a bit.'

'You want comfort. And reassurance.'

I turn to the boy. He must be around the same age as me, though a few inches shorter. His eyes seem to glow tonight as they take me in. He must be sensing my emotions. Damn these Mutare, can't a girl hide anything anymore.

'You can sense that?'

'Yes. And more. But I won't embarrass you by trying. Our powers should never be abused, and I never go too deep into people. Even surface sense can be feel like I've violated people.'

'It's okay, I think any old person could tell how I'm feeling. I'm not always the best at hiding it.'

'Nobody is. Trust me.'

I smile at him. He has already comforted me. Reassured me.

Reassured me that there are decent Mutare, worth helping. That what I do tomorrow will help Sense and others like him, come what may.

He puts his arm around my back, and I let him.

It feels good to be close to someone. I've felt so isolated, so alone since Pat died and having spent a week of training to put up ice shields, I finally let my emotional shield down and bury myself deep into Sense's shoulder.

Tears fall. I'm upset and angry that my little brother isn't here with me as I gaze upon the training lake, the moonlight smiling off surface and reminding me that water will always be there for me. My new best friend. And it can't be killed.

'Do you know I was confused and scared for so long?' I start talking to Sense, knowing he will listen. He won't interrupt or judge me. He won't repeat what I say. He'll just listen. I know this.

'I didn't know what was wrong with me at first. Weird things happened, like my mug falling over, or our washing water suddenly becoming cold. Nothing serious. I pretended I didn't notice but I did. But when it got serious, when I was older, then I just didn't know who I was anymore. My plan had always been to become a woodcutter, like Dad, but when I killed Gullan, my world crashed. My friends hated me, feared me, my parents became more and more distant. Scared. Only Pat, my brother, only he treated me like a person. He knew I was different, but he treated me the same. And that meant everything to me.'

I sit up and look directly at Sense. 'And that's why I'm here. That's why whatever I do for the Order, you must remember it's to help the little girl that I used to be. To help every person in this world who is different to be treated the same. And if that involves bringing down every rung on the ladder of this society, then I will take my axe and fell every tree in this forest of inequality.'

As I finish, I take a deep breath and try to slow my breathing. My heart is thumping so fast I fear Sense will think I'm dying.

'Sorry, I just had to say that to someone.'

'No problem.'

He continues to sit with me, in silence, and gaze at the lake, the moon and the stars. Tomorrow will be awful, but right now, next to this boy, I'm comforted and reassured.

'Sense, can you give me and Rime some privacy.' Cerebrum ambles down towards us.

'Sure.' He squeezes my shoulder as he leaves and I listen to his steps crunch the pebbles, before dying in the soft grass of the forest and being replaced with those of Cerebrum.

I shiver as he sits down next to me.

'I didn't know, Rime.'

I don't need to look at him to know he's telling the truth.

'Are you not in charge?'

'It's complicated.'

'Well, make it really simple for me.'

'Orochi and I've slightly different methods for getting things done. It was not my call to bring your parents into this. But I didn't stop her either.'

'Exactly.'

'I wanted to trust that you'd do it, but we didn't know if you'd go through with it. And you must. Everything depends on you doing it. We can't infiltrate the Golden Ennead without you.'

'And now I've no choice. I'm a slave to your ransom and I serve beneath two heartless tyrannies.'

'That's not true, Rime.'

'And I'm fed up with code names. I'm called Corena. That's what my parents named me. The people you stole from their homes to force me to kill someone. That sounds like a pretty heartless tyranny to me.'

'You don't understand what's at stake.'

I stand and move my face to within an inch of his. 'REALLY! I've no clue what it's like to be persecuted or mistreated for my powers? I've no idea how cruel they can be, do I? I only just watched my brother hanged because he inherited unwanted powers, but I know nothing of what's at stake, do I? You have no idea what I know.'

'I know that you are strong. And you are brave and loyal.'

'Yeah, unlike you.'

'And I know that you would do anything to protect people you love and that you are absorbed in the greater good. In freedom and equality for Mutare.'

'I'm having second thoughts, now. Why would I help people who would kidnap a girl's parents to force her to do their bidding? That sounds just like the current regime. Why replace one cruel Queen, just to crown another?'

'I don't expect you to trust us fully. Not now. But trust in your brother's memory. In his legacy, which could be our freedom from persecution. If you could save other children around the land from this, wouldn't you? Won't you? Rime, I just need your assurance that you'll do what you must.'

'I told you. My name is Corena. I give you no assurance. I make my own choices from now on. Not for you or your Order, but for me and those I care about.'

'Fair enough. I guess I can ask no more.'

'You can ask nothing of me now. You have forced me into becoming a killer. So, in that spirit, assure me now that my parents return home tomorrow after I've killed Orochi. Promise me.'

'I promise.'

'And if you forsake that agreement, it won't only be Orochi who will die tomorrow. You'll also die.'

'I will not forsake it.'

'Good, because if you do, this monster you've created...well, she won't be taking any hostages.'

Cerebrum looks hurt when I turn to face him, but I don't care. He brought my family into this. After he saw what they did to Pat, he brought them here to use as bait. I thought I could follow him and the Order, but he's not even strong enough to say no to Orochi, to tell her she's gone too far.

'I want to see my parents now. I want to speak to them before I do this.'

'That is reasonable. I will get them now. Wait here. We cannot let the others see you are close.'

He disappears off the shore and into the forest and while I wait, I practice at the water's edge, creating shards of ice just below the surface of the pebbles and thrusting them up in unison. I know I've not even begun to discover my powers, to see what I can fully do, but for my immediate task, I've learned enough.

Enough to kill.

To kill.

Kill.

The word permeates in my mind as I wait for my parents.

I drive it out to think about what I will say to them. After all that has happened. They won't know about Pat, except that he left. They have no idea what I've been through, what I've seen, what I've learned.

I'm not the same girl who left them, unsure of herself and her role in this world. I now have a purpose, whether forced or not, and I know what I am.

As I stumble through possible words, they arrive, led by Cerebrum. He stops at the edge of the pebble shore and urges them forward.

I make them come to me. I want them to close the distance between us. They created it after all.

They hold hands, unifying their guilt and sharing the shame. I watch the man that was once my hero amble towards me with his head lowered, his strong arms and back sagging. The man who taught me to read, to write and swim. He showed me the best way to climb a tree and sat by my bed every night for six months when I had the plague, falling asleep clasping my hand before getting up for work the next morning on only a few hours' sleep. But his eyes are fixed on the ground now. I'd be ashamed, too.

My mother at least looks at me. She seems lightened even

though she's lost all her children. Perhaps because I am all they have left; they will grow to love me. Before, it's been shielded by fear of the Kurikon. But they have lost everything and there is no need to hide from the shadow cast by the Kleriks over our land. Love, the one thing they can't control or deny. And I see it shining through again. There may be hope for them.

She wants to speak but doesn't. My dad finally lifts his head.

'Corena.'

That's it. That's all he says. After giving me up to the Royal Enforcers, abandoning me to certain death, all he can say is my name.

I want to hit him.

My mum's tears make me angry.

Shards begin to grow, the surface of the lake freezing.

Control.

'GET OUT MY HEAD!' I shout at Cerebrum because he's a traitor, but mostly because he is right. I do need to control myself.

I close my eyes, stretch my arms and breathe deeply.

'Corena, we're sorry.'

There, he finally got it out.

It's not enough, but at least he said something.

'Pat is dead.'

My words smack them.

Mum collapses onto the pebbles, her legs no use. Dad falls next to her and comforts her.

I stare at them, watching them transmit love to each other in a way they haven't done to me. Not for a long time. They remain entwined in each other's arms, Mum crying, Dad silent, me on the outside looking in.

Nothing has changed. They mourn their lost son, but still have no love for their only daughter. The hope of a moment ago, melted.

'He followed me. After you let them take me.'

'We know,' Dad says. 'I tried to find him, but I had to give up. How did he die?'

'He was hanged.' The words tear my tongue.

'Why?'

'For being like me.' I take immense satisfaction from those last words. Like me. My parent's worst nightmare. All they wanted was a *normal* child. I hope the words hurt them.

'Like you? He was Wiccan?'

'A Wiccan, yes. He was a Fire-Wielder.' I use the terms they will know, for maximum damage.

'Why didn't you protect him?' Dad's face is red. He stands up and leaves my mum on the pebbles.

'I tried to.'

'We tried to make him normal, but you always encouraged him. We thought that if you left, he'd have a chance. But he went after you. And you let him die.'

'I DID NOT LET HIM DIE!'

I move close to my dad, my fists balled with ice growing longer and sharper.

'I could do nothing. I tried to get to him, but I was too late. I did everything I could.'

'It wasn't enough. Now you've killed both of my sons.'

He turns his back to me, lifts my mum and walks away, dragging her behind him.

I want to scream at him. To hurt him. Even to kill him.

But I won't. I can't. They are family.

As I watch them re-enter the forest, I know I never want to see nor speak to them ever again.

I turn to face the lake and begin walking forward.

My body embraces the icy chill of the water as I move deeper and deeper.

When the water is up to my chest, I keep walking until finally my face submerges.

I begin swimming, deeper and deeper.

I use my power to create an ice-helmet, like I did in the sewer.

When I reach the bottom, I sit on the slimy stone and watch small, black fish swimming back and forth.

Rime, come back up. Please.

I ignore the voice. I need space. I need to be away from all these people, all these emotions, all this noise.

Then suddenly my helmet smashes and the water pours in.

CHAPTER 23

Soft lips press against mine, blowing air into my mouth.

Hands apply heavy pressure to my chest, forcing water from lungs.

My eyes spring open and Davin kneels over me, pulling her hands away and shaking her head.

My lungs and throat ache, my chest heavily bruised.

'That's two you owe me.' Davin turns and disappears, teleporting somewhere else. I'm glad she's gone. She's the last person I want to see right now. And I hate that I'm indebted to her for anything.

Corena, I am sorry.

I ignore him. I know he's standing a few metres away, but I don't look at him. Instead, I use the water around me to create an ice-cocoon. Nobody can get me in here.

Corena?

The cocoon shatters and I leap up and stride over to him.

'Get out my head. I hate you, Cerebrum. You are weak and you use people. I don't want to speak to you, so just leave me alone. I'll do your stupid mission; I've told you this already. Just leave me alone until I have to go.'

He turns away, clearly hurt, but I don't care. He hurt me by allowing my parents to be brought into this. I won't let him off easy.

As his dark figure disappears into the trees, I walk and I walk, glad to be alone for a while.

Eventually, I lie down on my back, shivering beneath the stars. Dad took Pat and I out one night to the open fields just outside our village. We lay beneath the stars, like I am now, gazing up and he described to us everything his dad had taught him. The one with the shape like an anvil, the one like a lion. And Pat's favourite, the ones he said were shaped like a ship.

I wake before dawn. Not that I got much sleep, tossing and turning with thoughts of Orochi's blood on my hands and parents I'll never see again.

Surprisingly it's that second thought that has eaten away at me the most. I thought I was over them, past caring, but I'm not. So, I push out of my sleeping bag and creep over to their tent.

I pull back the flap and I'm about to wake them, but they are already awake. In fact, with the lamp still burning, sleeping bags unused, it looks like they've not gone to sleep.

'You okay?' I ask, watching them tense.

'Fine, Rena,' Mum replies. 'I'm sorry about last night. We were just so shocked. We didn't know people like you…I mean, you know…well, that you could do things like that. The women appeared out of nowhere and took us miles away in no time. It was a shock.'

I take a deep breath. I need to remember that they are still taking all of this in. They are not deliberately being ignorant of me and my feelings.

'So, I'm leaving this morning.'

'You're what? We only just arrived.' Mum looks to Dad, then back at me.

'I know. But these people...my people...we have some things to do. Some changes to make. You won't understand what I'm doing, but I need to do it.'

'Rena, please tell us what's happening. We have been worried about you and your brother for weeks and then we're brought here, told our son is dead and that you are now leaving us, too. We deserve to know what has happened to our children. We may not have acted like it all the time, but we love you so much, Rena. We really do.'

I take a second to process her words. I can't remember the last time they said they loved me. Mum used to say it all the time, Dad much less. Neither in years.

It hits me at the back of the throat and a strange noise comes out my mouth.

'I'm not Wiccan,' I say, deciding to explain at least some of the truth. 'I'm a Mutare. A person with powers and abilities that very few other people have. So do the people in this camp. That's why Orochi was able to teleport you both here.'

Her blank face whitens, and Mum sits back down. Dad doesn't display any emotion, still focussing on his hands.

'I've to do something for the good of everyone and it will make me look bad, but I promise you it's for a good reason. I'm not a bad person, even if I'm different to you. And I love you both. Just remember that whatever you hear. I love you both and I forgive you.'

I turn and leave the tent as quickly as I can, surging through the dark, fallen leaves and branches to the meeting point, tears streaming from eyes, wondering if I will ever see them again.

I should have waited for their response. But what would they have said? They can't understand. I said what I had to. Now it's time to play my part.

Orochi waits for me on the pebbles. The sun peaks over the hills, glazing the dewy fields and making Orochi's hair appear gold on grey. One of her cheeks lift, as if surprised to see me.

'Are you ready?'

'I've one more thing to do.' I pick up a sharp-edged stone and start sawing at my hair. White locks fall upon the pebbles, the last of my outward female persona dying.

Orochi waits silently as I cut it close to my scalp.

When I finish, kneel over the water's edge. I search my face for recognition of Corena Storm, the Wiccan from the North.

And she's gone.

'I'm called Pat from now on.' I speak both to Orochi and to myself. 'If my Enforcer friends do decide to go to the Queen with news of me, they'll be looking for a girl, not a boy. This feels right. And I can honour Pat's memory by using his name to seek my revenge.'

'I've no objections. They logic is sound. But remember the mission. Don't let your own emotions cloud your actions. Remain focused at all times.'

'Yes,' I say, trying a slightly deeper than usual voice.

I splash my new, short hair with water and mess it up, like Pat used to.

'Now, are you ready?'

'Yes.' I take her hand.

The sensation of teleporting is no nicer this time around. When my feet hit the hard road that leads up to the gates of Rejik, my legs don't respond, and I fall to the deck. I didn't eat this morning, but my stomach is as unstable as my legs.

'Up.' Orochi holds her hand down to me.

I haul myself up. 'Thanks.'

But she's already walking down the hill towards the gate.

Rejik looms ahead, the city consuming the entire horizon and spreading out beyond what I can see. The buildings are taller than in Ghondulon and seem less industrial and more residential. In addition to the mammoth gate, there is a wall about ten times my height spread across the boundary. But very like Ghondulon, the walls are surrounded by fields containing crops and cattle, shepherded by farm hands and slaves.

Horse-drawn trade carts pass us, moving both ways in and out of the capital, and as we draw closer to the gate, we pass groups of people moving out from the city towards the fields to begin their day's work.

The vastness of the walls and city become overwhelming as we approach the gate. I could walk all day either side of the gate and remain at the foot of the wall. The gate itself is like a small town, many times larger than my village up north. The portcullis is up, the drawbridge lowered, and the cities moat wide and deep. No way in or out, except the way we're going.

Orochi slows when we're just short of the drawbridge. It's one hundred metres long, at least. On this side of it, small guard house flanks the bank to the left. Half a dozen Enforcers sit outside at a large wooden table, eating breakfast. Four more stand to attention, watching the trade carts and people moving past. Occasionally, they stop someone and question them, but the traffic is becoming so dense that most pass without interrogation.

'Put these rags over you. Make sure your hair is covered. White hair is very uncommon in these parts. We want nothing to draw attention to us until the time is right.'

She hands me some filthy, stinking material, which I drape over my shoulders, covering my hair. Fish and smoke stench almost makes me vomit everywhere, but I control my breathing through my mouth, making sure not to sniff. She didn't have to give me one this rancid, just dirty would have worked.

'Follow me and keep your eyes low.'

I walk after her, approaching the quartet of Enforcers letting people pass onto the drawbridge. One of them catches my eyes as I near him.

When I'm a few metres away he moves across my path.

'Stop there. State your business in Rejik.'

I keep my eyes on the ground, like Orochi told me to.

'Small trades.' I try to keep my voice deep.

'Well, you clearly ain't selling. What you buying?'

'Wood.' It's a stupid answer as there are trees very near the city, but it's what comes to me.

'Wood?' He lifts my chin, so I must look at him. 'Show me your coin?'

I realise I have none. My breath comes in short, sharp rasps. Think. Think. I'm going to get caught. I've ruined the whole thing already.

'She...he is with me. Here is my coin.' Orochi's voice cuts the tension with an easy, but deadly slice. She holds her hand out, a small collection of copper on display.

It's a meagre amount, but the Enforcer seems satisfied and grunts for us to pass. I lower my head straight away, eager for him to forget about me, but I feel his gaze follow us as we walk across the drawbridge, the wood echoing beneath many feet, hooves and the wheels of carts.

'That was close,' I say.

'It's fine. It won't matter if we get inside and to Freya Square. After that, you just need to kill me.' She gives me a smile, but her eyes look sad.

For the first time, I sense she might be having second thoughts about this. I've been the one doubting if I can go through with this all week, but I never thought she would waver. She seemed so solid before.

It's just going to make it all the harder for me. If she changes her mind, she'll be like a hunted animal fighting for her life and her claws are much bigger than mine.

The colossal gate draws both my eyes and mind away from my thoughts and allows me to only absorb its scale and its beauty. From this close, I can see the carved stone, etched with writing and images of the city's past. Famous quotes from old kings and Queens cover one segment, while depictions of renowned battles cover another.

Within the stone outline are several small pods that look like houses piled one on top of another. Each has a single window and through each peers an Enforcer, studying the movement of the incoming people. I spy several crossbows resting on the ledges of the windows, but most of them seem relaxed. There are so many of them, I'm sure they'd deal with any issues instantly. It makes me turn my eyes downward.

When I walk into shadow, I know we're passing beneath the portcullis, and I wish things were different and I could enter the city with my head held high, taking in the wonder and the magnificence of the capital, instead of creeping in like a thief.

The shadow is long and cool. I glance up once to see several layers of huge metal spikes high above our heads, ready to fall and pierce us. They remind of my own ice-blades. One of which I'll be using to kill the lady next to me in the next few minutes. I turn back to the ground, which is now stone, followed by earth after a few more steps.

We are inside. The sun hides for a long time as we move along the wide main avenue, the high walls shading us. People have begun their day here. Most of the buildings here look like Enforcer barracks and armouries and almost everyone we see exiting from the buildings is in the striking royal blue capes that Sorg and Hiro once wore.

I think about my friends momentarily as we move through the city. They must still be in the mines, breathing in poisonous fumes, each breath taking them closer to Ka-Ferno's gate.

'We are nearly there. Are you ready?' Orochi's voice shakes slightly at the word ready.

Is she ready?

'Yes.' My mind snaps back to the present and what I need to do. I try channelling my anger from Pat's death to solidify my resolve. I can't back out now.

The main avenue starts to widen and a few hundred metres in front, it opens onto a massive open space, packed with stalls and markets. This must be Freya's Square. It's ten times bigger than the square in Ghondulon.

The carts begin to diverge to different parts of the market, setting up for the day. Many have already begun their trade, and we pass the farm produce first, the number of stalls easily over a hundred, selling everything from maize to eggs to live cattle and fresh butchered meat.

The sight reminds me that I've not eaten today. My stomach responds, but today I won't eat until I've murdered.

In the distance, a large podium rises in the centre of the market, like a large mountain in the midst of many valleys. Orochi points to it and I follow her in that direction.

'Is now a bad time to tell you I hate heights?'

She gives me a weak smile but turns quickly and I must hurry to keep up.

The thought of all these people, many thousands, a large chunk of them Enforcers, focusses the reality of this ridiculous idea. How was this ever a good idea? Even if I kill her, what then? The mob will surely kill me before an Enforcer gets near.

As soon as they see my powers, they'll execute me. I've seen first-hand how quickly they do these things. Pat was dead within hours. I doubt I'd last that long.

A tight grip pinches into my arm and Orochi pulls me after her. I'd stopped and not realised it. Paralysed by fear I struggle to move one foot in front of the other. The crowd are dense either side of us, the noise deafening. And it's hot. So hot.

And dry. Where will I get the water to use my powers? The ground below is dry and lifeless. The sky is blue, no clouds or rain to aid me.

Somehow, I fight the urge not to pass out or vomit or run and when we reach the bottom stair of the high platform, I watch my legs take step after step, like they belong to someone else.

I fix my mind on Pat, wondering what he felt as he was led to his platform. Was it like this? Or worse? He'd have been terrified.

The noise I'd been blocking out suddenly returns.

'Ice the steps. Stop them.'

I turn and see a whole troop of Enforcers rushing up to us. But I can't do it. I can barely try to summon up the energy to work my powers.

Instead, Orochi pushes past me and makes a large wooden stall fly through the air and knock the Enforcers off the stairs sideways. The fall is so high, when they hit the ground, the thud confirms their instant death.

It makes me sway and my body moves close to the edge. The ground seems to be drawing me to it, and I nearly allow it, before Orochi's hand pulls my wrist up the last of the steps and onto the raised platform.

From here, the entire Square is visible, the thousands of people like small insects scuttering around beneath us. The biggest building I've ever seen sits a mile or so beyond the square, a large pyramid-shaped building. It looks ancient but strong, the peak as sharp as one of my ice shards. It must be the Queen's palace.

My head feels light. I stumble to one knee. All my energy is gone, the journey and the climb too much on an empty stomach.

Orochi pushes me aside again to take out another troop of Enforcers who climb up to stop us. This time, she creates a tornado of earth which whips through the air and sweeps them all off their feet. They meet a similarly horrible end as they hit the ground, over a hundred metres below. The wind from the tornado blows my rag away, revealing my white hair.

'It's time,' says Orochi moving past me and standing in clear view on the platform. 'It needs to be now. I've got their attention. They'll be baying for my blood, so you have a chance to be the hero. Do it.'

She turns to the crowd and shouts as loud as she can. 'I SERVE NO QUEEN. I PRAY TO NO GODS. I AM WICCAN AND I AM GOING TO KILL YOU ALL!'

I face her, getting back to my feet. I try to summon the sensation that I've practised all week, trying to draw water from some source nearby, but nothing happens. We stand, several meters apart staring at each other.

'DO IT!'

Her voice carries over the cries from the crowd below, who are cheering and whooping like they're watching some light entertainment.

But as I stand, unmoved, frozen at the thought of what I must do, Orochi throws the first blow.

A long fork if lightning cracks down from the sky, narrowly missing me.

The cheers turns to screams as the crowd begins to disperse and move away from our elevated arena.

But the electricity fizzes on the platform and she redirects a large dose of it to me. The shock causes a large spark that nearly knocks me off my feet. It's the jolt I need to act.

I attack. Orochi glances away my ice shards, my weapons no real threat to her, but she makes a real show of it, like she's struggling.

She makes a few weak replies, first whipping up some dust in my face, then makes a large rock zip towards my head. I manage to duck, just in time.

Annoyed, I lift my arms, forming a long, sharp blade of ice.

All I have to do is thrust it towards Orochi and I've passed the opening test. I'll have got the attention of the whole of Rejik. Which will hopefully get back to the Queen.

I stare at Orochi's eyes, so familiar in a way I've never been able to fathom. She's been a mentor to me and doesn't deserve an ending like this.

I can't. I've failed at the first hurdle. I can't kill her. I lower my arms.

The people shout and scream. They know what we are already, but most will never have seen one of us at work in their city.

A long shard of ice lands at my feet.

Orochi must have mastered ice, also.

'Now. Do it and help all our kind. Or I will kill your parents.'

I hesitate for a moment, watching the shard begin to melt.

The image of my parents faces pale and lifeless appears.

I've already said goodbye to my brother.

But this is his legacy.

I find the energy to lift the ice, and I hesitate...my arms shake...

The ice flies straight through Orochi's chest, her body falling backwards off the platform into the crowd below.

Then I collapse.

CHAPTER 24

A cheer from the crowd wakes me.

Tightly bound rope scratches my neck. The box I stand on creaks, the wood ready to snap under my weight. I try not to move, or even breath.

'SILENCE!'

The voice roars through the crowd, the air, the very earth beneath us. It's louder than anything I've ever heard. I'm certain that the people in Ghondulon could hear it.

I turn my neck to see the speaker. A huge woman looms over me, even raised on this box. Her hair almost blocks out the sun, the brown spirals weightless and erect. She is probably even bigger than Sway from the Order.

She must be Mutare, too.

The crowd become quiet at her command. Thousands more are packed into the square, eager to see what will happen. Many thousands more are watching from rooftops, walls and every other vantage point in the city.

I sense their hate burning into me. They want a hanging. And I think they're going to get it. The Order have betrayed me. I will not be escaping from this. I'm a murderer and Wiccan and in this world, both get executed. Nobody will know I didn't do it. Nobody will know why.

'FOR A DECADE, OUR QUEEN HAS BROUGHT PEACE TO REJIK AND TO THE REST OF OUR FAIR LAND. HER CRUSADE TO END THE RACE OF WICKED WICCE WAS SUCCESSFUL AND THE MAJORITY OF THOSE HATEFUL DEVILS HAVE LONG SINCE PASSED KA-FERNO'S GATE.'

The crowd thunder their approval. The Queen is much loved in Rejik. The Wiccan, the Mutare, are hated. For half a minute, the noise continues and escalates. The mammoth lady stands with her arms raised, encouraging their hate, inspiring their anger, uplifting their loyalty. She clearly does this a lot.

'YOU ALL KNOW ME. AMP, HEAD OF THE GOLDEN ENNEAD, AND TODAY WE WITNESSED THE MURDER OF ONE WICCAN BY ANOTHER. THEY BROUGHT THEIR FIGHT INTO OUR ARENA. ONE IS DEAD, NOW THE OTHER MUST ALSO BE EXECUTED. FOR PEACE. FOR QUEEN FREYA. FOR REJIK.'

Another long, loud boom of applause and cheering. Where is the Queen? She is supposed to be here to select me for her Golden Ennead. Or was this whole thing a trap? Perhaps Orochi tele-ported the moment she fell over the edge and left me here to take the loathing and punishment of our kind.

Or perhaps this is just the natural conclusion to my life. I've been dodging death for weeks now, lucky to make it this far. If it weren't for Pat, and my parents, I'd have given up by now.

The box beneath my feet creaks again.

'BEFORE THE WICCA IS EXECUTED, I MUST ASK THE TRADITIONAL QUESTION: DOES ANYONE PRESENT HAVE ANY REASON THAT WE SHOULD NOT EXECUTE THIS WICCA?'

The crowd are silent once more. I listen, hoping someone will defend me. Someone will stick up for me.

Corena, it's time to show the Queen why she must let you live.

I must do this myself. Nobody will help me.

'I have a reason.' I shout it as loudly as I can, despite the rope around my neck and my utter petrification.

'SPEAK IT,' replies Amp, moving round to stand in front of me. Now she blocks half of the city from my view.

'I BELIEVE THE QUEEN…'

I stop, starting at the volume of my voice. Amp must be making it louder, like she did with her own. I take a deep breath and continue.

'…I BELIEVE THE QUEEN WOULD VALUE MY SERVICE. I AM LOYAL TO HER.'

Amp starts laughing, the chuckle echoing all around the square and beyond. The crowd copy, clearly preferring a hanging to my serving the Queen.

'LOYAL? PROVE IT, WICCE.'

'THE WOMAN I JUST KILLED. SHE WAS A WICCE AS WELL. SHE WAS HERE TO KILL THE QUEEN. AND I STOPPED HER.'

The crowd erupt into a frenzied wave of gossip, rumour, and debate.

Amp simply stares at me, trying to work out the truth of it. I hope I don't crack, or show any sign of dishonesty, or this noose will get tight really quick.

Eventually, she turns to the crowd and holds her hand up to signal silence. The hush which follows is absolute.

'HE IS A WICCE AND HE WILL HANG.' Amp states is simply, without emotion. She nods to the Enforcer behind me, who crouches down, ready to pull the box from beneath my feet and to let me hang, like Pat did. Several moments with nothing below me, legs kicking frantically as the last bits of breath slowly exit my lungs and I die.

But I won't be joining him in the Haven. With everything I've done, the people I've killed, on purpose, I will descend through the Gate to join all the other sinners for eternity.

The box is pulled away and the rope becomes tight. The shock of it makes my brain light. I can't think, but instinctively I thrash and kick and grab the rope with my hands, trying to get my fingers between my neck and the rope. But it's no good, I'm too heavy. Gravity and a noose are the end of me.

Corena, you must show them your power. You can do it. I believe in you.

I try to summon some ice, but it's too late. I don't have the energy or the resources to do it.

The bright day slowly dulls.

Cerebrum's voice disappears.

Pat's face as he hung from that rope in Ghondulon becomes my world.

I failed you, brother.

My body feels suddenly light. The squeeze of the rope lessens. Air rushes back into my lungs and my brain reboots.

At my feet, a solid block of ice has formed, acting as a platform and saving me. I don't remember doing it, but it must have been me.

'GET HIM DOWN.'

Amp cuts the rope with one swift swing of her sword.

I crumple off the icy platform and onto the ground, grateful for the earth and dirt which I swallow. Grateful for the light which now streams into my eyes and blinds me. Grateful for the noise of the crowd which now blasts into my ears. And grateful that I've summoned up the power to let me live. At least for a few more moments.

'GET HIM UP.'

The Enforcers pulls me to my feet and holds me upright.

'Amp, let us speak for a moment, without your assistance.'

'Yes, your highness, it's done.'

I watch Amp and the Enforcer move to the edge of the platform, leaving me with my potential saviour. I need to be careful with my answers.

'What is your name, child?'

My instinct is to lie. I must.

'Pat.'

'And is what you said true? Are you loyal to me? Is that why you killed the other Wiccan?'

'Yes.'

'And why should I trust you? Why should I make an exception and keep you alive when all other Wiccan and murderers deserve death?'

I take a moment to respond, rubbing my neck as I carefully measure my words.

'You have no reason to trust me. But you've seen some of what I can do, and I have so, so much more...and once you see that, then you'll not just want me to serve you. You'll need me to.'

I don't know where those words come from. My brain is still hazy from the lack of air, but they don't sound like my words.

'We shall see. Strange that I was warned about an assassination attempt today from my very well-informed spies. And you suddenly appear to kill her. Convenient. But timely. And I must admit, I saw your skills and I was impressed, otherwise you'd be dead already. I'll give you a chance, and you can live. For now.'

With that, Queen Freya turns and walks away, her guard flanking her towards her carriage, which is waiting to return to the palace.

Before entering, she turns to Amp. 'Take him down below. See what he can do. Then report to me.'

Amp nods and the Queen disappears inside the carriage, which looks like a dark bubble. It immediately sets off, gliding along a wire that connects the platform to the tip of the pyramid. It's such an elegant and efficient way to travel.

'THERE WILL BE NO HANGING TODAY. THE QUEEN HAS

DECREED THAT THIS BOY IS LOYAL AND HER WORD IS IRREFUTABLE. RETURN TO YOUR LIVES.'

I watch as some of the crowd disperse, while others remain unmoved and mumbling in unison so loudly that I can hear the general noise up here, even without Amp's help.

'DISAPPEAR NOW.' Her voice is so full of threat that even I want to get away. If only I could. I've now declared my loyalty to the same Queen I vowed to kill.

The people go back to their stalls or houses. The roofs begin to clear, and eyes begin to move away from me and the platform.

'Okay, Ice-Wiccan. You've convinced the Queen. Now, can you convince the Golden Ennead?' She lifts me off the ground and carries me to the carriage platform.

She puts me down while we wait for it to return from the palace.

You did well, Corena. Now show them what you can do. Win their trust. I will not be able to contact you while you are in the palace. But I have a spy. Look out for them.

My head feels suddenly lighter, and I know Cerebrum has left it. He must have been in the crowd somewhere. I wonder if the other Order members were with them. I wonder if they watched me murder their friend and then pledge my loyalty to their enemy.

When the bubble returns, the doors slide open, and Amp directs me inside. There are seats all around the edge of the circular cabin. I move to sit on one of them, but the Enforcer pushes me to the ground. I expected this treatment. But I didn't expect what happens next.

Amp lifts the Enforcer with one hand and launches him back outside onto the platform, before slamming the doors shut. She pulls a lever, and we begin moving.

The bubble sways and I grip the edge of the seats, the thought of a hundred feet of nothing between me and the ground making me feel nauseous.

'Relax. Take a seat. It's all an act. We're not really that bad.'

Amp smiles at me and holds her hand out. She grips mine and hauls me into a squashy, purple velvet seat.

'Thanks.' I don't know what to do. Or say.

'You're welcome. Now enjoy the view. We are safe in here.'

I frown at Amp, confused and a little afraid. This is worse than if she were beating me and treating me like dirt.

'Why are you being nice? A few minutes ago, you wanted to hang me. Now you are kind and reassuring.'

'I told you. It's all an act. This is my job. I'm the voice of the Queen. Head of the Golden Ennead. And in case you didn't know, the Golden Ennead are all just like you. We are what the Queen and the rest of the land call Wiccan.'

I say nothing, wary that she's trying to trick me. To get me to disclose something that would reveal my true intention. But I won't give her it.

'I see,' I say, nodding slowly and looking out of the dark glass around us.

The city is receding, returning to its pre-execution state. There's a bridge in the distance, and the gate where we entered this morning, when Orochi was still alive. I relive the scene again and again, watching her fall over the edge many times, before the carriage coming to a halt brings me back to the present.

My stomach rumbles loudly, reminding me again that I haven't eaten today. Amp must overhear it.

'Before we put you through your paces, let's get you something to eat. The kitchens are also in the basement.'

I follow her out of the bubble, and we begin descending a long set of spiralling stairs, which get darker and darker, eventually lit by small, flaming lamps as the sunlight is entirely gone.

Finally, we reach the bottom, and we walk along a long dark corridor and enter the palace's kitchen.

'Go away Amp, I must prep the Queen's lunch. She has twenty important guests, and I need...'

'Flavio, take it easy, we just need some bread and water for our latest recruit. Meet Pat.'

The chef turns to me, his frown disappearing and holds up his hands. 'My apologies, lad. I didn't realise Amp had brought someone else. She usually just comes down here to steal some food.' He looks sidelong at Amp, before turning back to me. 'Now, I have some freshly baked bread just here and I'll get you some of my homemade fruit mix drink. Seriously, you need to try this...'

As he turns to pour the drink, Amp gives me a thumbs down and mimes vomiting. I snort, having almost forgotten what it's like to laugh, and a funny noise comes out.

'You okay?' asks Flavio.

'He's fine, Flavio, just get him something to eat. Then give him a check over.'

'A check over?' I ask, confused.

'Oh, Flavio is also our doctor and surgeon. He's a talented guy,' says Amp, winking at the chef.

I panic. What if he wants to check me...thoroughly?

'I wouldn't go that far, but I contribute any way I can. Amp and a few of the other Ennead's saved my life a while back. I've since vowed to serve them in whatever way I can. And feeding them and treating their numerous and wide-ranging injuries seems like the best way I can do that.'

'What's your power?' I ask him.

He turns away and starts slicing the bread.

I look to Amp, who just shakes her head, so I say no more.

'Here's your food, Pat. Nice to meet you.'

Flavio then disappears into a store cupboard and Amp nods to indicate it's time to leave. I follow her out, holding my plate of bread and my mug of Flavio's fruit drink.

'Eat and drink as we walk. Training will already have begun for the day. We'll join in.'

I've already started eating the bread by the time she speaks. It doesn't last long and then I down Flavio's drink, which didn't actually taste all that bad, if a little sweet.

We reach the opposite end of the corridor from the stairs and a large set of twin oak doors are closed in front of us.

'One bit of advice, Pat. Some of them can be a bit nasty. Particularly to anyone new. I love them all, but they can be horrible. Don't take it personally and don't answer them back. For now.'

She smiles, but I'm not encouraged. I'm about to enter the training room of the Golden Ennead. A group who hunts down Mutare, like themselves, and kill them in the name of the Queen. They are the enemy of the Order, and I will have to befriend them, then betray them, if I'm to achieve my objective.

I ball my hands into two fists, but even that cannot stop them shaking, so I bury them inside my shirt.

The doors swing open.

CHAPTER 25

Five faces look up.

They smile or nod to Amp, then every set of eyes study me. In particular, they roam over my white hair, unusual in these parts.

The room is huge, the roof domed, the walls curved, in contrast to the external shape of pyramid. A large space in the middle of the room is where the five stand, clearly in the middle of sparring with each other. All around the edges, various equipment, weapons and armour clutter the shadows.

And enormous, carved stone statues of the Ten. Each one peering down upon the room from up high. They look like they're spying upon us.

'Enneads. We have a raw one to put through his paces. See if he can make the grade. His name is Pat.'

I'm glad Amp doesn't magnify her voice in here as it would probably boom and echo for the rest of the day.

One of the Enneads moves forward. He is tall, nearly as big as Amp, and has a shaved head. His topless body, neck and arms are covered in tattoos.

His smile is warm and makes me shiver. 'I'm Kelvin. I'm a Flame.'

I take his hand, and it feels like my own is melting. But when I look at it, it's completely fine.

'Don't worry, I have that effect on everyone.' He winks and steps back.

I sense my face reddening, so I lower it and let my hair fall to cover me.

'Okay, Okay, Kelvin. Give him some space. He's only here a minute and you're hitting on him. About ten minutes ago he had a noose around his neck. The Queen spared him, so he doesn't need you lot on top of him. So, get on with training and I'll prepare him to be tested.'

'Target practice,' says a short girl with jet-black hair, shooting an imaginary arrow at me from her bow. 'See you in a second, gorgeous.' She blows a kiss and turns away to shoot at a target board at the side of the room. Predictably she smacks it right in the centre.

Amp places her hand on my back and leads me to the opposite side of the room where a huge pile of equipment and clothing hangs. It's organised chaos. But in its own confused way, everything here is deliberately placed.

'Pat, meet Leck. He's our equipment technician. Amazing guy. Best tech in the land and has invented more stuff than anyone in our history.'

'Nice to meet you, Pat. You joining this crazy squad?'

'Yeah,' I say, lifting my head to give him my best confident look.

He raises his eyebrows. 'I like your confidence, Pat.' He turns to Amp. 'So, what does he need?'

'He's an Icer, so a water suit and pack, just like an Aqua.'

'Gotcha. Take a seat Pat, I'll be a few minutes prepping that.'

Leck disappears amongst his equipment stores, so I turn and sit on the ground to watch the other Enneads training. Amp sits next to me.

'You know I think I might be able to like you, Pat. Let's hope you're as good as you say. It'd be good to have another boy round here.'

I look at the Enneads. Two girls, two boys. Aside from Kelvin and the arrow-girl, there is a second girl, about my height, with curly brown hair making objects move through the air.

'That's Loco, she can move stuff without touching it. We call them Telekine's.'

A second later, a levitating chair smashes into the roof and explodes into hundreds of tiny pieces.

The pieces fall, about to shower us all, when they stop in mid-air. Kelvin ignites some of them, turning them to ash in an instant. The rest float off to the side and fall safely to the ground, away from everyone.

A boy suddenly appears in front of us, smiles and disappears. He re-appears on the opposite side of the room, waving at me.

'He's a teleporter,' I say.

'Not quite,' says Amp. 'He's a Blur. He's so fast, he looks like he's teleporting. And his name is Bo...'

'...lt,' he finishes, appearing before us again. He holds his hand out.

I move to take it, but before I get there, he's gone again, my hand hanging uselessly where his was. A second later, he is back, taking my hand and shaking, while laughing hilariously.

'Sorry, can't resist. It's just too much fun.'

Amp swings a boot at him, but he's gone before she is even halfway through the motion.

'Damn nuisance. Never takes anything serious does that one.'

I smile at him as he appears, or stops, at various points around the room, disturbing the other's training with his speed.

He looks familiar, but there's no way I could have met him before. I'd remember him.

'And what about her?' I ask, pointing to the arrow-girl.

'Oh, that's Sinsi, she's a Percep. Her heightened senses mean her eyesight and co-ordination are so good, she never misses.'

'Never misses?'

'Not once.'

'Best avoid her then. She doesn't seem to like me.'

'Don't take it personal. She's like that with everyone. Except Kelvin.'

I watch Sinsi fire arrow after arrow at various targets, changing her angle, putting obstacles in the way, getting Loco to give her moving targets, but each time she hits.

The way the entire group work in unison, each working on their own abilities, but at the same time challenging each other. It's breath-taking to watch. No wonder these are the chosen Golden Enneads. How will I ever do enough to impress them?

'Here's your suit, Pat.' Leck passes me a sheer white, all-in-one uniform, with an open zip down the middle. 'Your pack is here, once you're changed.' He pats a slim backpack, also pure white, which rests against a box behind me.

'Thanks.'

He smiles and nods. 'Changing room is back there.' He points beyond his workshop, where two doors are clearly labelled male and female.

'See you in a minute,' says Amp, standing and walking out to the training area. 'And good luck.'

I nod and walk through to the changing area.

A surge of anger floods me as I have to make this decision. I know I should just go into the boys, don't make a fuss and keep my cover, but a large part of me wants to go into the girls.

Or neither.

To show them who I am, that I'm not defined by gender, or labels or anything the damn Kurikon has brainwashed them into believing.

But I submit. I do walk towards the boys changing room.

Now is not the time for this.

It's small, two benches and some hangers for my clothes, but I suppose there are only two boys, aside from me.

I change quickly, keen to get the Order's borrowed clothes off and into my cosy looking suit. It's made of a stiff, but elastic material that seems both strong and flexible. Perfect for fighting.

When I zip it up, it feels like it's moulding to my body shape, tightening all over, but remaining comfortable and easy to move. I study my chest, but fortunately I'm flat in that department.

But once the suit is on, the nerves of what's to come rush back. How am I going to impress them? All I've practiced with Orochi was defence, and this is a killing squad, each with their own offensive weapons.

I push myself off the bench, knowing that if I delayed any longer, I'd not be able to. My arms are shaking, and I hold them in front of me, squeezing my muscles, hoping to stop it.

'What do you think?' Leck asks me, as I step back into his workshop.

'Feels amazing.'

'Well, I do my best. Put on this pack.' He helps attach it to me.

It is extremely light. I can barely feel it.

'This is your water supply, which you can use for ice. It never runs out.'

'Never?'

'Nope. It has a special mechanism which extracts water vapour from the air. It can also cause a chemical reaction with the oxygen in the air to form water. Just press the button on the wrist of your sleeve and it should work.'

'Okay. Thanks.' I have no idea how this is going to work, but I can already feel the water building up in the pack, so hopefully I can control it.

'Now, go show them boy. Show them what you can do.'

I make my feet move forward despite almost every instinct saying I should run away from here. Try to escape. Anything but stay and face this trial.

But as I move further into the training arena, I relax my shoulders. They all seem less intimidating now that they've stopped using their powers. They are normal people like me, mostly my age. Only Amp looks older.

'Ready?' she asks.

I nod. 'What do I do?'

'Just...impress us. Enneads! Let's push him, but do not seriously harm. The Queen will want him alive after, either way.'

They spread out, forming a circle around me. I press the button on my sleeve and water circulates throughout my suit, being pumped round like my own blood. It feels great.

I fall into the defensive stance that Orochi taught me, ready to repel any attack or form an ice-shield if I must.

Sinsi attacks first, shooting her arrow at my back. I spin and manage to form a small block of ice front of me, which the arrow sinks into. The block falls to the ground, smashing and releasing the arrow.

'Good start,' says Amp. Sinsi looks furious, loading another arrow onto her bow.

Next a large wooden crate flies towards my head, Loco moving her hands in my direction and the object following. Kelvin thrusts a fire ball towards it and it erupts on contact.

I kneel, into ice-wall stance, quickly summoning the energy. I sense the icy layer forming in front of me. I make the part near my head extra thick. Just as the flaming projectile smashes into the ice-wall, a gust of wind blows my hair. I spin round, but nobody is there. Must be Bolt. Another gust, this time he sweeps my legs and crashes to the ground, winded.

He flies past me again, barely perceptible, punching me on the arm.

As I regain my breath, I realise just how to deal with him.

I place my hands onto the floor and develop a thin ice surface in a five-foot radius around me. I crouch, watching for the next attack, and when it comes, I only see a blur, but this time it misses me and he slides and falls onto his back with a loud thud.

Amp laughs. 'Now that was funny, Bolt!'

I smile slightly, but I've no time to relax, as another projectile smashes into my ice-wall and collapses it, exposing me to the other side of the attack.

Sinsi sends two more arrows at me in quick succession, but I'm able to block them with ice, like I did before.

Then I spot Amp giving a signal, touching her forehead and circling her finger. I've no idea what it means, but they all nod and move into different formations. Bolt gets back to his feet and takes his position.

I decide not to wait. If I do, I'll be beaten by all five of them, so I attack. Forming repeated ice-shards, slightly blunted so I don't kill them, I throw shard after shard at my enemies, making them dodge and back off. I make sure they move away from each other, trying to isolate them and reduce any effect of them working together. It's my only hope.

I'm careful to put one hand on the ground as I do it, to keep the area around me icy and eliminate Bolt's speed. When Sinsi sends her arrows, I make sure to encapsulate them in ice, so she'll run out. And even though Kelvin simply melts my shards when they come near him, I keep him busy enough that he can't attack me.

The two I worry about are the two doing very little, except dodging my shards. Amp and Loco are closing together and they make whispered exchanges, so I turn my focus to them momentarily.

I thrust a massive shard at the space between, hoping to split them, but instead my shard stops midway. It hovers for a second as I try to push it forward, but something is stopping it.

Loco.

She fights against my ice, but neither of us is gaining an advantage. Meanwhile, Kelvin and Sinsi close in on the opposite side.

I quickly form an ice-wall behind me while fighting against Loco who is gradually making my ice-shard come back to me.

But Kelvin melts my wall easily and Amp moves for the first time. She opens her palms towards Loco and when she does, the shard suddenly overpowers me and flies through the air so fast it hits before I realise it.

I'm down and I think my ribs might be broken. I can't breathe and a guttural moan comes out my mouth. I lie on the melting ice, knowing I'm beaten. They'll have closed in and will attack any moment, defeating me and confirming my death sentence.

I can't let that happen.

So, I summon every ounce of energy I can, close my eyes and try to encase myself. The ice-shields I spent all week developing need to work for me now. The ice forms, my muscles shaking with the effort and my head hurting. I open my eyes, and I'm sheathed with ice. Thick ice, too. I've done well.

But at one side, my worst enemy. Fire. Melting the shield. I reinforce that area, replacing the ice as it melts. It doesn't become any thinner.

At the other side, an object thunders into the ice, but it holds, and I reinforce it as best I can. I'm safe for the moment, but my arms are falling, and my head feels like it might explode with the strain.

The flames become larger, now entirely engulfing the ice shield. I struggle to stop it melting. In a few seconds, I'll be overcome and burnt.

With one final effort, I focus all my energy on one spot where I think Kelvin will be. A blunted ice-shard flies up from the ice-shield and he cries out as it hits him, and the flames extinguish.

But I'm done. The shield melts and I'm exposed, soaked and exhausted. My vision spins and my muscles fail.

'Do you submit?' Amp asks.

'He does,' replies Sinsi for me. 'He is finished; his efforts have exhausted him.'

'Then help him up, for goodness' sake,' says Amp.

Bolt and Kelvin move to lift, but Loco saves them the effort. I'm weightless as I'm transported across the room. Next to Leck's workshop is a small area which he must use for his medical duties.

Loco lowers me onto a bed.

Leck kneels next to me, checking my ribs. When he touches them, I want to scream at him, but I don't have the energy. Instead, I let out a hiss.

'Sorry. I think you have at least one broken rib. I'm going to put some of my healing salve on it. It will sting. Badly. But it will heal quicker.'

He unzips the suit and lifts my undertop, putting his fingers into a large bowl of brown gunge and massages it into my ribs. Every movement feels like a living hell.

And I'm conscious of my breasts, small as they are. If my suit slides off that part, they'll know what I am.

A few, long seconds later he finishes and pulls a blanket up to my waist. He hands me two pills. 'Take these to help you sleep.'

'I'm fine,' I mumble, pushing his hand away. I know better than to take random pills.

'You can trust me, Pat. I'm a doctor. They will help.'

Too exhausted to even lift my hand, I open my mouth, and he pops them in.

'Did I pass?'

The group turns to Amp. She looks unsure.

'I need to consult with the Queen. When you wake, I will tell you. Sleep now, boy.'

And she turns and exits the training hall through the doors we entered. Loco, Sinsi and Kelvin all disappear to the changing rooms, while Leck goes back to his workshop. I'm left alone with Bolt.

He squints at me and tilts his head. 'Do I know you?'

I shake my head. But at the same moment, a memory pops into my head. From the Kurikon, when I was being lashed. 'No, definitely not.' I smile. 'I'd remember.'

'Fair enough...I've got to admit, that was nice thinking with the ice. Nobody done that to me before. If you do get in, I look forward to working with you.'

I try to smile, but it's too much effort.

I want to say that I'm looking forward to working with him, too, but work involves killing innocent Mutare.

I turn to ask him if he's ever killed a Mutare, he doesn't seem like he could or would, but he's gone.

Seconds later, so am I.

CHAPTER 26

I wake to see Leck kneeling beside me again, checking my ribs.

'Sorry, didn't mean to wake you, Pat. Just checking on the ribs. How does this feel?'

He touches the area that was agony before my sleep. It's now a bit tender, just like a bruise.

'Fine. Your salve seems to have worked well. How long did I sleep?'

'Several hours. It's now evening.'

'Did they decide if I'm in?'

'Not yet. At least, Amp has not returned. Would you like some food? I could get Flavio to bring something along for you?'

'Yes, that would be great. Thank you, Leck.'

'No problem.'

I grab his arm as he's about to leave. 'Seriously, thank you. You've been very kind.'

He smiles and walks away, leaving me alone. He's the first person I've met in weeks who I don't feel has a hidden agenda.

I sit up and my head swirls. I grip the edge of the bed frame and use it to steady myself. I'm still sore all over, but without the pain in my ribs, it's just the same as after Orochi's sessions.

I zip up the suit, still arctic white despite the fight, and amble out into the arena. All evidence of the contest has now gone. No water, ice or fire. Not even the broken shards of wood from Loco's projectiles.

It's also eerily quiet. As I move towards the changing rooms, Leck shuffles about in his workshop area, hidden behind the stack of equipment and technology, most of which I don't recognise.

I push open the door to the male changing room and am grateful that nobody is present. I change out of my suit and leave it hanging up. Hopefully I won't need it again today.

As I change, I think about the Ennead. And how I hope to convince them all to trust me. I think I can get to them all, based on initial feelings. Except Sinsi. She seems to hate me already and I don't know why. But that's not what bothers me most. It's the fact that she looks so familiar, and I can't quite place it.

When I go back outside, Leck is waiting.

'Flavio's in a mood and won't bring anything along. So, we need to go along to the kitchen. The other guys are there already.'

'No problem, I'm so hungry I'd walk anywhere right now.'

He gives me a small nod and we leave the training area, walk along the corridor and enter the kitchen.

This time there's more than bread and fruit juice. The kitchen has clearly been busy all day. I remember that the Queen had important guests. Whatever they had smells amazing.

The other Enneads, minus Amp, are sitting at a large oak table, drinking wine from large glasses.

'Have a seat Pat, this is where you'll eat. If...you know...'

'Thanks,' I say again.

He nods to me and turns to leave.

'You're not eating with us?'

A snort comes from the table behind. No need to see who it was.

'No, I eat in my workshop.' He leaves without looking up at me.

The table has space for eight people. The large empty seat at the head of the table is clearly Amp's, so I move to sit in the one between Bolt and Sinsi, hoping to get talking to her.

'Don't even think about it…' Sinsi puts her hand on the seat.

I think she's just being a scutter, so I keep moving into it.

'Actually, I wouldn't mind if you'd sit in one of the other seats, either.' Bolt looks up at me sympathetically, but with conviction.

'Okay, sorry I didn't know seats were so precious around here.' But the moment I say it, I know I've made a mistake.

Kelvin takes a sharp breath in, Loco looks up at me and shakes her head and Sinsi leaves her seat. She's smaller than me by a head, but she doesn't let that stop her squaring up to me. Her growl is so fierce; it'd scare off wild animals.

I know I should be submissive and play it smart, but all I want to do is keep winding her up. Tick, tock. But Kelvin is out of his seat and places a warm arm on my cold skin.

The stimulus stops me, and I back off, moving to the seat beside Kelvin and the large one at the head.

As I sit, Flavio comes over, tiptoeing. He places a bowl of stew in front of me and some of his bread from earlier.

'Thanks,' I say.

'You're welcome. By all accounts you did well in the arena and this lot seem to think you'll be staying. So, I had best treat you like I would an Ennead.' He turns back into the kitchen.

'He ain't no Ennead. He doesn't deserve to sit at this table.' Sinsi still stands and leans over the table towards me. 'And you weren't all that good today. We took it easy on you.'

'Sure thing. How many times did your arrows hit me again?' I say, unable to help myself.

She leans back and slides into her seat, not replying immediately. Her cold eyes give me a non-verbal response as good as any words. 'Next time, Pat.'

'So, you must think I'll get in for there to be a next time? You need to remember what you're saying from sentence to sentence.'

Bolt's chair screeches backwards, anticipating trouble. Loco has her hands raised, ready to deflect anything that's thrown.

But Sinsi does nothing. She simply stands and leaves the room, slamming the door behind her.

'That wasn't smart, Pat,' says Kelvin. 'You ain't going to make friends here, if you act like that.'

'Like what?' I say, still in confrontation mode.

He places his hand on my wrist again and it has an instant calming effect. I turn to face him.

'Like insulting Sinsi like that. She isn't the easiest at first, but she's a damn good friend to us all. And that seat over there was her brother's. He was killed on our last mission.'

I suddenly feel smaller than a dung-beetle. Actually, I deserve to be in the dung alongside one. I can't believe I just acted like that. Kelvin is right, I was totally out of line. I need to make these people my friends or I'll never fit in here. And if I don't, I'm dead. So, screw your head on right, Corena.

'Sorry guys. I've just had a hell of a time. My head wasn't in the right place. I'll make it up to you. If I get in, then I'll show you I'm not always like that.'

'You'd better do. And Sinsi is the Queen's favourite, or used to be, so even if you don't like her, try to get along. She passes on reports to our Queen about what we do and how things are.' Kelvin gives me a last smile and leaves the table.

Loco follows him. I can't work her out. She doesn't seem annoyed or even bothered about me. I'll need to keep an eye on her.

Bolt stands last. 'You drink much wine?'

'Never had more than a glass on my dad's birthday. We didn't have much money.'

Bolt's grin spreads wide, every one of his pearly white teeth on display. 'Then I have an idea. I'll see you back in the arena.'

'I have to fight again?'

'No, but that's where we sleep as well. And pretty much everything else. We don't get allowed out much because we can't be seen performing any of our abilities. They accept that we exist and that we provide a service, but they don't want to see us too much. Freaks them out. You know, because magic is outlawed. All Wiccan get hanged. You don't want that, do you?'

'I might still be getting that.'

'Nah, Pat. You smashed it today. You'll get in.'

His smile does encourage me. Maybe he's right, maybe I have done enough.

'Anyway, see you when you've eaten. I'll have a surprise for you.' Then he's gone. The door slamming is the only evidence that he left the kitchen. If he didn't make a faint buzzing noise as he moved, then I'd think he teleported. This world is crazy.

I sit alone and enjoy my stew. It's the nicest meal I might ever have had. I think there's even salt in it. A small volume of wine remains in a decanter and an empty glass by my place, so I fill it up with the dregs.

I've either earned it, or it's my last meal before I'm hanged. Either way, I'm going to enjoy it. It's red and tastes a little bitter, but I enjoy the drink all the same, each mouthful making my general aches disappear and the whole situation seem marginally bearable.

Flavio clatters around in the kitchen, cleaning up for the night. When he bids me good night in a much politer fashion than when I greeted him this morning, I've had all my food and wine.

I follow him out the kitchen, but as he ascends the stairs, I move along the long corridor to the large doors where I will hear my fate. I hope Amp has returned because as I get closer to the mammoth oaks, I suddenly feel nervous.

Nervous that these are my last steps. But more than that, nervous that I might actually succeed and become a member of the Golden Ennead and have to serve the Queen by hunting Mutare.

I've come to the very edge of Ka-Ferno's Gate and must decide whether to proceed or stay in this world and kill more innocents in order to kill the Queen.

As I lift my arm to push open the door, it does so of its own accord. Or probably Loco's. I can't see her immediately, but she's probably close. Their chatter filters out from Leck's workshop.

They become silent as I walk in. Amp comes towards me, her face looking grim, a loose length of rope in her hand.

'I'M SORRY, PAT,' she says, voice amplified so loud it nearly knocks me over. 'THE QUEEN HAS MADE HER DECISION.'

CHAPTER 27

'WELCOME TO THE GOLDEN ENNEAD.'

They laugh at how shocked I must look.

'Do you do that to every new recruit?' I ask.

Amp nods while the others continue to laugh.

Amp drops the rope and holds out her hand. As I grasp it, I feel something I've not really felt before.

I belong.

Aside from Sinsi, who doesn't move from her seat, the other Enneads and Leck rise to congratulate me. It's official – I'm one of them.

I smile, despite this being a revenge mission, and only part two: infiltration, having been achieved.

I bury part one away for now.

There is still a long way to go.

I must get the trust of these people.

That's how I will get the Queen to trust me.

Before I kill her.

'Sinsi, come and congratulate Pat,' commands Amp.

She twitches in her seat, momentarily following the order, before her face darkens and she plants herself back down.

'Sinsi, you'll congratulate Pat, or you'll be suspended.'

She rises, walks over to me and taps my hand, before turning away and moving into the girls change room. At least her attitude is reminding me that she and they are the enemy.

'A formal ceremony will follow in the next few days, where you'll meet the Queen, but in the meantime, it's eat, sleep, and train for you.' Amp nods to me as she finishes, before also disappearing after Sinsi.

'Well, looks like we have a good reason to get stuck into this now!' shouts Bolt, holding up a bottle of wine. He points to five more on the table at the back of the workshop.

'Where did you get that?' I ask.

'If you don't ask, I won't lie,' he replies, winking.

I hate it when guys do that, like they just give you a wink and whatever they have done is forgiven. But in this instance, he is forgiven. I want to celebrate this moment and it's also a great chance to get them all drunk and find out what they're really like.

'I won't ask then,' giving him a smile and punching his shoulder.

We sit round a large steel table, the smell of welded metal, oil and wood burning engulfing us. I don't mind it because it helps to ease my nerves, particularly the burning pine wood whose scent I'd recognise anywhere in this world. it's from my homeland and it comforts me to know that our labour reaches as far as the capital. But my dad may never fell another tree, nor smell another pine if I don't succeed here. Who knows what the Order will do with them now, but if I fail, I can't see them just being released home, no matter what Cerebrum said.

I know my fate is entwined with theirs. They never saved me when they had the chance, but I can save them. I cannot fail here, and I don't intend to.

'So, you folks all know my story. Let's hear yours: how did you get here?' I look at each face in turn. Loco, then Kelvin, Leck and finally Bolt. Amp and Sinsi are still in the change room. We've all had a bit of wine and faces are flushing, tongues will be loosened.

'I'll go first, I've been here the longest,' replies Leck. That surprises me, but I guess it shouldn't. The guy looks like he can make anything from a few scraps of material.

'I was a blacksmith's apprentice down in Old Rejik. Was doing mighty well, too. Would have had my own place within a couple of years. But then old Garrick came to see me one day. Said he had a proposal for me if I'd come to the palace. Haven't left since.'

'So, you had a choice?' I ask.

'Of course. I loved working with metal and the materials I get here, and the technology passed my way makes it worth it.'

'Makes what worth it?' I know I'm pushing it so early in the evening, but I give him a big smile and sip my wine.

'Well, being stuck down here. No offence folks, but I'd like a wee bit of company beyond you lot at times and I wouldn't half mind going to my local inn and having some brews, but I know what I signed up for. Giving up your old life to serve for the greater good.'

'The greater good?'

'You know, helping you lot take out the last of the Wiccan that still menace the land. I remember as a lad, a young gal from along the street getting killed by a fire-Wiccan. But that's all above my head and thoughts. I just like making stuff in my workshop. That's what makes Leck tick.'

Leck downs his glass and pours himself another, offering top ups to the rest of us. I'm already feeling it, but I take more, knowing I've not even begun to gather the info I want.

'Bolt, what about you? How'd you get here? You always seem so chirpy. You don't strike me as the murderous kind of guy.' I add the last part to get under the skin, hoping for a bite. I recognise him from somewhere and want to find out more about him.

'I ain't a murderous kind of guy? You know what we do here, Pat? We protect the people. We don't kill, not unless it's necessary. So, don't get no preconceptions about us. We serve, we do what we can for the people we love and the innocent folks of this land. You got that?' His brow is furrowed, sitting forward over the table, pointing his wine glass at me.

I ignore his aggressive stance. 'Okay, so you're not murderous. But still, the work must be grim sometimes. Doesn't seem like it'd suit you.'

'Aye, well sometimes some light is needed when things get dark. I try to be the light, 'cos as much as Kelvin's your man for fire, he has got a real shitty sense of humour, eh Flame-Boy?'

Kelvin doesn't rise, remaining unmoved and composed. He takes a long swig of wine and places the glass on the table. Then, quicker than I can see, a flame is rocketed from him towards Bolt. Luckily, Bolt moves in time and the fireball smashes into a long, thick piece of metal and sizzles out on the sandy ground beneath.

'Too slow, Glum Bum. And you'll always be too slow for me.'

'One of these days, you're going to wind up the wrong person Bolt, and it'll be the last thing you do.'

'We'll see. Or you won't see, I'll be so quick.' He chuckles again, but Kelvin ignores him completely this time, instead turning to me.

'Do you know that Mr Protect the People, joke-a-minute, Bolt actually is here because he hurt some people. Tell him about it, comedian.'

Bolt gives Kelvin a death stare. 'Play nice, Flame-Boy or I'll spill all your secrets to Pat here. And then all your wit and charm won't seem so romantic to him.'

Kelvin turns the same red as the edges of his fire, but says nothing, his eyes remaining on Bolt.

'Anyway, I got into all this by a weird coincidence. Yes, I was a thief. I did occasionally hurt people, to get food and survive, but I never did it through enjoyment.'

'You assaulted some Enforcers,' shouts Kelvin.

'Yes, but only because I had to.'

'Likely story.'

'Besides, I ended up getting in with some crappy pirates, who caught me stealing from them once. I decided to drink some ale from the barrel and took a little too much. When I woke up, I was in chains. They said they would only release me if I worked with them. So, I did. And it went wrong.'

'What happened?' I ask. The mention of the pirates has my rapt attention.

'They double crossed me. They informed the Royal Enforcers about what I was and when I tried to steal from a trader in Rejik, they arrested me.'

'How did they catch you? The Enforcers.'

'They didn't. It was this lot. The Ennead caught me.' He lifts his trousers to reveal a large circular scar on both sides of his leg. 'Sinsi shot an arrow through my leg and slowed me down. That allowed the others to catch me. Trust me, if I was fully fit, and with all my training now, it could never happen again.' He stares at Kelvin as he says the last part.

'And they asked you to join up?'

'Yup. My speed is useful to the Ennead as you'd imagine.'

I nod, seeing just how normal this guy is. How he's not all that different to me. He's not here by choice, he was caught, and it was better than his life on the streets, stealing.

'What about you, Loco?' I've barely heard her speak, so I'm interested to hear her story. She's barely touched her wine.

'Not much to tell. Uncle was in the Ennead. He recommended me when he retired. I have the same skills, so it made sense.' She doesn't look at me as she speaks. Her head remains down through-out, and she says the fewest words that she has to. She's keeping a lot locked up, but there's something about her I like. Amongst these bravado Mutare, she seems very normal and down to earth.

I turn to Kelvin. 'And you?'

He is still red from before, still angry with Bolt. His face softens as he opens his mouth to speak to me.

'Time for bed, folks. We have a mission in the morning.' Amp appears at the doorway of the female change room.

'But look at all this wine. We need to celebrate Pat's acceptance.' Bolt pouts.

'That can be done another time. For now, get some rest and prep yourself for a sunrise departure. This is a big one. Four Mutare to capture.'

'Capture?' I say, surprised.

'Yes, capture Pat. Were you expecting anything else?'

'Your reputation is a little darker.'

'Maybe you should come along tomorrow. Just to observe. See exactly what we do.' She turns to the rest of table. 'Now off to bed. Good night.'

The table mumbles, Bolt loudest, but everyone follows the command.

I follow Kelvin to the bedroom, through a door at the back of the change room. There are six beds, each with their own curtains to make them self-contained. Bolt pulls it around his bed as soon as we enter. He is at the far end on the left.

Across from him, Kelvin gets ready to go to sleep.

'Take any of the empty ones, Pat. I put a spare pair of my pyjamas on the rail beside you.'

'Thank you.' My words seem inadequate. The kindness of his act hits me hard. So brotherly, or maybe something else, but unlike anything I've experienced. At least, not in a long while.

I pick up the pyjamas and take my place, closest to the door, on the same side as Kelvin.

Now the other two have pulled their curtains around their beds, I'm left alone in this strange bedroom. A shared, boys' bedroom...but at least it's a bedroom. My first after years of sleeping next to the fire.

The combination of the wine and the day's trials have exhausted me.

I've survived day one as a spy and as a boy.

I pull the curtains around me, change into the comfy, peach smelling pyjamas and fall fast asleep almost immediately.

CHAPTER 28

My mouth is dry.

'Time to go, Pat. We leave in five.'

I spring up. Amp stands beside me, a small smile on her enormous face.

'The mission?'

'Yes. Hurry, I want you to come along.'

'Yes, I'll be right out.'

I hurriedly throw on my white training suit, which has appeared at the foot of my bed, and run my fingers through my white hair. My new way of brushing it.

In the workshop Leck is attaching mechanisms to the other Ennead's suits.

He turns to me when I arrive.

'Sorry, Pat. I've not had time to work on anything for you, but I'll have something for you by the time of the next mission.'

I wave my hand at him, smiling. 'I'm just observing this time anyway.'

He nods and goes back to attaching funnel-like metal pieces to Kelvin's gloves and boots.

Sinsi winks at me. Why is she suddenly so nice? Or is she just messing with me?

Loco has her head down as usual, buckling up one of her boots. Bolt zooms around, a blur to us all, getting himself ready.

'Come with me, Pat,' says Amp.

I follow her out into the training arena.

'Okay, so you will stay in the aircraft when we go into Ghondu-lon. Leck is piloting, so you stay in the cockpit with him. Got it?'

'Aircraft? Cockpit?'

'An aircraft is a flying ship. Leck built ours. It's the only one in the world that we know off. Anyway, the cockpit is the place up front.'

When she sees I'm still confused, she adds, 'Just sit next to Leck and stay there.'

I nod, suddenly feeling entirely out of my depth. I've never heard of any of this stuff before. The suits and machines are one thing, but a flying ship is another. I wish Pat were here. He'd love the idea of a flying ship.

I return to the workshop, where a small breakfast awaits me. More of Flavio's bread and juice. I scoff and down both.

Then we move. The six of us walk across the training area to a hidden door in the opposite wall. It's only obvious now that I'm right in front of it. The outline is barely visible in the brick, because the door itself is made of brick.

When Leck presses one brick, the door swings open slowly, grinding as stone rubs against stone. Beyond the stone sits a museum of machinery unlike anything I could possibly imagine. This is Leck's showcase and when he sees the open-mouthed gaze on my face, he nods and pushes his shoulders back. He turns and gazes upon the room like a mother to her new-born baby.

Amongst a gallery of indescribable machinery and technology, sits three things I do recognise; a metal ship, shining immaculately in a narrow channel of water which spans the length of the vast room; a horse-drawn carriage, but composed entirely of metal and seemingly without any place to reign up the horses; and what must be the flying ship, the aircraft, also composed of metal, with vast wings, like a bird.

'Impressive, isn't it?' says Kelvin. 'Leck here is a master of small machinery, but an unbelievable engineer of larger machines.'

'Well, I do get a lot of help you from guys. Couldn't weld without you Kelvin. Or lift the heavier pieces of metal into place without Loco. And this would have taken me fifty years had it not been for Bolt, doing all the small tasks at super speed.'

The three Enneads blush. Amp also looks pleased. Sinsi does not. It's clear she feels left out, like her skills have a lower value. I enjoy watching her annoyance.

'Enough of the mutual love crap, let's get on with what we're actually here for. Let's catch these Mutare,' says Sinsi, striding towards the aircraft.

We follow her to the flying ship and climb aboard on metal ladders which extend into a long, metal tube filled with seats and a storage area at the back. I follow Leck into a separate area at the front. Here, the metal gives way to glass.

'You get the best views up here, Pat. I hope you like heights,' says Leck, pressing coloured squares on the metal panel in front.

The aircraft suddenly makes lots of noise and begins to vibrate.

'What's happening?' I ask, my hands tightening their grip on my seat.

'That's the engine. It's what powers the aircraft.'

'It makes this chunk of metal go into the sky?'

'Exactly.'

I have no idea how all this works, but nobody else looks worried, so I ask no more about it.

'Loco, open up the doors,' commands Amp.

This time, the doors are over twice as large as the aircraft itself, opening onto a long, smooth track which extends into darkness.

'Where does it lead to?' I ask.

'Out of the city. We can't take off in front of millions of people.

If people saw this, they'd want to know how we can build this and not feed most of the land. Plus, spies from the bordering lands are always canvassing the city for technology and information to use. This would be a big one for them, no?'

I nod, thinking about how I feel right now, then imagining millions of others thinking the same. They'd be scared and confused and worst of all, they'd feel betrayed, like they'd been kept in the dark about a large secret.

'Less chat. Hit it, Leck.'

'Yes, Ma'am.'

The engine increases in volume and the vibrations increase in intensity. The aircraft lurches forward at a terrifying speed, pinning me back into my seat as we plunge along the dark underground track.

After a minute or so, the speed seems to level off and while it's uncomfortable, my body adjusts. My stomach is churning and my head spinning, and I've never felt less safe in my whole life. But a small part of me starts to enjoy the sensation.

'How much longer?' I ask.

'Nearly there,' says Leck. 'But hold on. The next bit is the best.'

The tunnel starts to lighten, as daylight floods in from an opening that we catapult towards. Within seconds, we rocket through the threshold out into blinding light.

I keep my eyes closed due to the brightness, but I can't close out the sensation going through my body as the aircraft lifts and my body is pinned to my seat both from in front and above. I'm at a strange angle, so when I open my eyes all I see is a mixture of white cloud and blue sky.

We rise at this angle for the longest time, and I have to swallow back down several small mouthfuls of sick. I can't let them see me vomiting on my first mission. My body is soaked in sweat and I'm close to passing out. My head is light, and I've stopped taking in any other sensory information, like the sounds of the beeping buttons on the panel or Leck chatting to Amp.

Now my ears are hurting. Repeated small pops happen alternately in both ears, giving me a sensation like I'm deep underwater, at the bottom of the lake, when the Order kidnapped my parents to assure my compliancy.

Well, I've done all they've asked, even if they don't trust me. My parents should be safe if they keep their word. But I can't trust them. And now, here I am, trying to gain the trust of the Golden Ennead, so I can get close enough to break it, and kill their Queen.

A final pop and the ears hurt no more. The aircraft also seems to be levelling off.

'Are we as high as we're going?' I ask.

'Yes, we call the height altitude. We are at our flying altitude. We'll be in Ghondulon in an hour.'

'An hour?'

'Yes, we can travel much faster in an aircraft than by land or sea. It's why it's become so important for the Ennead. We can get to places where Mutare are reported before they move on. We have been much more prolific since we built the aircraft. You can go in the back and sleep if you wish. There are pull down beds in the storage area.'

I peer out of the window and now that we're level, I can see much of the land, and the sea, as well as the sky. I lean forward, feeling more confident by the second. There are villages and towns, small as insects on the ground, and ships upon the water, leaving tiny trails behind them.

'No, I'm fine up here. Can I stay and look out the window?'

'Sure,' replies Leck, smiling.

The rest of the journey is a wonder as I take in every small detail through the window and I begin to see the world in a whole new way: instead of a vast, immeasurable land, that no person could possibly see all of, it has become much smaller, much more attainable to go from one part to another. To cross a series of mountains, or cross seas and oceans or vast areas of land, that would take months or years in my old world. In this new world, it can be done in hours.

The world has shrunk.

'Two minutes to landing, Amp, if you want to get ready.'

'Got you, Leck, take us down nice and slow and do not be seen. We are very close to Ghondulon.

'Yes, Ma'am.'

The nose begins to dip and even more of the land is visible in the window.

Ghondulon: where Pat died, where I first met the Order, where we abandoned Sorg and Hiro to the sulphur mines.

I've only just left this town and now I'm back to face the demons of my recent past. But then again, I'm not leaving the ship. I'm staying behind like a little boy who needs protecting.

But I'm no longer that person.

I'm powerful and I can look after myself.

And I won't stay behind with a babysitter.

'I'm coming,' I say, turning around to Amp.

'No, you're staying this time, Pat. You can come next time.'

'No. I want to come. I need to. This place is full of my demons, and I need to face them. I can't wait until next time. It has to be today, or I'll forever be haunted by them.'

Amp looks at me for a long time. 'Fine but stay by my side at all times.'

'Yes, Ma'am,' I say, winking at Leck, who smiles.

Damn, did I just wink? Who am I?

You are the Ice-Wiccan of the North, the latest addition to the Golden Ennead, the unsure assassin of the Order. Whatever you are now, you are not the same person as before, so you can do new things. You can wink if you want. You can be the person you want to be.

'Prepare for landing, folks.'

I watch the ground get closer and closer as we approach a long strip of smooth land, which leads into a large hole in the side of one of the hills overlooking Ghondulon.

As we hit the earth, the aircraft bounces and has to hit the ground a second time, but this time it stays down.

I'm thrown forward as we begin to slow and pass into the tunnel in the side of the hill, the darkness engulfing us. We roll along for quite a while, longer than we did when we took off, until we reach a low-lit cavernous room.

It's rough and undecorated, almost like it's never been used before. But then I spot a single woman standing at the opposite side. It's too dark to make out who it is.

The aircraft turns in the space at the centre of the cave and comes to a stop facing back down the tunnel we just entered through.

'Okay, let's get moving Enneads.' Amp opens the door, and the others follow her out. I exit last with Leck, who remains at the top of the steps.

'Good luck, Pat. See you in a couple of hours. Stay safe.'

'Thanks, Leck. See you soon.'

In truth, part of me would like to stay in the craft with him but now is the time for action. I must show my worth.

Amp walks towards the lady in the shadows. She looks old, even from here I can see that.

The others follow, more warily. They must not know her.

'Enneads come around. I want to introduce you to our Ghondulon informer.'

We all move towards Amp and the informer.

'I'd like you all to meet one of our oldest allies. She is a Mutare as well.'

Amp raises her hands and the flames in the lamps suddenly brighten and the informer's face comes into clear view.

My breath catches and my lungs freeze.

My eyes refuse to close.

'Enneads, this is Orochi. And she'll be helping us track down and capture the Mutare.'

CHAPTER 29

Orochi holds out her hand, a neutral expression on her face.

She gives no indication that she spent a week training me to kill her, nor that she fell from the platform in the centre of Rejik just yesterday with a large chunk of ice in her chest. She must have teleported as she fell. But even that doesn't explain...this.

I take her hand, trying not to look shocked or surprised or terrified in the slightest. So many questions whirl, but I try to shut them out. I can think of them later. Just now I need to focus on this mission. Then I'll worry about who the hell Orochi is and who's side she is on.

'Orochi will come with us, locate the Mutare and help us with any local trouble we may have,' says Amp, once everyone has shaken her hand.

I wonder if Amp knows about Orochi. That she's really the joint leader of the Ennead's opposition. That she was chief in the plan to murder their Queen. I try to keep my eyes off her, but it's no good. I keep looking for an expression of acknowledgement from her.

It does not come.

We exit the mountain through a foot tunnel and when we emerge back outside, I instantly recognise where we are. We are in the hills beyond the sulphur mine. The smell is instantly recognisable. I hoped I'd never smell it again, but my path is taking many unexpected turns right now.

'Okay, we don't have much time. They rarely stay in one place in town for very long,' says Orochi, every word of hers a betrayal to the Order members we're about to capture.

'Bolt, how quickly can you get there?'

'A minute, maybe less. If I'm carrying someone, perhaps ninety seconds.'

'Fine, take Orochi first, drop her off and then come back and get us. We'll walk while you are away to shorten the journey a little.'

'Oh, gee thanks!'

He picks up Orochi and disappears in a blur of movement.

I consider telling Amp that Orochi is a double agent. That she is conspiring against the Queen, but I decide not to, as that would lead to questions about how I knew that. And Amp might even be in on it as she seems to know Orochi well.

We walk down the hill, but before we've gone very far, Bolt is back. He takes Kelvin next. Then Loco.

When he disappears with her, I'm left alone with Amp. We walk in silence for a few seconds before she stops me.

'Pat, I want to remind you again. Do not leave my side today. I will get Bolt to take you first, but then wait for me with Orochi. We'll not enter the house that the Mutare are in, unless we're needed. Do you understand?'

'Of course,' I say, trying to convince her beyond doubt. But I have no intention of doing otherwise.

I want to remain with the Ennead.

I want to return to the Palace without suspicion.

I want to be near the Queen.

I want to avenge Pat's death.

'Good. I do not want anything to happen to you.'

She walks ahead. I follow, wondering why she is so keen for

me to remain safe. Is she just genuinely being nice, or something else? I didn't suspect anything before, but Orochi's appearance changes it all.

Now I don't know who my friends or enemies are. I don't know who to trust.

Bolt reappears. 'Good to go, Icey!'

'Yes, but don't call me Icey again or I'll call you Quickie!'

'Gotcha, Frosty,' he says, winking. That's going to become so annoying.

But I ignore him and climb onto his back.

'Okay, hold tight, keep your head down to avoid whiplash and I'd suggest keeping your eyes shut. Most people are sick when they keep them open.'

'Will do,' I say, closing my eyes, gripping my arms around his neck tighter and burying my head into the top of his back.

When he starts moving it's ten times worse than the flight in the aircraft. Twice I nearly fall off, my grip slipping, but both times Bolt feels it coming and hauls me back on.

Then we stop. Bolt lowers me off his back.

'Pat, you probably don't remember me, but I've seen you before.'

I stare back at the Blur, glad I wasn't imagining that I recognised him.

'When?'

'Fort Lorn. I was taking a private message from the Queen to the High Klerik. You were being tortured to reveal your powers.'

Then it clicks. The dark face in the background. The one who objected to my whipping. Now I understand why. A fellow Mutare.

'I'd rather the others didn't find out just yet. Not while I'm trying to prove myself. Can we keep it between us?'

'Why lie about it? We know you are Mutare, so does Amp and the Queen.'

'There was a little more to it, but I'd rather not tell people about it. Not yet.'

He narrows his eyes, like he knows this is a bad idea. 'I hate having to keep secrets. I hate it.'

I can't resist asking. 'What other secrets do you have?'

'If I told you, they wouldn't be secrets.' His grin returns. 'And the secrets I have, the messages I've been asked to give from the Queen...they'd kill me if I told.'

'Well, if you tell mine, I'll kill you, too!'

'Ha, now who's joking, Frosty?'

And in one rapid movement, he guides me onto his back and we're off again.

When we reach the destination, a minute and a half later, I collapse to the ground and keep my eyes firmly shut. Even so, I end up vomiting my breakfast back up. Some of it lands on Sinsi's shoe.

'What the hell, Ice-Scutter?' she kicks her shoe at me, splashing me with small spots of my own sick. But I'm too dizzy, disoriented and disgusted to respond. Instead, I fall backward and land on the soft mud.

'This a new one?' Orochi asks.

I want to scream at her for her near perfect performance.

'Aye just joined yesterday. It's his first mission. He's impressed so far,' says Kelvin.

His warm hand grasps mine as he pulls me to my feet.

'I'm not impressed. Who spews on their first mission? Little newbie got a little dizzy.' Sinsi says it in a voice normally reserved for babies.

But I ignore her. Her little jibes are nothing in the grand scheme of things and while she's annoying, I can deal with her later. I don't need her for what I want to do.

'Go easy on him Sinsi, you've been at him since he arrived,' says Kelvin.

'We all know why you're sticking up for him, Kelvin, don't we?'

'Shut your mouth, Sinsi,' says Kelvin, his fists balling and turning red.

'Hey, stop arguing. I don't need anyone to stick up for me, Kelvin. Sinsi, you are being horrible, but trust me, I've had worse, and nobody is going to try it on with me, I assure you. So, you can stop all this right now. We have a mission to deal with.'

As I finish, I turn around and see Bolt has arrived with Amp.

'Nice speech, Pat. And he's right. WE DON'T FIGHT WITH EACH OTHER. It's all about the mission. Keep your squabbling for when we get back home.' Amp turns to Orochi. 'Okay, show us the place.'

'Just over here.' Orochi starts walking down a cobbled street, designed for walking only and no horse drawn carriages. The houses here are like I remember them, tall on either side, the air full of smoke from the factories.

'Here it is.' Orochi points to a large house at the end of the street. 'They are on the top floor, so it will be hard for them to escape. I'd suggest you keep a couple on the street in case they leap from the window. The only other way in is up the stairs, so the main attack should come from there.'

'Okay, you heard her. Pat, you're on the street with me. You four, take the stairs. Kelvin, you're in charge inside.'

'Yes, Ma'am,' he replies.

The four Enneads move inside the front door. Orochi remains with us.

'I should go,' she says. 'I'm no use to you if they see me.'

'Yes, of course,' replies Amp. 'Thank you again. The cave will be open to us when we return?'

'It will be as you left it.'

'Thanks, Orochi.'

'Anytime, Mira.'

I guess the unfamiliar name is Amp's real name. So, they must know each other pretty well. Orochi's face has reddened, embarrassed by her mistake. I really want to catch her out, but I just don't know if it will help.

Orochi disappears down a side alley.

'I didn't expect that we'd be getting help from people,' I say, trying to keep it casual.

'Well, we can't keep an eye on the whole of the land, so we have informers located across the country and when they spot anything suspicious, they send us a message.'

'I suppose so. Orochi sounds like she's been doing this a while?'

Amp stares at me for a moment. 'Yes, she has. Why the interest?'

'Oh, I just wondered because she was on first name terms with you?'

'Yeah, Orochi and I go way back. But it's not the time to discuss my friendships right now. Would you agree?'

'Yes, Ma'am.'

We turn our attention to the building in front of us. There is no movement at the windows upstairs, but I now realise, looking at myself and the others, that we hardly look like we fit in here. In fact, considering it's after sunrise this place should be much busier. On the morning I spent here before, it was packed.

Then everything happens at once. Every window upstairs shows fire. A body crashes through the window and falls three floors towards the stone cobbled street. But just before it hits the ground, Loco appears at the broken window and slows the fall allowing the person to rest gently onto the ground. More fire rages through the window. A great hole appears in the side of the building and rubble falls to the ground.

Amp moves before I do to see who it is and to get them away from the falling debris.

The body sits up and sees Amp approaching.

Kin, my old Order buddy, summons small turfs of dirt, then fires them at Amp, but Loco simply changes their course so they miss. Then Amp is on him. She pins the twin and manages to cuff him, despite his struggle. I notice the cuffs are metal, probably Leck's design, in which case Kin won't be escaping.

I try to avoid the eye line of the twin, knowing he'll give me away in a second. Amp drags him away from the building.

'I'll stay here in case anyone comes out.'

Amp nods and moves the captured Mutare up the street.

The blur of Bolt moves past the window. A second later, he emerges from the front door, carrying the other twin, Kei.

'Take care of him, Pat. I'm going back for more.'

And then he's gone. Kei is cuffed already, but he looks up when he hears my name. His eyes narrow and he charges for me, unable to use his hands to attack me with his fire.

Sinsi emerges from the building, aiming her bow at Kei's head. In that same moment, Davin appears next to Sinsi, with a long knife drawn, and slashes at her neck. I shoot a small, sharp shard which goes through Davin's hand. She drops her knife, curses at me, then disappears.

Sinsi's face is paler, her body very limp. She's lowered her bow and steps backward away from the knife that Davin almost killed her with.

Kei, temporarily distracted by Davin and Sinsi, lunges for me again.

I ice the cobbles beneath his feet, and he hits the deck hard. Blood pours from the back of his head. I rush over to check he's okay, but he's unconscious.

I turn him onto his side and use my iced hands to freeze the wound and stem the bleeding, but it's swelling fast.

'You little, traitorous scutter, I'll kill you.' I recognise Davin's voice in an instant and know instinctively to grow an ice shield around me.

She thumps it with all her might, but her powers are not in brute strength, and she can't harm me in here. Instead, she grabs Kei and disappears.

I re-emerge from the ice casing and look up. The fight is over. Loco lowers everyone from the burning building. Herself, Kelvin and Bolt.

'Bolt, to me,' commands Amp. 'Take him.'

The fast boy responds and within a second, he's gone with Kin in tow.

'To me, everyone.'

We move quickly towards Amp.

'Is that them all?' she asks.

'There was four of them,' says Kelvin. 'A set of twins, a tall lady and well…Sinsi?'

'My brother was with them. Alive,' she says. She's going to pass out.

'Your brother?' asks Amp. 'How?'

Sinsi shrugs and sits down. She stares at me, suddenly fixing her eyes on mine. Is she grateful that I saved her life, or does the look mean nothing?

But something else is now gnawing at me: her brother was in the Order.

'Okay, no time to worry. They had a teleporter, she attacked Pat and got away with the other twin.'

'What?' shouts Bolt, just returning. 'You let him get away, Pat?'

'He couldn't help it. He was attacked from behind. One will have to do.'

'We'll be punished,' says Bolt.

'Then we'll take the punishment. As a team,' says Amp, emphasising the last few words.

Bolt looks even angrier when he's told to ferry us all back to the cave in the hills. It's uphill this time.

We return in the order we arrived. That means a moment alone with Amp.

'Pat, we'll talk when we return to palace. Do not do anything silly, or you will be sorry. Do you understand me?'

I nod.

She heard.

She knows that I know the Order.

I'm done for.

I should run, but I don't. I will stay and prove my loyalty. Yes, I was with the Order and following their plan. But now I need to make my own plan to survive. And if I have to abandon the Order, and my parents, then I guess I have to do it. And hope Cerebrum will be able to convince the other Order members not to hurt Mum and Dad.

But if Orochi is still with them, then who knows what will happen next.

I avoid sickness on the return trip with Bolt. My mind is too preoccupied with what the hell I'm going to do next.

We arrive back inside the cave, about to board the aircraft, when Orochi appears again, this time holding someone by the collar, also in cuffs.

'Wait, Amp. I have a present for you. Fell right into my lap after I left you. Thought the Queen might like to question her. She is a known ally of the Order.'

'BRING HER.' The voice almost deafens us in this echoing cave.

Orochi approaches.

And she pushes forward the prisoner.

I gasp, almost giving the game away.

'What is your name?' asks Amp.

'No-One.'

CHAPTER 30

'Don't get wise with me, girl!' Amp slaps her across the face.

The echo silences us all.

'Slap me all you want. I have no name.'

And she does. Hard. So hard, that Elera flies across the floor.

I fight to silence the shards which are itching to birth from my hands. To puncture Amp twice. One in the heart, the other in the neck.

'Pick her up and put her with the Mutare prisoner. We can question them both back at the Palace.'

Loco lifts Elera into the back of the aircraft along with Kin. Kelvin and Sinsi guard them. My arms shake.

'Pat, a word. The rest of you get on board and prepare to leave.'

The other Enneads eye the situation suspiciously but do as they are commanded. Amp pulls me away from the aircraft along with Orochi.

'Is something happening here that I should know about Orochi?' she asks the informer directly.

'I gave you four Mutare. It's not my issue you only captured one, so don't take it out on me,' she replies, coolly.

'What's with the girl? She does seem like no-one.'

'She is closely allied with the Mutare you met today. If the one you captured does not speak, she will be able to give you valuable information.'

'Okay. Okay. We'll see what she knows, but if you're playing any games, Orochi, our alliance will end. Understand?'

'Completely.'

'One final thing...we left you in Ghondulon. How did you arrive up here so quickly with the prisoner?'

Orochi's fingers twitch. She takes one step back. Then disappears.

Amp turns to me, unsurprised. She must have known Orochi was Mutare.

'Pat, why did two of those Mutare recognise you back there?'

'Did they? I think they just attacked me because I was trying to capture them.'

'No, the other twin recognised you and attacked. Then the teleporter called you a scutter and attacked you also. They must have seen you before.'

'No, I have never seen either of them in my life.'

'Why would she call you a scutter? Is there something you need to tell me?'

I shake my head. 'No.'

She stares at me for several seconds, arms crossed.

Finally, she uncrosses them and turns away. 'If I find you've lied, you're expelled. Got it?'

'Got it.'

The journey home is a quiet one.

Sinsi paces back and forth, clearly disturbed by the sight of the brother she thought was dead.

Kelvin and Loco are guarding the prisoners in back. Neither prisoner is speaking, nor are their guards. It makes for a solemn atmosphere that even Leck cannot lighten.

Amp sits alongside the pilot in the front, so I'm now relegated to a seat beside Bolt. He is still annoyed with me for letting the prisoners go. His persistent scowls and tuts have yet to be replaced by his normal chirpy disposition.

'I gave you the kid on a plate, Pat. You just had to keep him for a few seconds until we arrived back down.'

'I'm sorry, Bolt, but there was a teleporter in case you hadn't noticed.'

'I did notice, she took Sinsi's brother and disappeared right at the start. You should have stayed on the aircraft.'

'I wish I had.'

He stops snipping at me, but he isn't happy for the rest of the journey and when we arrive back to base, he tromps off the aircraft and disappears.

Kelvin and Loco take the prisoners to another secret room located off the main training room, Amp following them in. The door shuts firmly behind them.

'Well, I better get this beauty refuelled. You go and get some rest, Pat. You had a big day. First mission and all.' He smiles, the only one still doing so.

I walk back to the boys' room, looking to do exactly what Leck suggests, but I have company.

Sinsi.

'I can't believe he's alive. Why didn't he contact me?' she asks me.

'I don't know.'

'And why is he with those Order troublemakers? We spent years together trying to stop them with their terrorist acts and he turns around and signs up with them.'

'I genuinely don't know Sinsi, but surely it's better he's alive and with them than dead?'

I remember the boy who comforted me. Who never spoke a word as I blurted out all my troubles. The boy who could sense anything.

I hope Sinsi isn't as perceptive or my whole act will be done.

But she doesn't seem to be bothering with me at the moment.

'It just doesn't make sense. I don't understand.'

'Maybe he just wanted a different life?'

She looks at me in a funny way, midway between a smile and confusion. Perhaps she's not as evil as I first thought. Or perhaps she is trying to trick me.

'You can't just have a different life, Pat. When you become an Ennead, you sign up until the Queen relieves you. You don't quit or else you face consequences.'

She turns to me and her face brightens.

'That's what he's done. He didn't want to face the punishment or for me to be harmed, so he faked his death. That's it. That's what he did. Oh, Sense. You were always too nice, always thinking of others first.'

'Your brother is Sense?'

'Yes. Why? You've never met him...have you?'

And suddenly her full perceptive force tugs at me.

'Oh, I just heard little comments from the others.'

'Really? Who was talking about him?'

Damn, she's going to find out.

'I can't remember, it was last night, when we were drinking wine, and I forget who said it.'

'Hmmm...you're lying.' She steps closer to me, studying my entire body. 'In fact, you've been lying about almost everything, haven't you?'

I freeze. It's not my ability, it's something else. My mind can't think up a lie.

'Yes, I have lied.' When I say the words, my body immediately thaws. The admission is freeing. I even smile.

'And why is that amusing?' Sinsi asks. 'You had better start telling me some truths, or I might let slip some of my suspicions about you.'

I need to make a call right now – either trust Sinsi and take a risk, or risk her raising suspicion about me.

'It's not amusing. I had a brother once. Two, in fact.' I don't know why I'm telling her, but maybe, just maybe if we could bond over something...even lost brothers...she could become an ally. And I definitely need allies right now. I've no idea who to trust. And I need someone to trust me if I'm to pull this whole thing off.

'You say 'had'. What happened to them?'

'Gullan was the eldest. We were out on the frozen river one day, messing around – well, I was messing around - melting and thawing the ice as he jumped from one block of drift ice to another, when the ice broke beneath him. He was gone before I could get to him. He was drawn downstream with the strong current. We never found his body. He must have been washed out to the sea. It was my fault. I couldn't control my powers back then.'

'And I lost my other brother. Younger than me. Recently...too recently to talk about.'

She places her hand on my shoulder. 'I'm sorry, Pat. But you can't blame yourself for Gullan. That sounds like an accident to me.'

'You're kind, but it's on me. I know it, deep down. If only I knew then what I know now. But thank you.' I place my hand on top of hers.

We sit for a moment in silence.

'I'm sorry, Corena, but I really need to know about Sense. Earlier, you said you knew my brother. How?'

I glance around, ensuring we're alone. I need to take a chance with someone and maybe if I explain it, she'll understand. Maybe even help me if I can use her closeness to her brother. 'Can you keep a secret?'

'Depends on what it is.'

'It's the biggest kind. One that, if you keep it, could change the world we live in. Change it to a world where you and your brother never have to hide again. You could be together without any need for faking deaths or secret Mutare groups fighting each other.'

'Now, that's a big secret. Tell me more.'

'Where do I start?' I ask, more to myself than Sinsi.

'With Sense?'

Good, I'd much rather talk about him than myself.

'Fine. He is a member of the Order of Mutare. I met him at their camp near Ghondulon. He was extremely nice to me, when I was very confused and upset.'

'He's always nice. Why were you confused? Worried about becoming a traitor?'

'Hey, back off. Do you want to hear about it or not?'

She shakes her head and her face lightens, the frown disappearing. 'Go on.'

'Well, he was the only one in the Order who actually wanted to know anything about me. The rest of them just wanted to use me as a weapon. Something to gain an advantage and do something they couldn't do themselves. He brought me lunch, when I was training. Nobody else thought to do that.'

Sinsi sits, but I remain standing. Somehow it seems to make it easier to talk on my feet.

'So, tell me why you are here? What is this plan that you're a part of? And tell me how you propose to be their *weapon*?' She looks me up and down.

'Sinsi, I know you don't like me...'

'I do.'

'What?'

'I do like you. I just never trusted you. Until now.'

'Seriously? I'd hate to see how you act with people you don't like.'

'Well, we all have our ways of surviving and mine is never to get too close to anyone. Because usually when I get close to people, they get hurt or disappear.'

'I know the feeling.'

We fall silent, occasionally glancing at each other.

Eventually I sit on the bed beside her.

'I think we have more in common than we both would like,' I say, expecting a witty or nasty backlash.

'Maybe.' She moves closer to me and stares at me in silence.

'Did you like him?'

'Yeah, of course. I said that. Everyone does.'

'No, I mean *like* him.'

'A bit, I guess. For a boy.'

I shift uncomfortably as those last few words come out. My eyes drift to Sinsi's and they meet mine.

'For a boy, huh? You're definitely different, Pat. I can see why my brother would be drawn to you. We are both exceptionally sentient and your emotions are not like anyone else's. Whether it's attraction or just intrigue, who knows.'

'What is it for you?'

She continues to hold the connection between our eyes.

For over a minute, she is silent.

I don't know why I asked her that or what I want her to say.

'I haven't decided yet.' She springs up off the bed and walks out, leaving me alone.

I just told someone the truth...well, some of the truth. I haven't done that in a while. That was weird. That was nice.

A minute later, Amp walks in, slowly closing the door behind her. Then it clicks. Did she just lock it?

I stand, sensing something different about her. She might have been listening to Sinsi and I. She might have heard it all.

Never have I had to be more careful about what I say.

'What did the prisoners say?' I ask.

'Interesting story,' she replies simply, taking slow, measured steps towards me. 'What do you think they told me?'

I swallow, knowing I've been found out. But, like with Sinsi, there must be an angle I can appeal to with her. One she'll understand.

'Did they tell you why they were in Ghondulon?'

'Perhaps. What else?'

A fragment of the truth...just a fragment...to buy time.

'Perhaps they said they had met me before?'

'Warmer.'

'Did they say something about me that would question my loyalty to the Ennead?'

'Warmer.'

'Did they say I was a traitor?'

'Why would they call you a traitor?'

'Because they tried to recruit me, and I refused. When I said I was leaving, one of them pursued me to Rejik, trying to get me captured and executed, so I was forced to kill her. Something like that?'

Amp studies me for a long time.

'Something like that. Don't go anywhere.' She leaves the room, locking it after her.

I could get out of here in a second, but then I'd look guilty... like a spy. I want to stay here and see this out. Running won't help me. Nor will it gain Pat's revenge.

Hopefully they buy that I genuinely killed an Order member. The only two who know different are Cerebrum and Orochi. Orochi, somehow still alive, who also appears to be working with the Ennead. To what end, I have no idea. And why has she brought Elera here. The assassin who abandoned my brother to save herself. She doesn't have the most blood her hands, I'm saving that for myself and the Queen, but she's up there. All I want to do is ask her what happened, what the hell she's here, what messed up game are we part of. But, of course, I can't.

I'm like a pawn in some kind of bigger game. But I won't become dispensable. I'm going to play this smart. Get through the next few days without getting found out by keeping a low profile. Stay out of people's way.

CHAPTER 31

Training is getting tougher.

Amp has really been pushing me. I think she wants to hit me so hard, that I'll eventually crack. That something will slip out. It won't. At least not to her.

Kelvin unleashes a tornado of flames, rising above him, spreading so wide that it heats the entire room.

But I know what he's doing. Heating the very air, trying to melt any weapons or defence.

So I play his game.

I place my palm on the wall, concentrating on making the ice climb and spread. It stretches across quicker than I'd hoped. This suit really intensifies my power. Soon, most of the wall and roof are covered. I layer it.

But Kelvin hasn't been idle. He detaches small tornados of fire form the main body, each quickly melting small sections of my ice-paint.

Every time he does, I re-ice, but then he hits another part.

We're just cancelling each other out.

I need to stop his focus. Distract him with something.

I readjust my focus to the roof and start to grow stalactite after stalactite. Ten. Fifty. A hundred. Then I make them fall.

As they hurtle down, Kelvin has to sprint away, dodging each as it crashes to the floor. And his tornado is lost, his concentration on evasion.

I ice the floor at his feet and he's on his back. As she slides towards me, I cocoon him in ice. It won't hold him long. Seconds. But it's enough.

I've won. I've beaten the Pyro.

The other Enneads clap. Amp joins in last, slow and hard. She continues on long after the others stop, and Kelvin has melted from his temporary prison.

'Very good, Pat.' Amp brings us all together at the side of the room, next to Leck's workshop. 'Impressive. Most impressive. Almost like you've been taught already. Like someone trained you?' She raises her eyebrows towards me.

'Just natural talent, I guess.' I smile at her.

'Aye, some folks got it, others don't,' jokes Bolt. He slaps Kelvin on the back, whose face has turned redder than his flames.

'Maybe.' Amp lifts her chin. 'Enough for today. Get changed and showered.' She strides out of the hall, towards the stairs to the upper Palace.

Bolt gives me a thumbs-up before following Kelvin to the changing rooms. He continues to jibe the Pyro.

Loco drifts off, silent as always.

I'm left with Sinsi. She stands with her hands on her hips, right hip out to the side. She tilts her head. 'Nice work. About time someone put him in his place. He always lords it about here.'

'I'm just training hard, doing my best...'

She steps forward. Places a finger on my lips. 'You don't have to spin me that crap. I know why you're here. But don't worry. I'm on your side. I want to see my brother again.' She walks away to the changing room. Then turns. 'Besides, there's something about you, Pat.'

~

I spend a little more time training, then hit the showers once I see Bolt and Kelvin re-emerge from the boys' changing rooms.

I've done this the last few days and I don't think anyone has noticed my tactic to avoid showering with them. Despite how well I'm doing in training, I'm pretty certain they'd quickly expel me from the Ennead if they knew what I was.

I head to the back of the changing rooms and through the door to the showers. I undress, keeping my underwear on. Just in case.

As I clean, my fingers touch the last of the scars on my back, almost gone. Ribs are also completely healed. Maybe I have some kind of healing power, too. Seems unlikely that I have more than one, but some mutare do, so why not me.

My hand moves over my small, aching breasts. Keeping them tightly pressed against my chest all day hurts but is necessary. Fortunately, I'm not big in that area, so it's not as bad as it could be.

I have to clean beneath my underwear, so I slide them off. I scrub down there, my boy and girl bits both. I was twelve the first time I saw the boy bit...well, I guess it's a penis, but it's far too small to be a proper one. I always thought I was a girl until then. Only boys have a penis and I'm not a boy. Or a girl. Now I'm something in between. I stare down, wondering what Sinsi would think if she saw me like this.

Would she still think there was *something about me*?

'Hey.' Sinsi's voice.

I snatch up my towel and cover myself, just as the door opens.

'Oh, nice...' She looks me up and down.

I'd enjoy it, if only I weren't terrified of her seeing what was underneath the towel.

'What's up?' I pull the towel tighter and step towards my clothes.

'Nothing. Just thought you might want to hang out later. Y'know, chat about stuff and have some fun.'

The word 'fun' causes me to stiffen. 'I'm not so sure, Sinsi. Are we allowed?'

'Well, I won't tell Amp, if you won't?' She does the hip-to-the-side thing.

'When?' I'm eager to get her out of here.

'After dinner. There's a praying area, just next to the kitchens. No-one ever goes in there. I'll leave the table first and you can follow me.'

'Deal.'

She smiles and darts away.

Once the shower door is closed, I quickly dress. If we're going to be alone together, I need to be extra careful. So, I put on the top half of my fighting suit, it's tight fit keeping my chest flat. Then I put another top on to cover it. I wear a belt with my trousers and pull it tight.

Then I return to the bedroom.

Bolt is lounging on his bed, reading something. 'Hey Pat, you love a shower, huh? Always in there ages. I don't blame you though, this is the only place I ever heard of with hot water showers. Wonder how Leck does it.'

'Not sure.' I hang my towel and get ready to go through for dinner.

'You're from up north, right?'

I nod.

'You got a sister, Pat? Just I saw a girl, looked just like you. Up in the Kurikon reformation center.'

'Nope.'

'Ah well. Wondered if that's how I knew your face. You know, they had that poor girl and they lashed her 'til her powers showed. And boy did they show. Ice shards everywhere. Little like yours, now that I think of it.'

My throat tightens. I can't speak for fear of giving myself away. The memory is the lashes is still fresh, even if the wounds are not.

'Must be a northern thing. With the ice, I mean. Not seen many that can do what you do.'

'Yes, there's a few up north, I knew a few...but they died.'

Bolt sits up. 'Unfortunately, they all do. But that's why we joined up, isn't it? Or we'd be dead along with them.' He walks to the door.

'Hey, Bolt. What happens to the one's we catch?' I think about Kin.

'They get a trial. Sometimes they're hanged but other times the Queen cures them and gives them mercy at the trial. The rumour is that she purges them of their power herself, returns it to the Gods.'

'How?'

'No idea. I'm not sure she does anything other than question them. Could you imagine if she was able to do that?' He leaves to go for dinner.

~

Dinner is a quiet one.

I look at the empty seats as I enter.

'Kelvin's ill apparently,' says Sinsi. 'Sitting in with Leck right now.'

'Reckon he's just embarrassed as Pat kicked his ass in training. Huh, Pat?' He elbows me and I smile.

A huge pot of kushari lies in the centre of the table. I ladle the rice and vegetables onto my plate and waste no time tearing into it. The intensity of training means we really have to fuel up at the moment.

Sinsi touches my leg with her toes, beneath the table.

I pause eating, glancing at Bolt and Loco. Neither notice.

I continue to eat, but the toes return moving up my leg. I spring up, banging my knees off the underside of the table.

'You okay, Pat?' Bolt looks confused.

'Fine, just thought a spider had crawled over my foot.'

He frowns at me.

'But it didn't.' I notice Sinsi sniggering behind her hand.

We all go back to our food. I'm not sure I've ever eaten as well as I do here. The thought of training all day, then eating here at night. Maybe flirting with Sinsi, or maybe more. All of this makes a small part of me want to stay. To keep things as they are. But if I do, then I will be serving the very person I vowed to kill. The Queen who ordered the execution of my brother.

Sinsi doesn't touch me with her toes again, but she does give me a flurry of furtive glances. I wish I didn't like the attention. I wish I could just freeze her out and not have any feelings.

'That was good.' Sinsi stands and leaves the table. She winks at me as she leaves the room.

I wait, continuing to pick at the food. Sipping wine. Just waiting long enough...

'Hey Pat, fancy playing some cards with me and Loco tonight. We often get a good game going with Leck after dinner. Sometimes Flavio when he finishes in the kitchen.'

'I'm okay.'

'Don't worry, we'll explain the rules and go easy on you if it's your first time.'

'No, honestly, I might just go lie down after this. Pretty tired.'

'Of course. You're still getting used to it. But you're doing great, Pat. Isn't he, Loco?'

She nods, a trace of smile creeping in.

'Enjoy your game.' I get up and take my plate to the sink.

'We'll walk along with you.' Bolt and Loco follow me out the dinner room.

Typical. Sinsi will just have to wait...unless...

'I need to pray for a bit.' I about-turn and head towards the prayer room.

'Really? You're religious?' asks Bolt. 'And didn't you say you were tired?'

Man, this is getting way too complicated. 'I pray to Suijin,

Goddess of Water and Ice, from time-to-time. After helping me as much as she did today, I better show my respects.'

'Fair enough, more of a Kami-no-Kaze follower myself, but we all have our different strengths. See you later.'

Bolt and Loco disappear back into the training arena, closing the large doors behind them. Meanwhile, I turn and enter the small door next to the dining room we've just exited.

It's dark, lit by only one candle. It sits upon a sunken basin in the center of the circular room. The Ten peer down on me, like in the training arena, but on a much smaller scale. I scan the room for Sinsi, but see nothing.

A giggle comes from across the room. Then a small gust of wind. And the candle goes out.

'Hello?' My voice is a little shaky, hoping this is just Sinsi messing around but worried someone else might be in here.

Someone taps me on the shoulder. I spin, but my hands grip nothing.

'Come on, Sinsi. Stop messing around.'

She laughs again, then she clasps my hand and pulls me to a cold, stone bench. We sit in the darkness. I imagine her face, looking back at me.

Then she kisses me.

But before it's really begun comes the dreaded, awkward nose-bump.

We both laugh.

Second time, our teeth clash. Kissing in the dark is hard.

'Should we light the candle?' I suggest.

'No, I like this. Just go slow.'

And we do. We kiss over and over. It reminds me of Asta and Elera. The same urge starts to stir down below. The boy bit in me gets excited.

I stop.

'Well, that was unexpected.'

'Really?' Sinsi places her palm on my cheek. 'After all that flirting these last few days, you really didn't see that coming?'

I laugh and we kiss again. Her hands move over my body, and I let her. I pray that the tight body suit beneath my top will keep my secret for a little longer.

But when her hand moves down to my stomach, I tense all over. And she notices.

'It's okay, we can go slow,' she says. 'Do you want to talk for a bit?'

'Yes.'

And we do.

The days pass and become weeks.

Each day is the same; train, eat, sleep, sneak out to the praying room with Sinsi. We spend hours and hours in there, talking and kissing. Kissing and talking.

But never more.

And we talk about everything. Very soon, she knows everything about me. From where I grew up and the cruel treatment of my village and parents, to my journey south and the horrific experiences I've suffered.

Sinsi hasn't had it easy either. None of the mutare have. Nor ever will. Unless things change.

We know almost everything about each other. But I still can't tell her my biggest secret. Not yet.

As usual, I slide into the praying room, unnoticed.

'Hey.' Sinsi's whisper helps me navigate to the stone bench in the dark.

We start by kissing. Get those in first. Don't want to ruin the best part by talking first. Imagine if we argued and never got around to it.

'We should do something soon.' Sinsi isn't asking.

'Do what exactly?'

'*Something*...we can't stay here forever. Not if we want to be together. And now I know that Sense is alive and elsewhere with the Order, I really don't want to be here anymore.' Her hand rests on my stomach.

'Just a while longer.' I can't leave yet, I've got a Queen to kill. Funny how that desire is just not as strong as it was.

'Okay, but not too long. I really hate hunting our own kind. And I *hate* having to sneak around with you all the time.'

'What would the Queen do if we were caught? The Kurikon would forbid this, wouldn't they? We'd be sinners.'

'We are Mutare. We are already sinners in their eyes. And the Queen? I don't know. I think she needs us. Otherwise, she'd have hanged us long ago.' She tilts her head.

'If you had choice, who would you want to destroy first; the Queen or the Kurikon?'

Sinsi smiles. 'They're the same thing, really. The Kurikon are much older of course, but the Queen controls them, to an extent. Possibly the Kurikon are more dangerous though. Most people in this world are under their sway. Destroying the Kurikon would be an impossible task, and even trying to would perpetuate the stigma that us Mutare already have.'

'What if we changed people's minds about us? What if we showed people that we are good? Or that the Queen or the Kurikon are bad? That way we don't have to destroy them physically.'

'How do you suppose we can change the accepted religion and culture of a whole kingdom? Impossible. Nobody has that power. Even the Queen would struggle to completely change the Kurikon's outlook.'

'But if she gave the command, maybe they would stop killing Mutare or seeing us as unnatural.'

'Maybe?' Sinsi shrugs.

The door swings open. A flaming hand lights up the room and Kelvin strides in. Followed by Bolt and Loco.

'I *knew* it.' Bolt punches the air. 'You owe me 3 coins, Loco.' He laughs.

'Amp isn't going to be happy about this...nor the Queen.' Kelvin also seems delighted. But in a different way. It's a sneer more than a smile.

'You won't say.' I know he will.

'You know what...I haven't decided.' He dims the flame in his hand.

'Who cares, Kelvin.' Bolt elbows him. 'They can be together if they want. You jealous or something?'

'I am not jealous, I assure you.' Kelvin stomps off down the corridor, footsteps echoing.

The room becomes dark again and Sinsi lights the one candle in the central basin.

'Don't worry about him,' says Bolt.

'He doesn't like either of us. Of course, he's going to say something.' Sinsi is right.

'Leave him to me. I'll speak to him.' And Bolt's gone.

Loco hovers at the door.

'You okay?' asks Sinsi.

She nods. 'I won't say.'

'We know. You've always been the nicest one.' Sinsi moves to her and gives her a small hug.

Loco follows the boys. Once the training arena doors close, I move close to Sinsi. I don't want anyone else to hear.

'We had better get our escape plans in place.'

Sinsi smiles and then kisses me.

I'm a boy, or pretending to be, and Sinsi is a girl. Even Klerik Anticus couldn't complain about that.

But something deeper inside me is gnawing, fighting its way to the surface. It's the guilt of not trying harder for vengeance. At fitting into this new life too well. *I haven't forgotten, Pat. I will avenge you. It's just so hard.*

As I'm about to leave, Sinsi laughs.

'What's funny?'

'I just remembered. Tomorrow is the Queen's Crystal Ball. How's your dancing?'

CHAPTER 32

'What about this?' Sinsi asks.

I shake my head.

She's shown me about ten outfits already. Not getting the message.

I wander over to the cupboard open with dresses. Sinsi took something from in their earlier.

I run my fingers across the clothes in the girl's cupboard and an instant surge of excitement runs from my fingertips to my spine.

'What are you doing in there?' Sinsi stands directly behind me.

'I like these much better.'

'Pat, have you never been to a ball before?'

'You know I haven't.'

'Girls wear dresses or gowns. Boys wear suits.'

'Well maybe I want to wear something from in here instead.'

'Pat?' She places her hand on my shoulder. It's a gentle caress, but when I ignore it, she spins me round. Her eyes are wider. 'You have to act as normal as possible. Blend in. There are already suspicions about you after what happened this morning. You don't need to draw more attention to yourself.'

I want to tell her. I want to be honest. I want her to know everything.

But what if I do, and she rejects me. Or tells other people.

I want to go to the dress cupboard and put on something bright and big, something pretty.

But I stay where I am, slowly turning back to the boy's cupboard.

A velvet waistcoat catches my eyes. It's a little like Terra's grand clothing.

I pick it up, stroking the textured material. We had furs and we had wool. Dad gave me my first furs when I was five. That was when he first showed me how to use an axe.

'I'm wearing this.' I hold up the waistcoat. 'And these.' I grab a pair of brown, leather trousers and hold both items against my body to allow Sinsi to inspect them.

She moves near to me, closing her hands around mine, which still grasp the waistcoat and trousers. She says nothing, gazing into my eyes, her usual fire gone, replaced by something else.

'You certainly are different, Pat Storm. I've never met anyone like you.'

And she kisses me.

Intense.

Not like Asta or Elera.

Her lips move quickly, but softly across mine. Warmth permeates from her mouth to mine. When our skin touches, a surge passes from me to her. She is extra-sentient, but I hope she can't feel how much I like her.

When we part, she takes a step away from me, smiling, glowing.

'Wear what you want, Pat. I'll be right beside you tonight, proud to be with you, no matter how you're dressed.' She smiles again, picks up her dress and leaves the room.

A tall mirror sits behind me. I've never had one. I've seen

myself reflected in water, ice and glass, but I've never seen myself as others do. And I don't need to. I now know who I am. I know what's inside of me and nothing I see in the mirror will change that.

I throw off my ice-suit and put on a smooth, clean white shirt with the velvet waistcoat on top. The brown, leather trousers match with the shade of the waistcoat. The finished result doesn't look bad at all.

A sharp rupture in my heart makes me sit. I grab my chest, still staring at the mirror.

Gullan. I look just like he did…before he died.

I will never forget his face as life left it.

I've often wondered what would have happened to Gullan had he survived. Would he have married? Become apprentice to Dad? It's what they both wanted but after the accident, my dad had to settle for me. He treated me like a son, tried to have me take Gullan's place, but when I couldn't, when my looks made society more likely to accept me as a daughter, it just made him resent me even more.

If he was here, perhaps he'd have powers too, like Pat and me. He would have stopped Pat following me. Or come along and protected him, like I could not.

'Ready?'

Sinsi's reflection watches me in the mirror. She stands by the door, dressed in a green gown. It's shoulderless and tight-fitting on top, flowing wider as it falls to the floor. I take long breath out before turning. My right hand shakes.

'You look great,' I say, as I turn.

'You, too. Come on. We don't want to be late.' She opens the door for me, and I move into the corridor, enjoying the rub of the leather on my legs.

'Looking good, Frosty!' Bolt leans against a wall in the corridor. His hands pull a long, purple robe tighter round his body.

I punch him on the shoulder. 'I told you not to call me that, Quickie!'

He laughs and walks away at normal speed.

Kelvin, in a deep red robe, nods and follows him. Loco smiles at me as she passes and finally Amp moves alongside Sinsi and I.

'You go ahead, Sinsi.'

She doesn't argue with the boss, giving me a smile and catching up with Loco.

'Why have you put *that* on? This is a ball.' Amp looks me up and down.

I return the look. 'I like it.'

'The Queen would not approve. Be sure to stay in the shadows tonight. I already have my eye on you.' She strides along the corridor towards the stairs at the end.

I bite down on my lip and stare at the ceiling for a moment. Now is not the time to fight back.

At the top of the stairs, Sinsi waits for me. The others have gone ahead.

'What did she want?'

'Just said she has her eye on me. And made a comment about how I'm dressed.'

'Told you.' She taps her temple. 'Just stick close to me.' She brushes her hand against mine as we walk along the new corridor.

Only one floor up, but it's obvious we're in the main part of the palace now. The blue carpets are clean and soft. The walls covered in decorated patterns of flowers intertwining clouds.

'It's nice up here,' I say.

'Nice? It's Haven compared to our dungeon down there. But I guess that's our place in this world. We're exactly where they want us.' Her fists tighten as she speaks.

'It will change.' My eyes narrow as the picture of Pat swinging returns.

'How? What can we do about it? There are so few of us, Pat. If we ever try to rise, they will stamp upon us. We are freaks to the rest of the world and nothing will change that.'

'But we must try.' I grab her arm and turn her to me. 'We must try.'

She nods and starts walking again.

This corridor leads to a much wider and grander one, furnished at intervals with silver and gold ornaments and suits of armour. Each corner has a silent Enforcer stationed.

'Lots of security tonight for the Queen,' I say, as we pass the tenth Enforcer.

'It's not for the Queen. She has us. It's for all her guests. Tonight, we're surrounded by the richest and most important people in the land. I even heard there's a prince here.'

I stop. 'A prince?'

'Yes, that's what I heard.' She narrows her eyes. 'I don't have anything to worry about, do I? You won't go running off with some foreign prince?' She laughs.

I force a laugh, too and squeeze her hand as I begin walking again.

'Careful with the hands,' she says. 'The top Kleriks will be here tonight, and I know the Kurikon would not approve of us. Whatever we have.' She tries to find my eyes when she says the last part.

I avoid them.

I'm too confused to label this. And I hate labels.

Ahead of us, two massive crystal doors lie open. The entrance to the massive room is flanked by four Enforcers and a short, pretty lady. She smiles at us as we approach.

'Good evening. Please take a drink.'

She holds a tray towards us. I take a small glass of red wine. I enjoyed it last night.

Sinsi and I enter the huge room, equivalent in size to our training room, but with a grandeur unimaginable. Crystal decorated lamps hang from the ceiling, the walls are painted with intricate and detailed depictions of banquets, feats and balls, just like this one.

Hundreds of people stand in small circles around the room, sipping their drinks, finely dressed. As Sinsi said, all the females are in radiant gowns or dresses. I look down at my own clothes and I do feel a little out of place. Even the men seem more majestically dressed.

'Let's move over there.' I nod to a dark corner of the room where the waiters and waitresses stand. Ready to move like shadows between the people and deliver fresh drinks.

Sinsi follows me as I find a spot next to a huge pillar. It rises, like many others at the edge of the room, towards the ceiling.

'I'm glad you're taking my advice about avoiding attention,' Sinsi whispers in my ear.

It tickles.

'I feel out of place.'

'But we are. As I said earlier, we always will be. But for tonight, let's pretend we do belong. Tonight is not the time to stand out.'

We watch the rest of the Ennead move to a table nearby and sit without speaking. Bolt tries to chat and make jokes, but nobody seems interested. They are all on edge, even Amp. I realise then, that while they have been here longer than me, serving the Queen loyally, they do not sit at ease with others.

Maybe it's the enforced isolation beneath the palace or only getting out when there's a mission. Or maybe they've always been like that, even before the Ennead. I know how they feel. They are more like me than I've realised.

I turn to Sinsi. 'We will rise. And I think the Ennead will help us. Look at them. They are as just as oppressed as the people they hunt. They just think their lives are better. I think I can convince them.'

'That would be a mistake. Amp would never give this up. And I don't think the others would either. You and me. We should leave

240

here. Find my brother. But don't involve the others. We can't be sure who to trust.'

'You can trust me.'

I jump at the new voice, so close.

I turn, but I know who I'll see.

I know that voice.

I turn to face Prince Terra.

A bell rings.

CHAPTER 33

We enjoy a six-course dinner, sitting with the rest of the Enneads.

Nobody talks much, except Bolt. He's had many glasses of wine and doesn't look like slowing down. Sinsi squeezes my thigh beneath the table. I don't stop her.

The Queen sits at a large top table, which faces out to all the smaller, circular tables around the room. Amp joined that table, taking her place as one of the Queen's top lieutenants.

I wonder how many people know that Amp is Mutare.

Terra is also at the top table, clearly an honoured guest. I remember the man who gave me food and let me ride his horse, when I was on the verge of collapsing. The kind man from the foreign land, who helped a slave girl. A person nobody else wanted. Even my own parents sent me away. I'll never forget his acceptance of me. His kindness, at a time when nobody else seemed to care.

And I'll never forget his broken promise. He said he'd take care of Pat. Get him back to me safely. And while Pat was captured and taken away to be hanged, Terra fled. He sits alive, while my brother is gone. He needs to take some of that blood from my hands, too.

The dinner bell interrupted us before, but I need to talk to him at some point tonight. And only talking will take every bit of self-restraint I have.

'Did anyone else find today's raid a little strange?' Bolt asks, out of the blue.

'What you mean?' Kelvin sits up.

'They seemed well trained. Almost like they knew we were coming. And that informant. Orochi. Her showing up with that other prisoner. It was all strange.'

'We shouldn't ask questions.' Kelvin goes back to his cheese.

Bolt looks to me. 'Something doesn't add up, that's all I'm saying.' He downs the rest of his wine and pours another glass.

Amp approaches our table.

'Pat, come with me. The Queen wishes to speak with you.'

'Me? Why?'

'Just come.' Amp turns and walks back towards the top table.

Sinsi shrugs her shoulders, while the rest of them glare at me.

I follow Amp, aware that many people are staring at me. It's either my white hair or my clothes, but I focus on where I'm going, wondering what the Queen wants.

When Amp gets to the top table, she continues beyond, to a door at the back of the room. She waits for me and directs me in when I arrive.

Two masked Royal Enforcers stand either side of the door. They look just the right size and build to be Hiro and Sorg, only they can't be here. They're still in the sulphur mines. And I can hardly ask them with Amp lurking and the Queen just inside this door.

I wonder if they would even recognise me now.

'You tell the truth now, Pat.' She opens the door and walks away.

The new room is much smaller, with a large, blazing fire in the far wall. It's the only light in the room. The faces of the Ten peer down upon us, their statues chiselled into the four walls.

The Queen sits on a gold chair, sipping a drink. Her gown

sparkles with crystal. Hundreds of small crystals. Must cost half the kingdom. More money than my family would make in a lifetime.

She waves her hand at a chair next to hers.

Every muscle remains tense as I sit on the puffy, cushioned seat. I wait for the Queen to speak, sweat coating my underclothes and the leather trousers. I'm regretting my wardrobe choices in a big way. I wipe my forehead.

Finally, she turns to me. Her mouth curls as she looks at me properly, taking in my hair, now stuck to my head, and my clothes, now stuck to my body.

'You are such an unusual one, Pat. Amp tells me you have made a promising start.' She smiles, becoming silent for several seconds.

I shift a little in my seat. My bum is becoming wet.

'But she has a few doubts about you, too. So, we should have a chat.'

Could I kill her now? There is plenty of water on my skin. But nothing else in the room to use. It's hot and dry. Almost like the Queen has adjudged the environment to make me at my weakest.

I could form a small shard, thrust it through her heart. End her horrible reign. But would it be enough. I'm not sure.

And even if I could, would it help us. Or would the murder further harm people's perceptions of the Mutare? Make them think even worse of us. They would know it was me and life would become worse for the Mutare, not better.

And I would lose Sinsi.

Now is not the time.

She pulls her chair a little closer and crosses her legs, the crystals catching the light of the fire.

'Do you realise I had been Queen for five years by the time I was your age, Pat?'

I shake my head. Thirteen is so young for such a big responsibility.

'Yes, my parents were killed. Assassinated. By a Mutare.'

She stares at me, waiting for my response.

Sweat continues to build as I squirm in the seat. It's so hot in here, it's like she wants it this way.

'I'm sorry to hear that,' I say, though I'm not actually.

'Yes, I was a scared little girl at the time, huge responsibility suddenly thrust upon me. I had to rule a kingdom, bury and grieve for my parents and fight a war Haras with before my fourteenth birthday. I grew up fast. I made a lot of mistakes in those early years. I trusted the wrong people.'

I remain silent, moving uncomfortably in my chair, trying to bury my feelings of sympathy for her. It's her fault Pat died. I repeat it over and over as she speaks.

'I know you have made mistakes, Pat. Perhaps trusted the wrong people, too. But Amp sees promise in you. And your ability...it's a new one to me. It's one which I will need to help protect our land.'

'Your Highness, why do you kill all the Mutare? Is it because of your parents?' I couldn't hold it in anymore. The heat is unbearable.

'Yes. Partly. But it's also for my people. They feel safer and happier knowing there is no-one out there with unexplainable abilities, who can kill hundreds in an instant. It's a necessity. I take no joy from it.'

She killed Pat.

'I wouldn't expect the Mutare to understand it. But I do it for the greater good. The Kurikon believe it's unnatural. Not me. Although, of course, I play along with their song. They are a useful ally. Faith gives the people something to live for, something to keep them in line.'

She stops speaking, staring at the ceiling.

When I shift again, unable to stay still any longer, she looks back to me.

'Can I rely on you to be loyal to me, Pat? I will need your abilities very soon and want to know I can count on you.'

'You can, your Highness.' Until I slit your throat.

'Good. I will call upon your powers in the coming days. Keep training. Keep getting them stronger.' She takes another drink. 'You may leave.'

I stand, grateful to escape the inferno.

As I reach the door, she speaks again. 'If I find out you're not loyal, I will kill you and all of your family.'

You already killed Pat.

I killed Gullan.

And my parents? Join the queue. It's no longer my family I fear to lose.

As I leave the chamber, I study the two guards. They've both lifted their visors slightly and I know it's them. My former captors, former disgraced Enforcers. Now reinstated to their former, glorious positions. They wanted to kill me at one point to get to where they are now. I wonder what price they've paid, who they've betrayed or killed.

Was it information about me? Or Pat? Or the Order members they met? The thought makes a tiny shard grow on my hand.

But before I can move or speak, Hiro silently pushes a note into my waistcoat pocket, and points her spear, indicating I should leave. The intrigue and surprise of the note has thawed the shard.

I do not return to our table, instead walking straight towards the bathroom. So luxurious, even the boy's toilets have individual stalls. And lucky for me as some important person follows me in. I step inside a stall and lock the door behind me.

Corena, we thought long and hard about the next step for us after we were left in the Sulphur mines. This is it; we have returned to the Queen's Royal Guard. We had to tell her about you to regain our positions. You seem to have settled into a new identity, and we recommend you keep it that way. Working this close to the Queen is dangerous. We are sorry for everything we ever did to you.

Please forgive us.

Hiro and Sorg.

You are forgiven. Both of you. I will never like you, but you're forgiven. I want to tell them so, but when I return to the dining hall, Amp is staring at me, so I can't do anything suspicious.

As I return to my table, I spot Terra. But he is not forgiven. A promise is a promise, and he broke it. The sight of him just reminds me of that broken promise and my dead brother.

I turn my back to him.

But he continues to watch.

Then comes the dancing. I've dreaded this and for the most part, I manage to stay away from the cleared space in the centre of the room, where everyone is pirouetting around. So fancy and pretentious, the way they all smile at each other and move rhythmically and in time with the music.

Prince Terra makes his way through all the important people present, dancing and chatting, drinking and mingling. Thankfully he doesn't approach me. I don't know what I'd do or say.

Finally, both Sinsi and I can sneak away. We get back down to our rooms and kiss goodnight.

'Maybe I can come into your room for a while? The boys will be up there for ages. Any excuse to drink and dance with girls.' Sinsi puts her arm round my waist.

Her touch makes me stir, down there, and I instantly pull away. 'No, I'm so tired. Maybe another time.'

She steps back, hurt scraped over her face, but she nods and heads back to her room.

I watch her leave. My insides are curdling with guilt and I'm about to go after her, when a strong hand covers my mouth, and the other arm holds my middle. I'm lifted from the ground and hauled into the boy's bedroom.

I tense and am ready to fight, when I'm released. I spin round. Prince Terra, looking handsome, with his sword at his belt and a huge smile on his face.

'Corena, please don't shout out or fight back...I am here to talk only.' He takes a step back.

I take a step forward. 'Talk? About Pat? About your broken promise?'

'I'm so sorry, Corena. I...I tried.'

'YOU TRIED? YOU PROMISED ME! You said you'd keep him safe.'

'I did all I could.' He kneels in front of me and takes my shaking hand into his. 'He was so brave.'

'You don't get to talk about him...you don't...'

'You'd have been proud of him. I saw him take on those Enforcers and it was incredible.'

'Did you see him hanging? His pale, lifeless body dangling from a rope...did you see that? Was that incredible? He's dead, Terra. And it's all your fault. You broke your promise and all your sorrys will not bring him back.'

I collapse on my bed, shaking. Terra gets up from his knees and sits beside me.

'I understand, Corena. I do.'

'How? How can you understand?' I sit up, anger returning, every part of my mind focussed on controlling myself. I want to send a thousand shards into him right now.

'Do you remember when we first met?' Terra waits for me to look at him.

'Yes, I believe I was tied up with the horses, trying to drink water from the ground.' I smile.

Terra laughs and brushes my hand with his. 'I knew immediately that you were different. Unique. I could see it in your eyes, actually. The eyes of someone repressing their true self. You had a mask on, then. But it's off now. Love can remove it. But so can vengeance.'

'But when we met, I'd stripped my mask off months before.'

Then a question I once wanted to ask bursts into my mind. 'You said you were here for a blood debt. Who were you here to revenge?'

He hesitates, taking a long breath. 'I lost my sister. She was killed by an older woman with powers. Like yours. And Pat's.'

'So that's why you helped me. You wanted to find out if I knew who killed your sister?'

'That was part of it, I'll admit.' He shuffles from side to side, looking at his hands.

'And have you found her yet? The woman who killed your sister?' I edge closer.

'No. But I have found out her name. I know you don't owe me anything, and you'll probably hate me forever, Corena. But I cannot return home until this debt is solved. I promised my father. I promised myself.'

I want to scream at him about promises. Instead, I take his hand. 'What's her name?'

'Orochi.'

Voices drift in from the training room.

'I must go.' Terra stands. 'Do not let anyone know I was here.'

'I won't.'

He sneaks from the room and closes the door, leaving me in a whirlpool of emotions, each so vast they threaten to drown me. So, I freeze them. And keep them locked away.

I must become like the very ice I can form. Outside and in.

CHAPTER 34

I'm confused about what to do. I'm under suspicion so it's going to be impossible to get to the Queen without anyone knowing and I must keep Sinsi safe. Now that people know about her, I can't do anything stupid. I'm stuck being loyal to the person who is responsible for Pat's murder. Some way to avenge him.

And after Terra's bombshell, and everything else I've found out about her, I know that Orochi is not to be trusted. I should warn the Order, but there's no way to get a message out while I'm being watched here. I must be patient.

As I form an ice-shield, I think about Sinsi sneaking into my bed late last night, long after Terra had left. Perhaps she can help me. Maybe together we could do something. But would she stay with me if she knew about everything. About what I am. Not Pat, but Corena. Would she accept Corena and like her?

'You have been summoned.' Sinsi stands behind me in the training room. Amp behind her.

'Huh?'

'To the Queen's court. You need to come with us. Don't worry.'

The Palace seems endless. Fifteen floors of lavish rooms and corridors longer than our entire village back home.

As I pass each, I take in as much detail as possible, trying to mentally map potential routes. But after a while, it blurs, like when I watch Bolt move.

Amp and Sinsi have come with me and although they seem chirpy and friendly, I can tell they've been ordered to accompany me. The illusion of freedom.

When we reach the last corridor, it's clear this is where the Queen will be. It's twice as wide and tall, laced with ten feet tapestries and paintings of the royal family, both past and present. I don't recognise any of them, except that they do have some resemblance to the Queen.

And to someone else.

I stare at one painting in particular, the face familiar.

'Wait here, Pat,' says Amp. 'The Queen is having an open court this morning, so there are a few people ahead of us.'

We sit on a row of gold-framed chairs, the backs and seat covers intricately weaved into scenes such as battles, coronations and funerals.

'Do you know what it's about?' I ask her.

'Yes.'

Sinsi keeps glancing at me, as she walks back and forth in front of my seat.

'Would you sit,' I say, eventually. 'You're making me nervous.'

She nods and sits beside me.

Amp alone remains standing, in a firmly upright and still manner.

As the seconds move on, my fingers twitch, the flow of energy through my body fluctuates and once or twice a small shard of ice falls from my hand.

Amp notices one of these. 'No abilities here, Pat. Not in front of the Queen or the crowd. That would be the end of you.'

I nod and smile to reassure her, but she doesn't seem convinced. She must have heard something from Kin or Elera that has raised her suspicions of me. But neither know my true mission.

I'll be seeing the Queen in a matter of moments, but this doesn't seem like the right time for the assassination. There is still too much for me to find out. And my connection to the Order as well as the Ennead would be publicised if I did it. That would probably have the opposite outcome that we're fighting for.

The tall doors leading the Queen's reception chamber open, with a loud click. Beyond the low murmurs of the gathered crowd filter out.

'Let's go,' says Amp, helping me to my feet but keeping herself close after. Sinsi follows and I can feel her trying to dig into my emotions, the same way her brother can.

I clear my mind. I won't let her know what's coming next.

I pass the threshold, the murmur silencing. Flanking the length of the room are Royal Enforcers. Either side of the crystal throne, Kelvin and Bolt. In the galleries, both above and to the side of the room, are hundreds of people, all in to hear from or ask of the Queen. But their time has passed. Now it's time for me to speak with her.

Prince Terra stands amongst the crowd on my left in his full uniform. He's hard to miss in any room. His suit of the night before has gone. His precious sword hangs at his waist. I wonder what his business was with the Queen. He could betray me at any time. Perhaps he already has.

I shake my head, wisely deciding now is not the time. As I continue to walk forward, his eyes burn into me, along with several hundred others. But the ones with the most heat come from the Queen.

Either side of her, both Kelvin and Bolt keep theirs' upon the crowd. Probably watching for anyone who might try to harm the Queen. Against those two, they have no chance.

About ten feet in front of the Queen is a white line.

'Kneel at the line,' Amp whispers to me.

When I reach it, I do.

'Rise, Pat Storm.' The Queen's voice is beautiful and full of warmth, not harsh or cold like I'd want it to be. I hate that there's part of her I admire.

I stand, pushing out my chest, like my dad used to when anyone important ever came to town. He said it makes you look more respectable.

'There has been a public accusation laid against you, Pat Storm. A serious accusation: treason against the crown.'

The crowd murmurs again, but the Queen thumps the base of her crystal staff upon the ground the room silences.

'It is within the right of the accused to face their accuser. Do you wish to do so?'

'Yes,' I say, immediately.

'Very well. Come forward.'

Davin moves into view. I look around for Kei, but he's not anywhere I can see.

Amp rushes to the side of the Queen, blocking her from Davin, the Royal Enforcers suddenly stand erect and focus upon Davin.

I don't move, fearing that I might set her off. She's not here for the Queen, she's here for me, but no-one else realises it.

She takes a step closer to me and nobody stops her. They all seem content as she moves further from the Queen.

'HALT!' The Queen's voice is amplified and echoes loudly around the chamber.

Davin responds by turning and smiling, putting in a small bow.

'PAT STORM. HOW DO YOU PLEAD?'

'I'm not clear what exactly I have done that is treasonous.'

The Queen turns to Davin. 'TELL HIM.'

'This *boy* is a double agent, a spy for the Order of Mutare, and is here to kill you, your highness.'

'AND HOW DO YOU KNOW THIS?' The Queen asks.

'Because I'm also a member of the Order.' As she finishes the sentence, she jumps to my side.

'ARREST THAT WOMAN. SHE IS MUTARE!'

But the Enforcers don't have a chance. They have no idea Davin's a teleporter and before they even get close to us, we've teleported.

But it's not just us.

As we reappear several floors below the chamber, in an empty room, Bolt and Sinsi are on top of us.

'Hold her Sinsi, don't let go!' Bolt shouts, pinning Davin, who struggles to fend them off and keep a hold of me.

She teleports again. This time, we're in the main reception to the Palace, surrounded by hundreds of people, including troops of Royal Enforcers. They all turn our way, but before they see who we are, we've teleported again.

This time, we land in the corridor beneath, which leads to the kitchen and the training arena.

'Separate her from Pat, Sinsi!' Bolt's voice echoes along the corridor.

Sinsi is on my arm, trying to prise Davin's fingers off my wrist, but she's too strong. Bolt has her pinned, but she's holding him at arm's length, so he can't get any blows in, and he doesn't dare let go of her in case she jumps again.

I do the only thing I can think of. I turn my arm into ice. Slowly Davin's hand is enveloped in ice and as it thickens, it moves up her wrist.

'You are a little traitorous weasel, girl. Why did you kill Orochi? Why did you abandon us after we saved you from the mines, huh?' Davin spits at me.

But I focus on growing the ice up her arm. Soon it will hurt. Soon it will be too much. And if she does nothing, I'll encase her.

'Pat, what's she talking about?' asks Bolt. 'Were you part of the Order?'

I can see the confusion on his face. He was so annoyed back in Ghondulon when Kei escaped, but now he seems more hurt by the truth.

'No, it's all a lie. Don't listen to anything she says. I'm loyal to the Queen.'

Bolt nods and focusses on keeping Davin still as she begins to thrash and struggle against my trap.

Sinsi raises her eyebrows at me. I shake my head. She tuts but says nothing else.

The ice is now at Davin's neck.

'Keep her alive, Pat,' warns Bolt.

'As if the girl could kill me,' replies Davin, suddenly swinging up and head-butting Bolt, who falls off her.

In an instant, we've teleported. We are outside Rejik, in the fields surrounding the capital's walls. A farmer is picking strawberries ten feet from us. He gets the fright of his life when we appear and runs away.

'One down, one to go,' says Davin, smiling despite the ice continuing to grow over her torso.

'Sinsi, let us go.'

'No. We can't let her get away.'

'I will deal with this.'

'No, she needs to tell me about my brother.'

'Your brother, huh?' Davin sneers. 'At least he had the good *sense* to join the right team.'

Sinsi starts repeatedly punching Davin wherever she can reach; her arms, ribs, legs and the occasional head blow. But Davin is strong enough to keep her from doing too much damage.

The ice now covers most of Davin's body and is now inadvertently on Sinsi, who has taken over Bolt's job of pinning her down.

'Stalemate?' says Davin.

'How so?' asks Sinsi. 'You can't go anywhere.'

As Sinsi speaks, I thicken the ice-prison I've covered Davin with.

'You really think I can't go anywhere?'

'Then, why haven't you?'

'I'm waiting.'

'For what?' asks Sinsi, looking around.

'Him.'

Kei comes charging across the field towards us, his right arm wreathed in flame.

'Sinsi, get out of here,' I say.

'I'm not leaving you. They'll jump you somewhere else if I do.'

'It doesn't matter. You have Kin.'

'Kin?'

'The other twin. They'll come for him. Go back to the Palace and guard him.'

'You have Kin?' Davin asks. 'You didn't kill him?'

'What do you think we are?' says Sinsi. 'We don't kill our own kind.'

'Oh, really? I don't believe you. What about the others you've captured? Where are they?'

'I don't know.'

'Exactly. Even if you don't kill them, someone does.'

A ball of fire smashes into Davin, melting the ice on her legs.

'Stop, Kei!' she shouts.

The twin comes to a halt, ten feet away, his arm still consumed by flame.

'Kin is still alive,' she says to Kei. 'Perhaps,' she adds, looking at Sinsi with narrowed eyes. 'I will trade you. Kin for the Ice-Girl.'

'No deal. I've sensed your intentions. You'll kill him...her,' says Sinsi. 'Take me instead.'

Davin eyes her warily. 'I can't trust you.'

'You trust my brother?'

She takes a few seconds to answer. 'Yes.'

'My word is as good as his. I assure you.'

Davin looks at me. 'Deal.'

'No, there is no need for this, Sinsi,' I say.

'It's fine, Pat. I want to see Sense anyway. There's no point in continuing with this. She's right, it's a stalemate.'

I relax my ability, letting the ice melt in the warm sun.

I turn to Kei who waits, still alert and ready for fighting, but I'm done fighting with them. They are not my enemy, not really. I need to get back to her.

'Okay, so how do we do this?' asks Sinsi.

'Corena will let go and Kei will take my hand. No funny business, girl,' she says to me.

'I'm not interested in you, Davin. Nor should you be interested in me. Whatever you think about me, we're on the same team.'

'I doubt it,' she replies. 'But I'd rather have Kin alive than you dead, so for now I'll compromise.'

'And the exchange?' I ask.

'I'll jump back to that last corridor in the Palace. It looked quiet and discrete. Be there at midnight with Kin. Alone. I'll return with this one, then.'

'What if I can't get Kin out?'

Davin smiles. 'Then we'll both lose a friend.'

Kei moves closer and takes her hand.

I release, the ice having finally melted, and roll a few feet away.

'See you soon, Pat,' says Sinsi, smiling.

'Thank you,' I say.

She nods and they disappear.

CHAPTER 35

'Pat, or should I call you Corena? Look nobody in the Ennead cares whether you are a boy or a girl.' Amp offers a small smile. 'But we need you to tell us what happened? Where's Sinsi?'

I'm in the prisoner room along with Kin and Elera, both of whom look thoroughly confused by everything. And I don't blame them. I have no idea what to say anymore.

'I told you before. I don't know. The teleporter took us through several places, Bolt can vouch for that, then she got him off and took us outside the city. I got free of her then, but she teleported away before I could do anything else, so I returned to the Palace.'

'So you say.' Amp paces back and forth outside the room. I can see her through the large, wall-sized window, made of some weird material. Probably another of Leck's inventions.

'But what I don't understand is why she took Sinsi? She was only interested in you upstairs. What was that all about anyway? Are you a spy?'

I shake my head. 'This is getting tiresome. I'm not a traitor. I just changed sides. I'm not in contact with anyone in the Order anymore, and I think you can see from Davin's reaction that they hardly want me back. I'm here to stay. With the Ennead.'

Kin shakes his head at me but doesn't verbalise his clear

disgust. Elera is also silent, but she refuses to even acknowledge me. She sits in the corner, biting her nails, staring intently at the smooth, marble wall.

'I want to believe you, the rest of the Enneads are happy to trust you, but the Queen ain't having it, so you're going to have to stay in here until this is all over.'

'When what is all over?' I ask.

'When Sinsi returns. Or we hear why they've taken her.' She turns from the window and walks beyond a second door, out into the training area. The door thumps shut after her.

I notice the shadow of Loco, sitting just outside the view of the window, her outline illuminated on the wall from the lamp on the table. At least I know she won't speak to me.

I turn my attention to my fellow prisoners.

'Look, this isn't what it looks like.'

Kin shakes his head again.

'So, what is it, then?' asks Elera. 'Last time I saw you, you were hell-bent on finding your brother.' She pauses and finally turns to me. 'I'm sorry about what happened to him, darling. He seemed like a good kid.'

I nod but can't speak. I clear my throat.

'So, tell us what this is?' she continues.

I take a long breath. 'I can't say.'

Elera turns away.

'No, trust me. Please.' I stand and face them both. 'I was instructed not to tell by Cerebrum. I'm here on his orders.'

Elera looks up. Kin also gives me a glance.

'But you can't say any more?'

I shake my head.

'Makes it real hard to trust someone when they say nothing. Wouldn't you agree, darling?'

'Yes, but you must. You know me. You trusted me before. Can you do it now? I'm going to need your help for what I must do.'

Elera paces the cell, glancing at me every few seconds.

I don't want anyone to die, Ennead or Order. But to save people I need to abandon my mission here. And that means missing out on the Queen. It's an impossible choice: the long-term good that will result from killing the Queen versus saving my fellow Mutare here and now.

The image of Pat swinging blinds me again.

'Can you assure me that what you are doing is worthwhile?'

'Yes, it is. For everyone.'

'It's not just some kind of revenge mission?'

'At first it was. But now, I've seen the bigger picture. This must be done. Will you help me?'

'Fine. But once we're done, I have my own business to take care of with Orochi. The scutter tricked me.'

'You're not the only one,' I say, walking to the window.

'So, how do we get out of here and do whatever needs to be done, darling?' Elera stands with her hands on her hips, tapping her fingers.

Kin looks attentive now. Perhaps he could be convinced to work with us. If I could offer him a way out.

Out of the window, Loco paces, moving her chair high above without concentration. She's focused instead upon making six stones move in an intricate and co-ordinated way. As I stare at the stones, I have an idea.

'Kin, can you dig us a tunnel in this dirt?'

He nods.

'Okay, get going. In that corner, there where she won't be able to see it. Make it go right under the room next door and into the main training area.'

Again, he nods, moves into the corner of the cell and raises his hands. As he does, the earth begins to lift and form a small pile, leaving a person sized hole, which gets deeper and deeper.

'If they catch us, they'll kill us,' says Elera.

'Not if we're in the main hallway by midnight.'

'What happens then?'

'You'll see.'

Elera shakes her head but takes a seat. I join her and we sit silently watching Kin dig our escape route.

'So, what happened to you after the inn?' Elera asks me.

'I left. I needed to find Pat.' I stand, the memory triggering movement. 'I found him. Hanging there from the rope like the rabbit or deer we used to trap. His pale face was so calm and peaceful. And lifeless.'

'He was so brave, you know,' Elera says. 'He didn't cry or plead or anything.'

'Brave? I wish he'd been less brave and maybe he'd still be alive. Burning those Enforcers cost his life. I'd take coward and alive over brave and dead. You said you'd protect us. And after all that talk, when it really mattered and you could have helped him, you didn't. You let him be taken.'

'We had to leave. Terra and I would have been killed. There were too many Enforcers and more on the way.'

'I suppose I shouldn't have excepted much more from an assassin. Despite your promises.'

'I'm sorry, darling, I was just trying to help.'

'You can't. Not with the past. But you can now. Just trust me and do whatever I say. Can you do that? Maybe you can honour his memory by helping me avenge him.'

Elera nods slowly, lowering her head.

The door to the adjacent room slams open. In from the training arena strides Prince Terra, his cloak floating behind him. His gleaming sword swings from his belt and his eyes find me in seconds. Then he turns to Loco.

'I have been granted an audience with the prisoner. Stand aside.'

But Loco does not move. She doesn't need to. Instead, the floating chair moves swiftly between the Prince and the door to our cell. Then the six stones begin to circle Terra's head, moving too quickly to watch.

'A Telekine?' His eyes widen. 'It's a pleasure.' He holds his hand out to Loco.

She looks suspiciously at it and shakes her head.

'I mean no harm to anyone,' Terra adds, turning to the window of our cell. 'I'm only here to talk to an old friend and check on her well-being. Things have changed significantly since we parted.' He moves closer to the window. The stones continue to orbit his head but do not come any closer.

'Well, well, Corena. What are the chances that we would meet again in these circumstances?'

'Can you get me out?' I ask, taking a step away from the corner where the hole is.

He shakes his head, glancing at Loco. 'No. I'm lucky to have this much. But you serve the Queen now. I'm sure this misunderstanding will be resolved soon enough. A member of the Golden Ennead will get a fair hearing, I'm sure.'

'Then why are you here?' I say, conscious of the spectators.

'I needed to see you Corena. I haven't stopped thinking of you since we parted. Once I regained my sword, I abandoned my intended journey to reconnect with you. I knew you were coming to the capital and here you are. And I see that Miss Elera has stuck with you. That is pleasing.'

'So, you've seen me. Anything else?' I sense Kin continuing to work slowly on our escape route. I need to get rid of the Prince in case he sees it.

'Corena, are you not happy to see me?'

'Prince Terra. You were kind to me, and I thank you for that. But I'm now in prison and unless you are going to get me out, I don't see what else we have to discuss.'

The Prince stands in silence, staring at me. Clearly, he was expecting a different outcome with his visit.

Amp bursts into the room.

'WHO ARE YOU? AND WHAT ARE YOU DOING IN HERE? NOBODY IS ALLOWED DOWN HERE!'

Prince Terra jumps, the window vibrates and even Loco's stones move in the air.

'I have permission,' says Terra, stepping backwards towards the window.

The stones circling him move closer.

'FROM WHO?'

'The Queen herself. She said I could have an...'

'STOP! I HAVE JUST SPOKEN WITH HER AND SHE SAID NOTHING ABOUT IT!'

'She did. I am a man of my word.'

'I DON'T BELIEVE YOU. LOCO, KNOCK HIM OUT!'

Terra draws his sword and falls to his knee in one rapid movement. The stones fly towards where his head was, missing their target and crashing into the window.

The glass breaks into thousands of pieces, scattering across the cell.

I form a thin ice-shield to protect Elera and I. Kin dives into the tunnel he dug.

When the shield melts, Terra's sword clashes, deflecting the various objects that Loco directs towards him.

Amp has gone. Perhaps to tell the Queen, perhaps to get reinforcements.

Either way, we have little time.

'It's time to go,' I say to Elera, pulling her through the gap where the window was.

Loco notices us and projectiles begin hurtling towards us. I form a shield over my right forearm, extending it out to cover us, but keeping it transparent.

'Terra, come with us. We are leaving,' I shout over the destruction.

'Why? I'm having fun!' he replies, ducking under another rock.

We reach the door leading to the training arena.

'It's locked,' says Elera.

'Damn, we'll need to take her down before we can get out, then,' I say.

The bench from our cell zooms towards us. It collides with my ice-shield, shattering it upon contact and the follow through knocks Elera and I off our feet. Terra leaps over us and deflects the next few smaller projectiles.

'We won't last long against her. We need to get out,' says Elera, pulling me to my feet.

I form a new ice-shield just in time to deflect shards of glass which soar from the cell floor. Some of them catch Terra. He falls to one knee.

I move forward, shielding him.

'Are you okay?'

'Yes, just a few scrapes. I'm fine,' he replies, standing and charging Loco.

She spots his attack and the large bench, in two pieces, crash into his back and floor him. The back of his skull leaks blood.

'You killed him!' I shout.

Every projectile in the room falls to the floor.

My shield melts, reforming as a shard in my right hand.

I hurl it at Loco. It's going to hit her between the eyes.

Then she reacts, redirecting the shard. It shatters on the wall behind her.

'Loco. Look at what you are doing. Is killing people part of your job?'

She stares at me blankly, shaking her head.

The door behind us clicks open.

I turn, readying a shard, but it's Kin.

'Help us with Terra. He's hurt.'

'He'll slow us, Corena. Leave him,' says Elera.

I turn to her. 'Really? You'd leave him behind to die?'

'It's him or all of us. This is our chance to go.'

'No, he came here to help us. Even if he didn't say it, that's what he intended. Help him, please.'

Elera tuts but grabs him under the arms. Kin grabs his legs, and I hold his middle. I touch the back of his head with my open palm, freezing the wound to stem the flow of blood.

'Loco, are you coming? We are getting out of here.'

She remains unmoved. Her eyes meet mine. Then she shakes her head.

'Fine, but don't be used by the Queen to kill people. Use your powers for something good.'

We carry Terra out of the room into the training arena. When we're halfway across, Leck spots us from his workshop.

'Stop, Pat!' he shouts. 'Stop!'

He runs towards us.

'Leck. Don't come any closer. I don't want to hurt you. We are leaving, so go back to your workshop.'

'Pat? You are one of us? Why are you helping...them?'

'There is no 'us' or 'them', Leck. That's the problem here. We are the same. Please, just let us go.'

He takes a step backwards, watching us move to the exit.

'STOP!' Amp's voice is louder than ever.

The doors bang open. Standing in the space leading to the corridor, Amp is flanked by Bolt and Kelvin.

'IN THE NAME OF THE QUEEN, DO NOT MOVE. ALL FOUR OF YOU ARE UNDER ARREST FOR TREASON AND PLOTTING TO ASSASSINATE THE MONARCH, AS WELL AS ATTEMPTING TO ESCAPE PRISON AND ASSISTING IN THE KIDNAP OF A SHIELD MEMBER.' She turns to the boys either side of her. 'ALL IN ALL, ALL FOUR OF YOU DESERVE TO DIE. TAKE THEM DOWN BOYS.'

Kelvin looks to Bolt, who shrugs. A large piece of flat metal moves through the air. I turn and see Loco behind us.

Trapped.

'We should surrender,' says Elera.

'No,' says Kin. 'They'll kill us anyway. May as well go down fighting.'

I nod.

'Fine,' says Elera, pulling Terra's sword from the sheath.

I scan the room, looking for any advantage.

'LOCO. BOYS. GET THEM.'

In a flash Bolt has us all on the deck, barely a second passing. I hit the ground hard on my back. When I look up, Kelvin is close, fire swelling in his fists. He takes aim and creates a circle around us.

'Kin, dig under and get them from below. Bolt can't move on ground that isn't there. I'll deal with flame-boy.'

Kin nods and the earthen floor starts to swirl in a chaotic and random way all around the arena. He leaves the small patch at our feet unmoved.

I extinguish the flames, drawing water from Leck's workshop and the changing rooms beyond. The air has become so dense with earth that it's impossible to see, hopefully nullifying Loco's projectiles and Kelvin's flame. Bolt won't know where we are, so that takes him out, too. Only problem is how do we get out.

Kin, Elera and I stand back-to-back, prepared for the next attack, when everything suddenly stops.

Everything.

The ice melts. The earth returns to the ground. The flames die. The projectiles fall. Bolt is unmoved. Amp's voice has returned to normal volume.

'My Queen,' she says, kneeling.

Loco, Kelvin and Bolt follow. I notice Leck sliding back into the workshop.

The Queen strides from the corridor into the training arena, still dressed in her grand and formal way, completely inappropriate for the surroundings and for us.

I attempt to summon a shard to pierce her heart, but the energy has gone, my powers muted.

It seems absurd that she's here.

But here she is.

And everyone is powerless.

'Please stand.' She waves a hand at the Ennead's as she passes, before coming to a stop in front of Amp, Kelvin and Bolt, facing us.

My heart races at the sight of the two Enforcers who accompany her. Standing either side of the large doors are Sorg and Hiro. There's no time to even contemplate how they got here. The thought that they may have sold me out definitely crosses my mind.

'Do stop these silly games. I don't want valuable people to die.' She smiles in a sweet and fake way.

'Let them go,' I say, my hands shaking. 'They've done nothing wrong. You can have me. Whatever you want to do, I'm yours.'

'No,' she replies. 'You're all mine. Except the Prince and the assassin. They're not needed.'

She flicks her hand towards Elera, who looks confused for a second, before her right arm, holding the sword, jerks towards Terra.

I swipe my own arm out and knock the sword from her grip. Elera breathes out and relaxes. At the same time, I lose control of my own body.

My right arm picks up the fallen sword.

'How are you doing this?' I shout.

'Relax, Corena. You pledged your allegiance to me, so you can carry out the task. It will be over soon,' replies the Queen. 'In fact, I need one of them to be publicly executed and take the blame for the disruption upstairs. You can choose which one dies now and which is executed later.'

'You can't make me choose. You don't need to kill either of them.'

'How poorly you know me, girl. I once had to watch my parents die and could do nothing. At least, you get some choice. Now, choose quickly or I'll choose for you, then I'll make you kill your other friends, too.'

I fight against the power she has over me. But no matter what I do, I've lost control of my own body.

'Time up. Decide now or others will die, too.' She smiles and closes her eyes.

'Prince Terra.' It must be him. He promised he'd keep Pat safe. He didn't.

My body turns to towards to the unconscious Prince. The man who showed a slave so much kindness in her old life. Who was only here to repay a blood debt. To Orochi. He came down here for me, knowing the consequence if he was caught.

I've forgiven him. But if I kill him, will I be able to forgive myself.

'Don't make me do this!' I scream.

People shift uncomfortably, but nobody tries to stop it.

I fight against it, but I have no control.

Then I'm free. I'm back in control and I lunge towards the Queen.

But before I reach her, Terra grabs me roughly and throws me to the dirt. He raises his sword and thrusts it towards my chest.

I produce a quick ice-shield and crawl away on all fours. As I turn, I leap to my feet and prepare for another attack. Terra comes again.

The Queen must be controlling him.

His eyes are lifeless, focussed only on killing me.

I parry blow after blow, but each time his sword shatters my weaker ice-shards. And he's showing no signs of tiring, despite the blood pouring from the wound on his head.

'Why?' I scream.

'A chance to assess your powers. Before I take them,' shouts the Queen.

Her arms move through the air, like the conductor at last night's ball, moving Terra around.

'Why are none of you helping?' I shout to my friends.

'We can't move, Corena,' replies Elera. 'Just take him down, go for his legs. They'll heal.'

I take her advice, glancing a powerful swing away, rolling to the ground and thrusting an ice-shard deep into the back of Terra's leg. I withdraw it and bound away to a safe distance.

He crumples but makes no noise. He swivels instantly and swings his sword at me again, missing by a long way.

'Stop this, surely I've shown you enough.' I face the Queen, my hands lowered in surrender.

'What good are your powers if you cannot kill with them? Either you kill him, or all your friends fall right now.' She motions to Kelvin, Bolt and Loco.

The three Enneads move into position near Kin and Elera.

This is impossible. I know what Terra would say if he were himself. He'd tell me to kill him to save the other lives. His eyes are vacant. He's become a vessel, used by the Queen.

Elera smiles. 'Don't worry about us, darling. I'm long overdue anyway. I thought I'd die in the prison. You gave me more life than I thought I'd have. I'm ready.'

I stride towards the Queen, but when I do I see flames erupt in Kelvin's hand. He holds them an inch from Elera's face.

'Do it, Corena,' the assassin shouts.

But I turn away from the Queen. I stride over to Terra, still on his knees, swinging wildly.

'Sorry,' I whisper.

His movements are slow. He's weak now, despite the Queen's intervention. I knock the sword from his hand and pick it up.

I stare at each face around the room. I want them to know the kind of person they serve. But I always want them to know who I am.

That I can do what must be done. That I am strong, like Terra. That I am stronger than the Queen.

I count to three and close my eyes.

Then throw the sword to the ground.

I face the Queen, opening my eyes. I've damned us all, but I'm not a murderer. I may have killed but I won't choose to kill.

'You have lost, your highness. You are wicked and cruel, and your games will not work on me. You can kill us all, but that will only highlight your true self to all your closest followers. Your move.' I turn away to help Terra.

But she's controlling me again. My hand moves to the sword, grips the hilt and holds it pointing towards Terra.

'No. STOP!'

My shout wakes Terra. His eyes widen at the site.

Then he nods.

I try with every bit of strength I have left to move, to do anything but this. But I can't stop it. 'I'm sorry.'

Weirdly, he smiles. 'Remember my blood debt.'

The sword slices into his chest, burying itself deep. Blood gushes from the wound and he lets out a short, grunt before falling motionless.

When the Queen releases her control, I drop the sword and fall to the floor.

I look up at the face of everyone who stands opposite me. My eyes drift from Bolt looking at his feet, to Kelvin, who locks me in his gaze. The Enforcers, my friends who knew Terra, look to each other, but not at me.

Each of them is just as responsible as I am.

Their inaction as bad as my action.

My hands shake as I punch the dirt beneath me.

'That's better,' says the Queen. 'I knew you had killer potential.'

CHAPTER 36

'YOU'RE SICK!'

'Corena, you have no idea how sick I am or what I'm capable of. Very few do and even less live to ponder it.'

'He did nothing wrong. He was your guest. He didn't need to die.' My arms shake and my legs are jelly, as she finally releases her puppet-like grip on my body.

'On the contrary. I can't have stories going back to his father. We struggle to maintain peace between our kingdoms as it is.'

'Don't pretend you did that for peace.' I turn away from the strained face of Terra, his last painful moments etched on his face, and forever in my heart.

'I did that because he came into my palace and betrayed my hospitality and tried to cheat me of my prisoners. I cannot allow that.'

'So, instead of sending him away, exiling him from Skolway, you killed him.'

'No, you did, Corena.'

'You made me.' If I had any energy, any power right now, I'd fly a sharp shard through her head.

'You made the choice. It could have been the assassin that died. Let's be honest, she probably deserved it.'

I look around the room. The Enneads stand in formation, their bodies alert but powerless. Sorg and Hiro glance at me but say nothing. They must have been reinstated but what did they give to the Queen in exchange? Information about me, more than likely.

I look beyond the traitors.

The door lies open. Davin will be appearing in that corridor any time now, waiting to make the trade.

She takes a few steps towards us. 'Now, what shall I do with you, Corena? You're too much trouble to keep alive, but your ability is too valuable to kill.'

'You're not going to kill me.'

'Sure about that, are you?'

'Yes. I'd already be dead if you were.' And for once, I'm completely confident I've read the situation right.

'Perhaps. Or maybe I'm keeping you alive for another purpose.' She turns to the workshop. 'Amp, what's the technician called again?'

Amp scurries forward. 'Leck.'

'Call him.'

'LECK!'

The technician slowly emerges, his head down.

'Get the conduction engine ready,' the Queen commands.

He turns without looking up and returns to his workshop.

'I'm going to kill you,' I shout, stepping towards the Queen. I won't let her use whatever contraption Leck is fetching on me.

Instantly she controls me, and I stop, unable to move my legs.

'No, you're not. You're going to make me stronger. I'm going to add your ability to all the others I possess. Then I'll take your young friend's.' She nods to Kin.

'How?'

Perhaps I can distract her with questions. It's what Susanoo-no-Mikoto would do. Pat and my favourite, always playing tricks on the other Gods.

'The conduction engine. It allows the transfer of abilities.

Every Mutare we've ever captured has been brought here and their abilities transferred to me. And now I will add yours.'

'And then what? How much more power do you need? You're the Queen!'

'I want...no, I need the power to never lose someone I love again!' She immediately covers her mouth, regretting the outburst.

She strides towards the workshop, moving on from her moment of vulnerability. 'Bring them.'

'What about the spare?' asks Amp.

'She is to be publicly executed and used as the face of the disturbance today. We don't want people thinking that Mutare can enter the palace. Much better to blame an assassin. Kelvin, hold her for now.'

Kelvin tries to summon a flame, but nothing happens. He opens his mouth but doesn't know what to say.

The Queen turns. 'I sometimes forget how powerful I am.' She clicks her fingers and Kelvin's hand ignites.

Bolt blurs around us once, then comes to a stop, a frown on his face.

I try my ability, but she's still blocking it. And my legs are still fixed. I'm useless against the Queen, she's too powerful for me.

I turn to Kin, but he shakes his head.

Bolt ties Kin's hands and my own in an instant and carries us both to the workshop. He dumps us on our bums next to it, before the Queen even gets close. I watch her approach, my legs still incapacitated, dreaming of every possible way to gain revenge for Pat. She's so close. I could end her. Images of ice-shards piercing her head or heart consume me.

But outside, nothing. I'm the weak, wood-cutters daughter who kisses girls and boys, and sins. I'm the daughter who was sent away and treated like an animal. I'm going to have my powers taken from me and then killed, like Pat. And there is nothing I can do about it.

Leck pushes out a large machine on wheels from deep inside

his workshop. He moves it next to where Kin and I sit. It has two seats, connected to each other via lots of coloured bits of string. At the top of each seat is a metal helmet. It doesn't look comfortable.

'Bolt. Put her into the seat and secure her.'

The Blur nods and I'm unable to resist as he places me into the left seat, securing me into it with leather straps around neck, chest, waist, thighs, wrists and ankles.

'Does it hurt?' asks Elera.

The Queen turns to her, and she replies with a wide grin.

'Bolt, Kelvin. Does this seem right to you?' I look at both the Enneads, seeking some understanding. 'One person taking all our power.'

'Shut up, girl.' Amp slaps me across the jaw and my skull clatters into the head rest behind it.

Bolt looks uneasy. Loco takes a few steps away from the machine, like she's afraid. Bu Kelvin looks like he's enjoying it. Sicko.

The Queen moves to the other seat, but no straps are placed on her.

'Rest easy, Corena. If you wish, you may die afterwards. Most beg for it. They can't stand to live without their powers.' She grins and sits back.

Again, I search the room for help. Sorg and Hiro remain at the door. Kelvin guards Elera and Kin, his hand engulfed in flame. Leck is behind us, clicking something on the machine.

Amp moves close to me. 'I always did suspect something. The moment we went to Ghondulon, you didn't add up.' She moves away, shaking her add. 'You could have been a great addition, Corena.'

'A great addition to a murder squad? I'd rather die.'

'Precisely,' adds the Queen.

Leck pulls the two metal helmets over both our heads. I can't see anything, my head entirely encapsulated.

'Relax, Corena. It will be okay,' whispers the technician as he moves away.

'Are you ready, my Queen?' he asks.

'Yes, get on with it.'

A loud buzz tells me this machine runs on the same thing as the plane. Electricity.

Leck told me one thing about electricity. It doesn't mix well with water.

I try to summon the feeling, to somehow draw some water from anywhere. But I'm still power-dead. The Queen has a hold on me, but surely she can't do that during the transfer.

Then agony hits. My head jerks back, my neck muscles contracting involuntarily, my arms and legs straining against the straps, every part of me flooded with energy. But not a kind I can control. It must be the electricity.

Every second that passes makes my mind weaker. It feels like everything; my memory, my personality, my consciousness is being drawn from my brain.

Don't fight it Corena. It hurts more when you do. Relax and let the power leave you. Then it will be over. No more pain. I will end you myself if you want.

But the voice makes me fight harder. I strain and I concentrate. She won't take it from me. I can't let her win. She's abused the Mutare for too long.

I'm impressed. You are fighting harder than I thought you might. But it's pointless. You cannot defeat me. In here or out there. I'm stronger than you.

My hand tingles. It becomes cold. A tiny shard forms on my right hand, and I waste no time. With every last bit of energy, I force the shard into the coloured wires, severing as many as I can.

The electricity stops.

'What happened?' screams the Queen.

But all that can be heard are cries and screams.

My power floods back and immediately several small shards are cutting the straps. I push up the helmet and stand.

The room is in chaos.

Kelvin stands in front of me, shielding the still helmeted Queen with walls of flame. Kei and Kin are working in unison, Kin extinguishing the flames with earth, Kei redirecting and manipulating Kelvin's flames.

Davin appears beside me. 'Time to go.' She puts her arm around my waist but before she can teleport, she is hit on the head with a chair and falls limply to the ground.

The Queen's grip takes me again and she throws me back into the seat, using her powers to hold me rather than any straps. I can't even shout. She's silenced me, too.

She turns to the room and holds her hands high.

Everyone becomes powerless in an instant. Projectiles fall, earth floats back to the ground and fire is extinguished.

I spot Amp unconscious on the ground near me, her head bloody. When the Queen sees her, she screams. The noise that echoes in the room causes the walls to shake and large blocks of stone fall to the ground. For several terrifying seconds, I think she's going to bring the whole roof down on us, but then she stops. And so does the shaking and the falling blocks.

Everyone takes their hands away from their ears.

The Queen shakes, her arms still high. She turns to me and I'm shocked to see tears. She falls to Amp's side. Slowly, she strokes her lifeless face with her hand.

'Who did it?' she shouts, standing and looking around the room. 'Which one of you did it?'

The room, so loud and ruckus a moment ago, is now silent.

'Then you will all die.'

She lifts her arms and ground shakes. Large cracks appear on the floor, gradually widening.

People start running, but she still has me. I'm not going anywhere.

More slabs of stone fall from the roof and the wall, the entire room too unstable to stand.

A large fissure appears in the centre of the floor.

Elera and Kei fall. Their screams echo up from the depths, but then stop abruptly.

The shaking also stops.

I can move.

Without thinking, I form a small shard in my hand and leap towards the Queen, but I stop mid-motion.

Hiro lies dead at the Queen's feet, but behind her Sorg stands, still gripping a long sword which he has buried deep into her lower back.

'Go, Corena. Now,' shouts the large Enforcer. 'Forgive us.'

The Queen twists, the sword coming free of Sorg's hand. 'You?'

With one swift movement, the sword slides out her back and flies through Sorg's throat.

'NOOOOOOOOOOO!' I scream, surging at the Queen, shard formed in my hand.

I thrust it at her chest, but an inch from penetrating into her heart, she stops it. It falls to the ground, as does she. Blood streams from her wound. She is weak.

Beside her lie Sorg and Hiro.

Dead.

Fighting for me against the Queen they served.

Someone grabs my hand and drags me away from the Queen. I try to resist, but I'm powerless again. The Queen doesn't attack me, but she won't let me finish her.

'Leave me. I need to kill her,' I shout.

'No. Time to go.' Leck's voice is authoritive and his grip strong. Sinsi is at his side.

'We need to kill her now, Sinsi.'

She ignores me, pulling at my arm. Her touch takes away all my anger. She must be an emoticon like Sense. Leck grabs my arms and together they haul me away.

A shower of brick falls from the roof, separating us from the Queen.

'We need to go, or we'll die in here,' Sinsi says, looking at the large pile of fallen rock. 'I'm not losing you. I know everything now, Corena. Everything.'

They pull me past Davin.

'Wait, she can get us out,' Sinsi says. 'If she's still alive.'

'She's unconscious,' replies the technician. 'She's still breathing, but she won't be taking us anywhere.'

'Well, wake her up. She got me in here, she can get us out.'

'Not like that. she won't. Anyway, I've got a better way.'

'How else will we get out?'

'The plane.' Leck nods to the hanger where all his vehicles sit.

They wrench me away towards the door leading to the plane.

'Wait, we need to bring her,' I say, resisting their pull.

'She'll slow us down,' says Sinsi. 'Leave her.'

'No,' I free my arm from them and run to her side. I try to lift her but she's too heavy. I turn to Leck and Sinsi. 'I need help.'

Leck grabs her legs, and I get her arms and together we haul her up. Sinsi tuts and finally helps. We move amongst the rubble and the large cracks in the floor, looking out for anyone else, but the dust in the air makes it impossible to see much beyond a few feet.

'Do you know where the door is?' I ask.

'Yes,' replies Leck. 'I live here, remember.'

We reach the door, but it's blocked by a large pile of rock.

'We're not getting through that anytime soon, unless you know a secret way out, Leck.' Sinsi gives the technician a hopeful look.

He shakes his head.

We lay Davin down onto the ground.

'I should go back and finish her,' I say to Sinsi. 'She'll only come back and kill more of us if I don't.'

'Corena, we're getting away. Isn't that enough?'

'No. She has killed too many. Pat, Terra, Hiro and Sorg. I need to end this.'

'You'll die if you go back. She is too strong.'

'Look.' Leck points into the dust.

Two bodies float through the air, followed by a third just behind.

'Loco?' Sinsi runs towards her.

I tense, ready to fight her if I need to.

She lands and hugs Sinsi. Kei and Elera are lowered gently to the ground.

'How did you escape her?' Elera asks me. 'I thought you were dead, darling.'

'Well, I'm not, but no time to explain. You need to get to the plane. Loco, can you clear the rubble?'

She nods.

Block by block, she clears the area around the door. When it's finally done, Leck pushes the doors open. Beyond everything is in ruin.

'Well, we won't be flying out of here.' Leck shakes his head as he stares at his collection of vehicles, every one of them destroyed by falling stone or fallen into a chasm. 'All those years of work. Gone in an instant.'

I look behind us and see the dust beginning to clear.

'Just as well I'm awake, then.' Davin sits up, rubbing her head. 'Let's get the hell out of this hole.'

CHAPTER 37

'I need to end this. Now.'

'You'll die,' says Sinsi. 'She's too strong for you.'

'For me alone, yes. For all of us, together, we could do it.' And for once, I believe it. I believe in them all, and one thing the last few weeks have taught me is that working with others is always better than working alone.

'You saw what she did before. She can cancel our powers.'

'She's weak. Sorg stabbed her. And you don't need powers to kill someone. Just a sharp blade,' I say, nodding to Terra's sword.

The Prince's body lies motionless, his treasured blade next to him.

'We also need to take his body. It needs to go back to his father.'

'Corena, don't be ridiculous. We are leaving right now,' says Sinsi, turning to look at the others for support.

Davin nods. 'Yes, I'm not dying for some Prince I ain't ever met before.'

'That Prince saved my life.'

'What's that to me? If you want to get his body, that's your business. But if you do, you can find your own way out,' says the Teleporter.

'Davin, we can't leave her,' says Kin.

It's the first I've heard him speak. His twin nods next to him.

'Yes, if she's not leaving, we help her. Then we get everyone back to Cerebrum,' adds Kei.

'You two are a real pain in my butt,' Davin says, shaking her bleeding head.

'Davin, you take Leck and Terra's body and get them back to the camp.'

She nods, grabs Leck's arm and disappears. We see her flash into sight next to Terra, then they, and his body, disappear.

'We're going to need all of us to take her on,' I say.

'Don't forget Kelvin and Bolt,' says Sinsi.

'They can't still be defending her after all that?' says Elera.

'You'd be surprised.' Bolt appears beside us. 'That flame-head Kelvin is over there helping her as we speak. But Amp is dead and she's the only reason I was loyal. Plus, there ain't much left here for me, now.'

'So, you're with us?' I ask.

He nods. 'Aye, what's the plan, Icicle?'

'Loco we need you throw everything you can at Kelvin. Keep him busy. Bolt, help her. Keep him away from the Queen.'

'Gotcha,' he replies. 'Come on Loco, let's find some junk for you to hurl.'

'Sinsi, can you get a bow from the armoury?'

Bolt re-appears next to us. 'Here you go.' He hands Sinsi a bow and a quiver of arrows, then disappears.

'Okay, Elera, you take the sword. You're the assassin. If me and the twins distract her, could you sneak up and finish her?'

'Absolutely, darling.'

'Stick with Sinsi until the chance comes.'

The girls nod and move towards a large pile of rubble to take cover.

'Boys, you ready for this?'

They nod in unison.

'Good, but if she's strong enough to silence our abilities, you get back. Alright?'

Again, they nod. I smile back at them.

We move back towards the workshop. Most of the training room is covered in fallen brick, but we navigate back towards the conduction engine. Those few moments in that machine still make me shiver.

Loud thumps and streaks of flame tell us that Loco and Bolt are fighting Kelvin.

'We need to get her now,' I say. 'Flank out and approach from either side. Hopefully she'll only see me.'

The twins nod and move in opposite directions, walking through convenient paths between the rubble. I walk straight ahead, the top of Leck's now ruined workshop helping me navigate.

'You must really want to die.' The Queen moves slowly towards me.

I'm next to the main door leading to the corridor and the rest of the Palace. I stand between the door and the Queen.

'Brave, but stupid.' She holds one arm up, grimacing, and my power has gone, just as I hoped.

She holds me rigid and moves closer. Her expensive, white gown is rich red and torn across the stomach.

'Hurt, does it?' I ask.

'Not as much as what I will do to you. Come.' She moves past me and makes me follow.

I catch the twins moving in sync either side of us, peering from behind large stones and moving quickly between them.

'Why did you do it?'

'What's that?'

'Kill all the Mutare. Why hunt them all down and kill them? Was it just for their powers?'

'The answer is too long and complex to tell you, Corena.' She stops and faces me. 'Tell your friends to move away or I will end you right now.' She uses her telekinesis to lift a large slab of stone ten feet over my head. It would crush me.

I notice her arm shaking. She must be weak. Her face is even paler than usual. She's lost a lot of blood.

'Kei, Kin. Go. I'll be fine.'

I hear nothing.

'GO. Or you can see what will happen. I will be fine.'

Scuffling footsteps move away, back towards the hanger door.

'A wise move. You just saved their lives. Nobody else is helping you. Except the ones that Kelvin is taking care of. Such a lovely, loyal boy. Despite everything that happened, he remains loyal to his Queen. The perfect soldier.'

'He's not a soldier. None of us are. What you are doing, outlawing the Mutare, it's wrong. And you're such a coward that you won't even be open about it. You're a liar, a murderer and worst of all, a hypocrite.'

'Okay, I'll bite. How so?'

'You claim you are helping to rid the kingdom of dangerous people, to make it safer, but all you are doing is discriminating against a group of people who have no choice but to fight back. Your hunt is creating war, not peace. Death, not life. And worst of all, you are getting fat on that death, like a crow feasting on those fallen in battle.'

The Queen stops and faces me again.

I want to strike her, to bury a shard of ice deep into her black heart, but weak as she is, she has total control of me.

'Nice speech, Corena. I have become fond of you, you know. When I shared your brain just now, I saw a lot of your thoughts, fears, memories...it was enlightening. I can help, you know?'

'Help with what?'

'Your *confusion*? Your *unnaturalness*? I can help your mind become clear about your gender identity. I can remove that which makes you feel different. In exchange for your powers.'

I stare at her, disgusted that she's raked my personal thoughts.

That my own memories have been violated. I might once have been tempted by her offer. But now I know I'm neither a boy nor a girl. I'm happy that I'm just a person, one that doesn't need the labels of the Queen or the Kurikon.

'No.'

'Fine. It's a pity but I do have to kill you.'

I spot a shadow moving just behind the Queen, but keep my eyes fixed on hers.

'I welcome it. You took away from me, the most precious thing in this whole world.'

'Did someone you love die? Yes, I saw that, too. Well, dry your eyes, it happens to us all.' She turns to exit the training room.

'My brother Pat.'

She turns back, smiling widely, her eyes bright again.

'He was hanged in Ghondulon on your orders. That's why I'm going to kill you.'

She laughs but stops short and holds her stomach wound.

But it's enough. Her grip on me is released for a moment and I rapidly grow a short, sharp shard and thrust it up towards her throat.

It stops.

Then it turns, moving towards my left eye.

And it keeps going.

I force both eyelids shut, squeezing them tight.

A rush of warm blood smothers my face.

The Queen screams.

CHAPTER 38

The Queen falls to her knees and rips the ice-shard from her eye socket.

I have no idea how that happened. I touch my own eyes to ensure they are still unharmed.

The remains of her eye and a stream of blood follow, sliding down her face and onto the ground.

'MY EYE!'

Her scream reverberates through the corridor and into the training room. Her fists are clenched in arms which thrash blindly at whatever they can touch. Deliberate or accidental, the ceiling, walls, floor and even the foundations shake.

'FINISH HER!' Sinsi approaches, her bow bent. An excited arrow shakes between her fingers. 'Or I'll do it myself...with pleasure!'

A stone falls from the ceiling of the corridor.

'Finish me then, Sinsi! Do it. You've always been such a madam but at least you were loyal.'

'Until you lied to us about Sense. You made me believe he was dead.'

'He was getting too close to the truth. Too perceptive.'

'Well, now we all know. And it's time for you to die.' Sinsi pulls her bowstring tighter.

'I should have killed you before now.' The Queen flicks her hand and one of the fallen stones crashes into Sinsi's skull. As it strikes her, she releases the taut arrow, and I watch it fly past me and into the Queen's chest.

I dive towards Sinsi as she falls, eyes closed. Blood floods from the left side of her head and coats her face.

She remains still.

Elera also falls to the ground next to her. 'Finish the Queen off. I'll get Sinsi.'

'No, we need to get her to out of here. I can come back and finish it.'

Together we gently lift her lifeless body and move back towards the training room. As we pass through the doorway, I turn to see if the Queen was killed by the arrow.

But she's limping out of sight at the far end of the corridor.

Alive.

If she gets away, there won't be another chance as good as this.

She's vulnerable and wounded.

But I can't do anything about it.

I need Sinsi alive more than I need the Queen dead.

But this is about more than just us. If the Queen lives, the rest of the Mutare will forever be in danger. I must end this. Now.

Mustering every ounce of power, I sense for every source of liquid in the palace. It's everywhere, I've never had this range or control before. I focus on concentrating it all onto one spot.

The tunnel where the Queen limps away.

As if sensing what I'm doing she turns and faces me. She smiles.

And then I do it, every atom in my body exerted to bring the water racing to that tunnel. As it rushes in, I insta-freeze it, mixing up sharp shards with large blocks of heavy ice and crashing them together on that one focal point.

And to make sure, to finally end this, I flood the whole tunnel from one end to the other, again freezing it the moment the water arrives, locking the Queen in a tomb of ice.

'Bloody heck, darling. No one could survive that. Not even all the Ten put together. She's gone. Let's go.' Elera lifts Sinsi under one shoulder. I grab the other.

I've done it. I'm a murderer. It had to be done, but the thought nauseates me. Crushed and buried in a frozen crypt is no way for anyone to die. Even her.

But I did it for love and I just hope I can live with that. That the light of my love can burn away the darkness in my heart.

I put my fingers to Sinsi's neck and check for a pulse.

Slow but strong.

'Davin had better come back,' says Elera. 'She's losing a lot of blood.'

I increase my pace in response and Elera stumbles.

'Sorry.'

A wall of flame suddenly looms up in front of us.

Kelvin appears next to it.

'Where are you going, traitor?' he says to me. 'And what happened to Ms Happiness? Such a shame, she was always so nice to me.' He laughs, but the smile doesn't go higher than his cheeks.

His eyes are locked on mine, burning with hate.

He thrusts a ball of flame at Elera, and I have no choice. I drop Sinsi.

In the same movement, I extinguish his fire with an ice-shield in front of Elera's face.

'Defending criminals now, Corena? Although that actually makes sense, seen as you are one.' He thrusts a double-handed burst of fire at me this time, but again I'm able to block it, the instantly formed ice-shield melting upon contact.

'I'm fed up playing now,' he says, moving to block our path. 'In fact, I'm...'

I thrust two ice-shards, and he doesn't finish his sentence. He melts one of them, but the other passes through his left arm.

He falls to the ground, groaning.

I encase him in ice, thickening as quickly as I can.

Kei and Kin sprint towards us. Kei's clothes are burnt and completely disintegrated in places.

'Take Sinsi back to the meeting point. If Davin is there, get her back to the camp. She's hurt.'

The twins nod to me and pick her up, swiftly moving away through the rubble.

'What are you going to do with him, darling?' Elera points to the iced Kelvin with the point of Terra's sword.

'Take him with us.'

'What? The guy who just tried to kill us.'

'He didn't try to kill us. And he's not a bad person. He's just very loyal.'

'No way. Kill him or at the worst, leave him here. But don't take him.'

'I have to. I must try with him. If we can convince him to be on our side, then we become all the stronger.'

'I can't see those others being too happy with you for this.'

'Better that than forsaking a good person without even trying to help them see the truth about the Queen. Help me lift him.'

Together, Elera and I lift the huge ice-encased boy up and struggle back with him. The training hall is a wreck now and a small part of me is sad that it is. It's here that I learned so much about myself. It feels worse than when I left my childhood home in the north. I don't know what that says about me.

We approach a small group huddled together. Bolt appears next to me, helping to support the block of ice containing Kelvin. He tries and fails to melt the ice case. He's weak, bleeding and unable to move. He's not getting out there.

'Are we taking the Queen's loyals now?' Bolt asks, raising his eyebrows.

'Don't you start. You were on the Queen's side until very recently.'

'Yeah, but I saw sense. I saw what she tried to do to you. I honestly never knew...'

His eyes are swimming.

'I believe you.'

As we place the block down, I squeeze his shoulder. 'You joined the right side in the end.'

'Unlike this hot-head. What are you going to do with him? He won't change. He tried to melt us just now you know.'

'Everyone deserves a second chance to make up for mistakes. I've certainly had them. And you, too.'

Bolt nods and stays silent, sitting on a fallen stone from the ceiling.

I fall next to Sinsi, still unconscious. Loco is next to her, holding a cloth to wound on her head.

'I've got it, Loco.' My hand replaces hers. 'And thanks...for everything. I'm glad you're with us.'

She nods and sits beside Bolt.

We wait in silence, each of us deep in our own thoughts.

I think about how I finished the Queen. She was vulnerable, wounded and on her own. There wouldn't have been a better chance. I made the right choice.

Sinsi stirs and opens her eyes. 'She dead?'

I nod, unable stop smiling. Sinsi's going to be okay. I place my hand onto the wound, trying to seal it and stop the bleeding with a little ice.

'That's nice,' says Sinsi, placing her hand on top of mine.

Bolt and Loco move down next to us.

'How you feeling?' he asks.

'Pretty crap, but glad you're not protecting that scutter anymore.'

Bolt reddens a little, but smiles.

'So, we getting out of here soon?' Sinsi asks. 'I know this was home, but I really grown to hate this place.'

'Yeah, Davin's coming back for us any minute now.' I say it with confidence only because Kei and Kin are still here, and she wouldn't leave them here. The rest of us? That's a different matter.

'Corena, the ice is melting,' says Elera.

I leap over to the block and place both hands on it, reinforcing and thickening the shell.

'You gotta admire that he's still fighting, huh?' Elera raises her eyebrows. 'Doesn't seem like someone who's suddenly going to have a change of heart.'

'Well, we have to try,' I say.

Davin reappears next to us.

'About time,' says Bolt. 'We were...'

But he doesn't finish his sentence.

Davin is covered in blood.

CHAPTER 39

'What happened?' asks Bolt.

Kei and Kin leap to their sister's side, helping lower her to the floor.

She wipes blood from her forehead. 'We were ambushed.'

'By who?' I ask.

'Enforcers. Loads of them. And Orochi. That was the worst. The Order were putting up a good fight against the Enforcers. But against Orochi, they had no chance.'

'We need to go back there and stop her,' I say. 'Davin takes us there.'

The teleport shakes her head. 'No way. I only just got away alive.'

'We have to help them.'

'I tried, Corena. But you'd die if you went back. They weren't leaving anyone alive.'

'Did you see Sense?' asks Sinsi.

'No. Cerebrum wasn't there either. Unless I missed them. There were bodies everywhere.'

'Leck?' asks Bolt.

'That guy I took? Dunno, we got separated in the panic.'

'You let him go? He doesn't have any abilities.' Bolt advances on Davin.

Kei blocks him, his fist lighting up.

'You should have seen it. It was chaos from the second I jumped. I barely made it out myself.' Davin coughs and winces. Kei falls back to her side.

'We need to go back. My parents were there, too.' I hate them, but a small part of my heart remains unfrozen, still connected to them.

'I don't even know if I can. It took all my strength to get back here.' Davin moves her hand, pressed hard against her side. A stream of blood spills from a deep wound. 'That traitorous scutter got me. Had to jump or she'd have finished me.'

'No, you can't move with that wound.' Elera tears material from her sleeve and wraps it tightly around Davin's middle.

'I can get us there quickly, but I'm not sure where it is.' Bolt moves away from Davin to face me. 'I can get you there, Corena.'

'How many can you take at once?'

'I've only ever taken two before. But I could take three, if someone goes on my back. They'd have to hold on pretty tight.'

'Okay, take me, Loco and Kei.'

'No, I'm not leaving my sister.'

'We need you to show Bolt where the camp is. Kin can stay.'

'It's fine, Kei. Go and give them some Joshi-family havoc.' Davin fist pumps her younger brother, and he nods.

'Elera, we need to get the rest of you out of sight. Enforcers will be on their way down. Get inside one of those vehicles and block the doorway in. Hopefully the Enforcers won't know about that room. Bolt will come back if he can. If not, wait until Davin is able and jump out of here.'

'Where should we go?'

'Do the Order have any other hideouts, aside from the one near Ghondulon?' I ask Kei.

'Yes. We have another near Trihelm. Davin can take them there.'

'Good. Bolt, let's go.'

Bolt takes me in one arm, Loco in the other. Kei is left to climb on his back.

'Ready?' he asks.

'Yes.'

Loco nods and Kei gives him a thumbs up.

'Good luck,' says Elera.

'Be safe,' says Sinsi.

'We will,' I reply.

With a blur of rock, then darkness we fly through the secret underground tunnel that we passed through in the jet.

For a horrible minute, I keep my eyes closed and hold in my vomit. Twice it comes up into my mouth and both times I swallow. But the second time, it comes straight back up, splattering who knows what or who.

A jerk of the neck and a drop in nausea levels tells me we've stopped. I open my eyes. Even though I'm still, everything around me seems to be moving forward.

'Where are we?'

'Just outside Ghondulon. I need Kei to direct me now, so I'll slow down and make a few stops. Go ahead, kid.'

Kei points up beyond the hills that overshadow Ghondulon. As my vision returns to normal, I take in the city of Pat's death, my imprisonment in the Sulphur mines and my eventual escape to join the Order. All of that seems so long ago.

In a series of very fast episodes, we arrive in the woods around the Order's camp.

It's silent, except for the odd crackle of still ablaze trees.

'They burnt everything,' says Bolt, looking all around us.

'Hopefully not everyone, though.' I move forward through the charcoaled forest, towards the spot where we slept.

My foot catches on a loose branch, and I fall, face first, into the ground

I spit out ash as I wipe my face and the front of my suit.

'You okay, Corena.' Bolt kneels beside me.

'Yeah, just tripped on a branch.'

'Eh, that's not a branch,' he replies.

I spin round and stare at a charred human body. It's so badly burnt, there's no way to recognise who it is. I retch but bring up nothing, my stomach empty. Bolt pats me on the back. Loco and Kei look on, faces pale and disgusted.

'We better keep going.' Bolt helps me to my feet.

I grow two ice-shards, ready to kill whoever I find.

The forest floor becomes covered in a sheath of ice, that spreads out from my steps.

Bolt slides to his knees. 'Hey, keep control, Corena.' He points to the ground beneath him.

'Sorry.' But I'm not. However, I do reign in my power for their sakes. They'll help me gain revenge on Orochi and whoever is with her.

If they're still here.

I see the place where our tents once sat.

In their place, melted canvas and more bodies.

I run forward, but I arrive after Bolt, who's already on his knees, trying to clear the faces of the dead for Kei and I to identify. 'You know any of them?'

As I look at lifeless face after lifeless face, spotting Order members that I recognise, but never spoke to in my short time here.

But I don't find my parents.

Or Sense.

Or Cerebrum.

And I don't find the murderers.

They've gone. The forest around us is empty.

'Bolt, see is they're still anywhere now. Now.'

He disappears.

Kei moves from corpse to corpse, his hands shaking. Both are fully alit and every few moments a blaze of fire is jettisoned into the air.

But neither Loco nor I stop him. I can completely understand.

Finally, I recognise a face. Her eyes are wide open. It's the water girl. I squirm with guilt as I can't remember her name, but I close her eyes for final time. She's passed onto the Haven now and won't have to suffer in this harsh, discriminating world.

'We should bury them,' I say.

Loco nods. Kei says nothing but begins to gouge out holes in the scorched earth. Loco uses her power to lift the earth and to lower the bodies into their graves.

I leave them to the burials.

I need to be sure that my parents are not here. Or Sense, Cerebrum and Leck.

I shouldn't be glad at the moment, but not finding their bodies is the only reason I'm holding myself together.

My ice-blades are still formed and ready in my hands as I delve through the forest. When I find the occasional body, I shout out and Loco moves it back towards the gravesite.

My feet take me to the small lake where I trained with Orochi. As I step over the pebbles, where I fell and gained bruise after bruise under my mentor's attacks, I wonder how long she had planned all this.

And how long had she planned to use me as a pawn in her plan? I think of all her involvements; from training me, the fake death and infiltration of the Ennead to planting Elera in that palace and the murder of her own Order.

Was she in league with the Queen or out on her own, trying to kill the Queen for her own gain? Whatever the reason, it's not worth this. Nothing can be worth all of this.

Deep in my thoughts, I haven't realised that I'm now waist-deep in the water. The lake is frozen, my hatred fuelling my ability to uncontrolled levels.

I allow the anger to pass through me, out into the now-frozen water and I watch jagged stalagmites rise from the surface, a mini-mountain range growing from the lake.

I close my eyes and imagine every one of the sharp peaks driving right into the heart of Orochi, over and over. Then through each of her eyes, like I did with the Queen, over and over, destroying her traitorous, cruel body and sending her screaming through Ka-Ferno's gate.

'Corena?'

I open my eyes.

Hundreds of sharp icy spikes fall from the air and smash through the surface of the ice-covered water.

My arms fall to my side.

I turn and slope out of the water, traipsing across the pebbled stones.

'There is no sign of them. They must have teleported or used a vehicle or something.'

'Bolt, she needs to die. Orochi, she's betrayed everyone.'

'I know. But the people here. This is going to continue. They will hunt and kill the Mutare until we're all dead.'

'We won't let that happen.'

'We can't stop them. The Queen had an army of Enforcers and if Orochi has control of them, then we have no chance. They are the strongest of us.'

'But there are only two of them. The Ennead is disbanded. There are still lots of us standing. And many more Mutare we don't even know about. It's not just us, you know.'

'Yeah, you're right.'

'I know I'm right. Now, get up. We need to get to Trihelm and meet the others.'

'If they got away.'

Bolt take us back to the graves.

Kei and Loco stand silently, all the graves now filled.

Twenty-four.

'Leck?' Bolt asks Loco.

She shakes her head.

'Cerebrum? Sense? My parents?' I ask Kei.

He shakes his head.

My shoulders relax, but my hands still shake.

'We should go now.' I place my hand on Kei's shoulder. 'I'm so sorry. I know you knew them much better than me. But we'll get Orochi for this.' I turn to Bolt and nod. 'We'll kill her for this.'

CHAPTER 40

'I can't wait any longer,' says Bolt.

He and Kei have not stopped pacing for the last hour.

Trihelm seems uncompromised, but none of the Order are here. Either those from the burnt camp or from the Palace.

'I want to go back as well, but if we go and they arrive here, we could end up in trouble ourselves. The only sensible thing to do is remain here. Where we said we'd meet.' I remain seated with my head lowered. I know they're both probably glaring at me.

'You made me bring you here and for what? To bury some people. It was pointless. We should be back at the palace helping the others escape.' Bolt's voice is calm, but he thinks I made the wrong decision.

Maybe.

As he whizzes back and forth, carrying out repeated perimeter checks, Kei ramps up the intensity of the fire. This part of the country is usually warm, but tonight it's cold. The extra heat hits my back and chases the chill in my spine.

Loco sits next to me. She lifts my chin.

'You did good.'

I stare back at her, looking closely for the first time. She has silver flecks in her eyes. So pretty. When she smiles, I can't help but mirror her.

'It doesn't feel like it.'

'They'll be safe. They can take care of themselves.'

'It's Sinsi I'm worried about. I hope she's okay.'

'She's tough. Don't worry.'

She places her hand on mine.

'I wanted to thank you for showing us the true nature of the Queen. I've been miserable for a while, suspecting that what we did was wrong. And when you came along and questioned it, we all began to do the same.'

'Except Kelvin, it seems.'

'He's been with her a while. The loyalty is deeper. And she likes him. Always treated him well. Anyway, thanks. That could have been one of us on her horrible machine if it weren't for you.'

'There are more people to thank than me. My friends died tonight. That's on me.'

'Sometimes sacrifice is necessary to stand for what's right. They all made a choice to be there for you. You'd have done the same in return.'

We grow quiet as I think about Sorg and Hiro and Terra. All dead. Once, the four of us met on a dusty road when I was drinking trough water. Our worlds have changed so much.

'I hope their sacrifice has earned them a place in the Haven.'

Loco pats me on the thigh. 'I'm sure it did. All worthy lives, full of good deeds that are rewarded so.'

She walks outside, probably to talk with Bolt. Hopefully convince him to calm down a little. Kei sits opposite me, staring into the fire.

The room temperature and light intensity fluctuate. He's taking out his emotion on the fire. I don't mind, it's keeping me warm and giving him a release. We all need a release sometimes.

Loco races back into the house. 'Someone approaches.'

We all run back out to the front of the house. I search the surrounding countryside and see the light approach.

'Wouldn't mind a bit of help if you're not too busy,' shouts Davin from the darkness.

Even I smile. We run towards her.

When I arrive, Bolt has already passed me going to the house with someone.

'Did you all get away?' I ask.

Davin nods. On the grass next to her, Sinsi lies unconscious. I fall to her side and check her pulse.

'She's alive. Just passed out with all the jumping,' says Davin. Kei and Kin together help her back towards the house.

I put my hand on Sinsi's forehead. It's soaked and her skin burns.

'I'll help you carry her up.' Elera gets down to her knees and helps me lift Sinsi gently.

We move back to the house in silence. I can't breathe. Not Sinsi. After everyone else I've lost. Not Sinsi.

'I brought back Terra's body. And the Enforcers. Davin didn't want to, but I convinced her brother, so she agreed.'

'Thanks.'

'No problem, darling. After all they did, they deserve a proper earth ceremony. But flame-boy got away.'

'Kelvin?'

'Yeah, we didn't have the time or the energy to go after him again.'

I wanted to convince him. I know he's a good person, but he's run beyond my help. Back to her.

We place Sinsi down in a bedroom at the back of the house, away from the fire.

'We need a wet cloth to put on her head,' I say.

'Got it.' Elera disappears to find it.

I use my sleeve to wipe away the sweat from Sinsi's face. I chill my hands and place them on her forehead and on the wound. I place a gentle kiss on her cheek and whisper in her ear.

'Stay with me. Fight, you stubborn scutter.'

Elera returns with the cloth and places it on Sinsi's forehead. I touch it to chill it even more, an icy layer forming.

'She's going to be okay, Corena.' Elera places a hand on my shoulder.

'She better be. If she dies, I'll never forgive myself.'

I remain by Sinsi's side, watching her small chest rise and fall.

Bolt and Loco come in and nod encouragingly to me but have nothing to say. They knew Sinsi for longer than me, but they have become distant from each other lately.

As I sit beside her bed, I slip in and out of sleep.

A boy hanging. A bleeding eye. A prince murdered.
   A boy hanging. A bleeding eye.
   A boy hanging.

Sun streams in through the shutterless window, waking me from another nightmare.

'Morning, Rena.'

I jerk my head up and see Sinsi. Alive. Smiling.

I grab her and hug her tight, then suddenly let her go. 'Sorry, you're still hurt...'

'It's fine. Only really my head hurts. You can crush my chest if you want.'

'Sorry.' I move over and give her a kiss.

'That was nicer,' she says.

'I didn't know if I'd be able to do that ever again.' I've lost so much already; I can't lose her. The thought of never touching those warm lips again makes me shiver.

'Oh, don't be dramatic. It wasn't that bad.'

'You weren't in a good way last night.'

'I'm fine now. Where the hell are we?'

'In an Order house. Somewhere called Trihelm.' I point vaguely outside as if I know the geography any better.

'Oh, that's right. We're working with them now, huh?'

'Looks that way.' I lean back on my chair, relaxing for the first time in...well, a long time.

'Did everyone make it out?' Sinsi asks.

'Yeah.'

'And the camp?'

'You should rest. I'll tell you later.'

'Tell me now,' Sinsi says, sitting up in her bed. She immediately grabs her wound and slumps back down. 'That was silly. But tell me. Please.'

I help position her head on her pillow again before sitting back down.

'A lot of them were dead. As Davin told us.'

'Did you find anyone alive? Did you find Sense?'

'No, but people must have got away. There weren't enough bodies. Sense was not there.'

She slides into her pillow a little deeper. 'Did you get that scutter, Orochi? The traitor?'

'No, she was gone, too. We buried those bodies we could find.'

We fall into a short silence. I don't want to push her. She needs more rest.

But her voice has clearly carried.

'Hey there, Sinsi. Glad you're well. You had us all worried for a bit.' Bolt appears on the opposite side of the bed.

'I'm fine,' she replies. But already the little colour she had is fading.

'Okay, we need to leave you to rest a bit more,' I say, standing up and pulling Bolt to the door.

'What did I do?' asks Bolt.

'Nothing. She just needs rest. I'll close the door, Sinsi.'

She nods and pulls her blanket up to her neck.

I move back into the main room and find everyone sitting down to breakfast.

'How is she?' Loco asks.

'Better. She's just getting more rest,' I say.

'Good. We need to talk,' says Davin.

'About what?'

'What we do next.'

Next? I can hardly cope with now.

'We need to find Cerebrum. And any other Order members that survived. Where would they go?' I ask Davin.

'Here.'

'Then we stay here. At least for a day or two. If they don't show, we leave and try to find them.'

'What if the Enforcers show up? Orochi knows this place as well.' Davin grimaces as she adjusts her position on the bench.

'Well, then it's going to be one hell of a fight.'

'Are we really in a good position to fight her and an army of Enforcers?'

'I'm ready,' says Bolt.

'Of course, you're ready,' replies Kin. 'You can get away if it all goes badly. The rest of us are risking a lot more.'

'You're just scared. Too much time hiding with the Order.' Bolt purses his lips, like he's sending the twin a kiss.

In unison, Kei and Kin go for him. But he's too fast.

He re-appears in the opposite corner of the room. 'Come on boys, you'll need to be quicker than that.'

'Stop it,' I say to Bolt.

'Enough,' Davin says to her brothers.

Both parties stand down.

'Corena is right. We need to be ready to fight if we must,' Davin says to the group. Kei and Kin shake their heads, narrowing their eyes towards Bolt.

'But we should also be prepared to disappear if we need to.

The Order and The Ennead need to work together on this. If Corena and I can get along, so can you.' She looks to her brothers, then Bolt. 'The three of you can get to work securing the perimeter and putting up warning traps. Loud ones to give us enough time. One hundred metres out.'

'What if she teleports right next to the house?' asks Loco.

'Good point. Do a second circle of traps ten metres from the house. Be sure we know where they are if we step outside.'

The boys go outside in silence.

'This is going to be hard. They've been brought up to fear and hate each other,' I say to Davin.

'I know. But unless we come together and fight against those who marginalise us, we'll all be destroyed.'

CHAPTER 41

We must leave in a few hours.

Time is up. They haven't come. I said we would leave and now we must.

Sinsi sleeps.

Her colour has returned. Her personality, too. Much to Bolt and most other people's annoyance. But not me.

I drift in and out of sleep, dawn creeping over the hills that surround us.

I dream that Elera stands over Sinsi, a sharp blade in her hand, hesitating before she kills her.

It's okay, nobody who dies in a dream is really dead. It's only if you die, that you die. Pat told me that just a few months ago. He heard it from someone else, I think. I wish he could tell me more... about anything.

And as she raises it to kill Sinsi, I think that perhaps I should wake up now.

But I am awake.

I leap across the bed, a shard forming as I dive. I plunge the ice-blade deep into Elera's stomach. Her blade sinks into my shoulder, which lies directly over Sinsi's heart.

Sinsi shouts out, but I make no noise. Elera is also silent. Neither of us can believe what has happened.

Then the pain hits and I know I'm not dreaming.

Sinsi holds me close to her, tying her bed sheet around my shoulder. The blade sits there at a funny angle, the handle towards my legs, like Elera tried to pull it away at the last second. Perhaps she did.

But she was going to kill Sinsi.

Elera is my friend. I'm alive because of her.

I turn to my friend, lying in a pool of blood, the shard slowly melting from deep within her stomach.

'Sorry, darling' she says. 'Orochi paid me to kill you. Right after you'd killed the Queen. I'm an assassin, after all.' She spits out a mouthful of blood. 'But I'd fallen for you. I was going to rescue you. Convince you to leave with me. Then, when I found out about her.' She points at Sinsi, groaning. 'She had to die for us to be together. I'm not sorry about what I tried to do...just that I failed.'

Then she dies.

I hold her, a fusion of anger and pity, of love and hate, tumbling through me. I did love Elera, but not like I love Sinsi. She was a true friend; she was brave, and she saved me more than once. I only wish I'd told her. We kissed and then we didn't speak. Maybe if I'd spoke to her about Sinsi and I, about how I felt.

Perhaps she could have accepted that. Perhaps we'd have become friends and allies. Or at least parted ways. Both of us alive.

By now, the room is full of people, but I only have eyes for Sinsi. She carries me away from the bedroom and into another one down the hall.

It hurts being carried.

'You saved me,' Sinsi says simply.

'I did.'

~

The funerals.

Terra. Sorg. Hiro. Elera.

My friends.

Each dying for me in such different ways.

I regret Terra.

I will every day of my life.

At least the others made their own choice.

'I should have been stronger, my Prince. If I had, you would be riding back to your father and your future kingdom. I will return your sword.' My words are the only ones spoken as his body is lowered. The rest did not know him.

'Sorg and Hiro. You tore me from my home with the worst intentions. But then you saved me in the darkest moment. You sacrificed yourselves and showed the kind of bravery that belongs in stories. If I can be a fraction as brave as you, then I will have the courage to continue in this life. Thank you again, my friends.'

I stare at their faces, Sorg's now revealed. He was a handsome man, his features large and prominent. Hiro's perma-frown has gone, her face peaceful.

I swallow.

I never had a chance to speak to them after we abandoned them in the sulphur mine. I have no idea how they got the capital. I never will.

They are lowered, one at a time, by Loco. Kin neatly piles earth above them.

Elera is last. Sinsi leaves and returns to the house. As do the rest, except Loco.

'Elera. You were my friend. You saved me. I'd be dead if I hadn't met you. Despite what you did...what you tried to do...I know it came from a place of love. Your life was dark for so long, stuck in that hole, and you came back into the light, even if it was only for a while. You shone brightly in this world for a small time once more.'

My shoulder pulses with pain, the wound now cleaned, and

the knife removed. 'Goodbye Elera. I will remember you as the lady who saved me from the dark.'

Loco lowers her body and floats the earth on top.

She leaves me at the foot of the four mounds. They don't get a gravestone, but I won't forget where they are or what each of them did.

'Time to go.' Davin stands out front of the house, the others assembled around her.

'I know,' I shout back.

I stare at the mounds a final time.

I'm ready.

I walk to the others. The remainder of the Ennead and the Order. Together. United against the Queen and the Kurikon, which sought to destroy one using the other.

And the worst of us all. Orochi. The double-faced Mutare, manipulating both sides. We have all vowed that she will die.

But first, we must find the few friends we have left.

'Are you sure about this, Corena?' Davin asks.

'Absolutely. The Kurikon control this kingdom on behalf of the Queen. If we destroy them, then we weaken the kingdom.' I turn to Davin. 'And I know exactly how to get their attention...we spread the word, we make ourselves more public and we show people the way we're treated. We need people to know what it's like.'

'This isn't likely to end well,' Davin says. 'It will be hard to convince people about all of this, considering what we are. It might just look like more Mutare causing trouble. They may hate us even more if we do this.'

'Perhaps. But we've ended the Ennead. We've destroyed the conduction engine, so a new Queen cannot rise in her place. And we know exactly what we must do. We might not change this world. But we've got to try.'

I might not know how this will all end, but I do know one thing now.

The Queen, the Kurikon: they cannot tell me who to be or how to live or who to love.

I grab Sinsi's hand and kiss her.

A loud crack frissons through the air, snapping me away from the kiss.

Orochi appears in front of us.

'Hello, Corena. Disappointing to hear that the Queen is still alive. It seems you have failed your assignment.'

CHAPTER 42

Orochi has one hand on her chest, breathing heavily.

'I'm tired of lying. Tired of all these games. So now I'm going to get straight with you.'

I surge forward, ice forming into a long, sharp shard on my right arm. As I thrust it towards her head, she disappears.

I lose my balance and fall to the ground as I miss my target.

'You do not want to kill me, Corena,' shouts Orochi. She's now at the opposite side of the graves. 'I'm here to help. We both want the same thing.'

'You're a liar. You betrayed us all. You killed half the Order. You killed Terra's sister.' Spit flies from my mouth. 'I hate you and I will kill you.' I push myself up with my shaking arms.

I run across the ground towards Orochi. Sinsi shouts at me, but the buzzing in my ears blanks her out.

But before I even reach her, she disappears again.

'This is pointless. You're going to forgive me, or at least tolerate me and we're going to work together.'

'I will never forgive you.'

'Once you know the truth, perhaps you will.' She holds her hand up to her heart.

'I won't believe a word that you say. You deserve much worse than death. You deserve to be dragged through Ka-Ferno's gate and burned for eternity.'

'Ah, you are quite right, my child. I probably do deserve that. You don't agree with my approach, but we do want the same thing.'

'So you've said. But I will never work with you, so either fight me or go away. I've hurt enough today.' I turn to Sinsi, tears beginning to form.

'I see I have no choice. If you won't work with me as an enemy, then perhaps you'll work with me as family.'

'Family?' I turn.

'Yes, Corena. I'm your grandmother.' She walks slowly towards me.

I put my hands up, blocking her from sight. She can't be related to me. She can't. She's abominable. A demon in human form.

'Don't fight it, my child. It's true. Accept it and we can move on. Work together.'

'No...no...' I continue to stumble backwards, away from her.

'I have your parents. Your father, my son. And Cerebrum. They will work with me.'

Sinsi grabs me round the waist and helps me to the ground. My head is light. The sun becomes dull.

'Peton never told you because I told him not to. I wanted you all safe, in the north. How did I know you would end up involved? But when you did, I knew you had to be trained. You are like me Corena.'

'I'm nothing like you...' My face is scrunched. I don't want to look at her.

'You are. And both of us, we're the same as the Queen. We are all Absorbers. This is why I've come for you. It's only us that can kill her. Only us that can end the hunt of the Mutare. Whether you like it or not, you need to work with me. If you want to change this world, you need my training. And my help.'

'I want nothing from you.'

'Maybe not today, but you will.' She walks over to the graves. 'I'm sorry about Elera. She was a good assassin. She liked you, did you know?'

I shake my head, unable to begin processing this. 'She said you paid her to kill me.'

'Yes…yes…I didn't want to. You must know that. But at the time, the plan was different. I hoped you would be able to kill the Queen. And once she was gone, I couldn't have you around, with potential power to match me. But now…well, now it's different. Now we must bury old grievances and work together. At least until the Queen is gone.'

'Liar! She is gone…I killed her.'

'Did you? Did you see the body?'

Suddenly, I'm full of doubt. Orochi could be messing with me, but she could also be right.

At my back, I hear people emerging from the house. Their voices are panicked.

'Are you okay, Corena?' shouts Davin.

I raise my hand and wave it. 'I'm fine.'

'Partners?' Orochi moves closer, holding out an old, wrinkled hand. As I take it, a familiar feeling drifts through me. Stirring a memory from long ago. By the fire, my grandmother singing, the cold hands. It was her, all those years ago. When she still had some love in her. Maybe it's not all gone.

'No. But if the Queen is still alive, I will work with you to take her down. But you will not stay here. And you will bring my parents and Cerebrum to us.'

She shakes her head. 'One day, you will look at me as your ally and grandmother. But for today, I accept your terms.' She disappears.

Sinsi turns my head, her hand soft on my cheek. 'You can't do this, Corena? She is a liar and a murderer.'

I smile, despite the shock and the upset that today has brought. 'She is. But right now, I need her. We all do. But the moment we no longer need her, she is dead.'

CHAPTER 43

Sinsi watches me from the side of the bed. 'You had something to tell me.'

'Yes.' I don't want to keep secrets from her anymore, but I'm scared of losing her. Of scaring her away. And right now, I need her. More than I need anyone else.

'Well, best hurry. We leave very soon.' She smiles but her finger fidgets.

'I've never told anyone outside of my family. I don't want this to ruin what we have.' I can't stop pacing back and forth.

'It's okay, you can tell me anything. You know this. I didn't care when I found out you were Corena and not Pat. I won't care about whatever it is you have to tell me.'

I want to believe it. Outside the window, the others are assembling. Ready to be jumped away to our next hideout. We can't have Orochi telling others where we are. We may have to work with her in the future, but for now, we need to be safe.

I sit beside Sinsi on the bed. Then I stand up and walk away.

'Come on. It really can't be that bad...can it?' Sinsi stands also. 'Just tell me.'

'It's better if I show you.' I remove my trousers. Then my underwear.

Sinsi stares at me.

I search for any expression that tells me what she feels.

She remains silent. Unmoved.

I pull my clothes back on.

She's disgusted. Or afraid. Or both.

I storm out of the room and find another empty one. The bed explodes with dust when I collapse on it. I knew it was a stupid idea. I knew I risked losing her. She thinks I'm unnatural, she's just the same as my parents.

Three small knocks at the door.

I jerk my head round. Sinsi steps towards me, her hands held out. And then she hugs me, squeezing me tight. Still silent.

We lie for a few minutes, and each second, I'm more relaxed but also more terrified. Is she accepting me or is she being sympathetic? I wish I had her power. I wish I could sense what she does.

'I will always love you, Corena. For the person you are. You can be boy, girl or anything you want, for all I care. I love you. Every part of you. You no longer need to hide it. Not from me.'

The tension drains from me, and I could lie with her forever. I can't speak, I know if I do, I'll breakdown.

'That took the most incredible amount of courage, Corena. Even more than fighting the Queen, even more than lying and infiltrating the Golden Ennead, even more than choosing to save me over getting your revenge. You are the bravest person I've ever met. And we will take on this world. Together.'

She cups my chin. And we kiss.

---The End---

ACKNOWLEDGMENTS

Firstly, to my ever-enduring family who have to sacrifice time with me, to allow me to write. It's an impossible situation and I grow ever more guilty of my writing time as you get older but I hope you'll understand one day why I spend so much time at my computer, when you read a life-changing story yourself.

Thanks to Kesia Lupo for your editorial insights - it's made the book much, much stronger. I hope I get to work with you again on another book.

Thanks to Rio Bagoes Nugroho for the cover work - I think it looks great and you've done such a good job capturing the story from so little information from me.

Thanks to everyone who has helped me with this book - it's been through so many drafts and iterations over the years, with many pairs of eyes reading it and giving me feedback - thanks to all of you.

ABOUT THE AUTHOR

Stuart is an award-winning author and secondary school teacher. He has a Masters Degree in Creative Writing and founded, and now runs, WriteMentor. In 2020 and 2022 he was placed on the SCBWI Undiscovered Voices longlist and named as an Hononary Mention for his novels 'Ghosts of Mars' and 'Astra FireStar and the Ripples of Time'. In 2023, he won the WriteBlend award for his middle grade debut, Ghosts of Mars.

Stuart was included in The Bookseller's 2021 list of Rising Stars in the publishing industry.

You can follow Stuart on his newsletter https://stuartwhite. substack.com/ or his website https://stuartwhiteauthor.co.uk/ or any of his social media channels.

Also by Stuart:

Ghosts of Mars: https://amzn.eu/d/d3YHR3A

The Nameless: https://amzn.eu/d/icm4Iwj

Astra FireStar and the Ripples of Time: https://amzn.eu/d/ 1NcTDuo

APPENDIX OF RECURRING CHARACTERS

In the North and the Journey:

Sorg and Hiro: disgraced Royal Enforcers

Pat Storm: Corena's younger brother

Prince Terra: Terra Scorpa, Prince of Haras

Corena's parents: Peton and Lila Storm

Elera: assassin for hire

The Order of Mutare:

Orochi: Leader of the Order

Cerebrum: Deputy Leader of the Order

Sense: brother of Sinsi - a percep

Davin: a teleporter

Kei: twin to Kin - Kei is a flame

Kin: twin to Kei - Kin is an earther

The Golden Ennead:

Queen Freya: Queen and Ruler of Skolway

Amp: Head of the Golden Ennead and mouthpiece for the Queen

Kelvin: a flame

Sinsi: sister of Sense - a percep

Bolt: a blur

Loco: a telekine

Leck: equipment technician